THE SORCERESS

Second book in *My Paranormal Files* series

BISWAJIT BANERJEE

ISBN-13: 978-1514829721
ISBN-10: 151482972X

Visit the principal blog of the author at
http://realmofbiswajitbanerjee.blogspot.in
For information on his books visit
https://www.amazon.com/author/biswajitbanerjeepage

DEDICATION

I dedicate this book to the advent of humans, an invaluable stage in the process of evolution of consciousness.

CONTENTS

ACKNOWLEDGEMENTS

The first credit for all my literary works goes to my loving father S.B. Banerjee and my loving mother Rama Banerjee. Without their constant support none of my works would have been possible. Their love is like an unceasing stream of nectar. And their presence makes my existence complete.

My brother Debjit Banerjee and my sister in law Debjani Banerjee have always been great pillars of strength. I have learnt a lot from my brother who also happens to be a great chess player and a brilliant writer. Many of my ideas in Physics, Mathematics, literature, Philosophy, and Spirituality evolved because of invaluable inputs by this great brother of mine.

The encouragement and support of my wife Ruby Banerjee is crucial to my literary endeavors. *The Sorceress* needed a lot of time for research, writing and editing. This necessitated stealing minutes, hours and days away from the time that rightfully belonged to the family. She has been very kind to allow all the liberties I needed to complete this book. Besides, her suggestions for the book have been of great value.

My niece Arunima Banerjee and daughter Madhurima Banerjee have been of tremendous support. Although they are little girls but their unceasing interest in my works acts as a great source of inspiration. Both of them read my stories and often come up with very useful suggestions. I feel so secure in their presence.

I simply want to say to my family members that I love you all and that my life has little meaning without you.

I convey my heartfelt thanks to Saonli Hazra, litterateur, writer, corporate trainer and my very dear friend for editing the manuscript. With someone of her caliber in charge of editing, the writer could take it easy. I am so happy for her ingenious contributions to the work. I look forward to more such creative associations with her.

Credit is due to Sandeep Mukherjee, my friend and colleague around whose personality the character of Saikat Mukherjee has been built. Sandeepda, as I call him, has always encouraged me to pursue my literary ambitions. Despite being a very senior functionary in the Government of India with tons of responsibilities, he always finds time out to listen to my stories and objectively analyze them. I am so glad to have a friend like him.

Credit is also due to Arvind Pokhriyal, again a senior functionary in the Government of India, and a very close friend of mine. He also has been very supportive of my efforts. Arvind's words also fuel up my creative spirits.

I do not have enough words to thank Sunita Gupta, my hugely talented personal assistant. She takes care of the nastiest works and does them with impeccable precision. In the context of *The Sorceress*, she has been by my side right from the stage I conceived the story to the point when I published it. I am also indebted to her for going through the manuscript and making useful suggestions.

I tremendously respect the efforts of my other friends and colleagues including Sudipto Banerjee, Priyadarsi Dutta, Rajib Roychowdhury, Amitabha Bandopadhyay, V.P. Rajvedi, Ravindra Kumar, Manisha Bhatnagar, Uday Sankar Chattopadhyay, Sushil

Kumar, Kirti, Shibu, Dr. Bikram Kesharee Mohanty, Sanjeev Kapoor, Soumitra Basu, Rajesh Saraswat, and Padmini.

I am nothing without my readers and students … it is they who make my works complete. Thanks to all of you all over the world who exude interest in my works. Doesn't matter whether you praise my writings or make the bitterest of criticisms, it is you I write for.

Last but not the least, I would like to express my love and admiration for Lord Krishna, the Supreme Personality of Godhood. It is He I seek through my works!

FOREWORD

The Sorceress is the second book in the series *My Paranormal Files*. I hope it finds the same degree of acceptance amongst my readers as did *The Bureau*, the first book in the same series. Like *The Bureau*, *The Sorceress* also, amongst other things, deals with the gamut of consciousness. I would rather call it a paranormal adventure with consciousness as the central theme. This must not lead my readers to think that this book is a continuation of the story of the first book. Well, it is not. It is an independent story although it does at times refer to the plot of *The Bureau*. However, the reader needs no knowledge of the first book to understand the storyline of the present book.

The Bureau met with very good success. It was the number one best seller in the genre of Horror amongst Kindle books in Amazon.in for a good number of days. Even at the time of writing this Foreword, *The Bureau* figures amongst the top hundred Kindle books in the same genre in Amazon.in. I thank all my readers for this stupendous response.

In *The Sorceress*, I again dealt with trans-textual characters and I found the entire exercise immensely enriching as a writer. Although the protagonist of this series viz. *Biswajit Banerjee* is not me, I share some traits with him and the process of spiritualization he has been subject to in this story has also in many ways pushed my spiritual growth.

From the multitude of emails and calls I have received from my readers, it appears that some are not quite clear that the *Biswajit Banerjee* of *My Paranormal Files* and I are not the same. Let me clarify again that *Biswajit Banerjee* who is the protagonist of the series is just a character and although he and I have the same name, he is not me. I must further clarify that these stories are not all real accounts. While it is true that many of the elements in *The Bureau* as well as in *The Sorceress* are derived from real life events, these books are essentially works of fiction. Let the reader not make the mistake of treating them as pieces of creative non-fiction.

Certain portions of *The Sorceress* are expositions of some of my ideas on consciousness and I wondered if they could be too heavy for my readers. But then it struck me that these portions are keys to progression of knowledge and therefore I decided to keep them as parts of the story. After all, my idea is not to tell a plain story but to tell a story steeped in spiritual and philosophical themes. I hope my readers find these portions interesting as well.

With these words I now offer *The Sorceress* for your reading pleasure ... happy reading.

BISWAJIT BANERJEE

PROLOGUE

At the centre of one of the prominent crossroads in my city stands a beautiful sculpture on a high pedestal. I can best describe it as the surrealistic impression of a woman. One day it shed tears – tears of blood! People watched the spectacle in awe. Ideas of all kinds made waves in no time. Some of them sounded intelligent while others utterly asinine. Some felt the sculpture was possessed. Others thought that the tears were God's explicit disapproval of idolatry. Then there were some who saw the signs of a doom in the near future in the tears. And of course there were some who dismissed the tears as the mischief of a man or a group of men with no better thing to do. By late evening that day, the sculpture had become the focal point of all attention. It is then that the officials of the municipal corporation woke up. They cleaned the tears and dispersed the crowds around the sculpture. Some journalists had also taken note of it and the event found reasonable coverage in many a news channel.

The next day the White Lady shed tears of blood again. News spread like wildfire and people from all directions thronged the place again. The authorities were quicker that day and the tears were soon cleaned. Yet again, the sculpture with blood tears made headlines in various electronic and print media. Most, however, including the media houses, governmental agencies and so-called rationalists made light of what they had witnessed. It was suggested that some prankster was behind the blood tears. Little did they know at that time that what they dismissed as a mere prank was to confound one and all for days to come.

Fresh tears of blood were sighted the next day again … and then again the next day … and then again the next day … the phenomenon was now too blatant to be ignored. The authorities surrounded the pedestal and deployed some guards over there. A couple of Closed Circuit Television Cameras were also installed with one of them firmly focused on the face of the sculpture.

Then it became clear. No, there was no prankster behind what was happening. The camera covering the face of the sculpture clearly showed the tears of blood oozing out of the corners of its eyes. A team arrived at the spot for scientific investigation of the phenomenon. Samples of tears were collected and sent to the National Chemical Laboratory for tests. The tears were cleaned again and the barricades around the pedestal were fortified.

Every day tears of blood would flow from the eyes of the White Lady and soon it figured as one of the principal news items in the international media. More investigation teams arrived from various scientific agencies to find out what was going on. Some of the rationalists opined that the sculptor might have cleverly installed a circuit of tubes inside the White Lady and that the red liquid or blood, whatever it was, flowed from a secret reservoir through the tubes either by way of some remote mechanism or as a result of changing temperatures and pressures of the atmosphere.

News arrived shortly that the red liquid flowing from the eyes of the White Lady was human blood. The phenomenon was further sensationalized by the media when it was declared by the investigating agencies that there was neither any secret reservoir nor any circuitry of tubes inside the sculpture.

Ideas of myriad kinds took rounds again. Religionists tried to have us believe that some kind of divine mechanism was at work. And those who are never willing to accept the existence of any possible phenomena that defy scientific logic, the ones whom I often refer to as the *so-called rationalists*, offered one scientific logic or the other as to why human blood was oozing out of the sculpture. Those in the middle of these two extremes also came up with various kinds of explanations. None of these ideas, however, sounded convincing and had to be dismissed when strong arguments were offered by some researchers to counter them.

The phenomenon had by now become nothing less than an obsession for the international media. The city of ours witnessed a sudden boom in domestic and international tourism. Documentary filmmakers and news gatherers also thronged the city. The White Lady had become a household name everywhere. Visuals of tears being cleaned and fresh tears appearing filled up most of the television space.

Many agencies also investigated into the paranormal phenomena, some of which are in professional partnership with the Bureau for Advanced Paranormal Research & Investigation (BAPRI), which is being run by me and Saikat Mukherjee, my adorable friend and co-researcher. The two of us now share the same apartment which I have been living in for more than a decade now. We have converted its living room into our office. The Bureau is indeed doing very well. Coming back to the White Lady and her tears, most of these agencies concluded that the phenomenon could be classified as a paranormal activity of the highest order which could not be explained with the tenets of known science. The remaining investigators could not arrive at any conclusion.

One day, as miraculously as it had begun, the statue stopped shedding tears of blood. The crowds kept a close watch for several days, and then their interest petered off. All except my own levels of curiosity. Thousands of questions continued to gnaw and nibble at the deepest layers of my senses. I pored over the collection of reports I had amassed over the days. A collage of explanations, all attempts at unearthing the truth. The White Lady continued to occupy my mind and no explanation seemed sufficiently agreeable to me. It was several months before I too gave up all attempts at piecing together the puzzle. Truth has a way of eluding itself to seekers…till the time is right. Unknown to me the truth about the statue was lurking in the shadows, waiting to be discovered and it would be time that would finally lift the veils off it.

For now I would have to wait…

1 A MYSTERY IT IS

It was an exciting day for me and Saikat as Neha paid her first visit to our bureau. She appreciated the way we had converted the living room of the apartment into a professional looking office. She was happy to see our huge collection of books on paranormal activities, science, philosophy and spirituality. She pulled out some of these books and skimmed through the pages quickly.

"This is indeed a great collection," she smiled.

"Thanks Neha," Saikat responded and looked at me. We exchanged smiles.

Meanwhile, Mrs. Veena Kapoor, our housekeeper came over and served tea and snacks. We settled down on our chairs and an interesting conversation ensued.

"What exactly is your bureau doing?" Neha said sipping tea.

"That is very difficult to tell," Saikat explained, "we don't have a very strict mandate. All I can say is that we are attempting to understand the unknown. The unknown, as you would appreciate, could lead us to understand hitherto unexplored realms of the universe. It is possible that what we call *paranormal* today might appear perfectly normal tomorrow in the context of the fresh knowledge that we unearth in the pursuit of the unusual and the unknown."

"That's very interesting. Do you also go on ghost hunts?"

"No Neha, we don't," I said, "but we are in touch with a number of ghost hunting agencies. Sometimes these ghost hunters conduct the preliminary investigations for us."

"Is ghost hunting a popular vocation in the city?"

"O yes," Saikat replied, "there are plenty of agencies that are involved in ghost hunting activities. The ones we work with are equipped with the latest of gadgetries to detect unusual presences such as EMF meters, motion sensors, EVP listeners and infra-red thermometers."

"They conduct preliminary investigations for the bureau, you said," she looked at me, "do you engage one or the other agency for every case you deal with?"

"No, not always, only when a case requires the kind of investigation they conduct," I responded, "these agencies come in very handy in cases of reported ghost sightings or unusual disturbances."

"What is your usual approach to a case?"

"Whenever a case comes to us, the first thing we need to do is to decide whether or not we should accept the case. Some of the cases that come to us are very shallow in nature. We do not accept such cases. We take up a case only when it feels meritorious enough for us to intervene. If the case in hand feels weighty enough and if it relates to paranormal phenomena such as ghost sightings, we usually engage a ghost hunting agency with a good track record. We ask the agency investigators to find out if the place we are supposed to look into is really haunted or not. We also tell them that if they find a place haunted, they should research into the history of the place and the possible reasons as to why it is haunted. Usually the reports they submit are very comprehensive. We go through those reports and make our own deductions. Thereafter, we undertake several visits to the place and try to help our clients in whatever way they want us to help them. More often than not, they want us to rid the place of ghosts. Now, we do not ourselves perform any ghost cleansing activity. We engage the spirit mediums and other people who have specialized in such activities to do the needful. Sometimes, although that happens very rarely, the clients want us to investigate into and report on aspects of history of the place far deeper than those that had been looked into by the ghost hunting agencies. Then there are some clients, again very few, who want us to research into the paranormal activities in question and come up with plausible philosophical explanations. However, these are not the only activities our bureau is involved in. Saikat had rightly pointed out that it is very difficult to explain as to what exactly the bureau does. There are far subtler activities that we undertake than the ones I just described. It perhaps would not be wrong to say that our research, which is more spiritual in nature than anything else, is the mainstay of the bureau."

"Hold on now, Biswajit," Neha said, "I would certainly like to know more about the research BAPRI is doing. But first tell me more about the ghost hunting agencies that work for you."

"I have already told you. We engage them, as and when required, to conduct preliminary investigations for us."

"That's fine, I understand that but what I don't understand is how do you deal with the biases that creep into your minds?"

"What biases are you talking about?" I asked though I could sense as to what she was referring to.

"From whatever you have said, I gather that you lay a good deal of importance on the reports submitted by the ghost hunting agencies in cases of reported ghost sightings. Is that right?"

"Yes," I nodded.

"But don't you think that such reports can make your judgment biased? It is possible that the ghost hunting agency that you have engaged tells you that the place in question is haunted whereas in reality it might be a perfectly safe place without any ghosts. Even the reverse could be true – the concerned agency might declare a place to be devoid of ghosts while the truth might be otherwise. So every time an agency's findings are at variance with the truth, you could be approaching the case with preconceptions."

"Having a degree of preconceptions in our minds cannot be ruled out," Saikat responded, "but we do not place absolute trust in the reports submitted by these agencies. There have been some occasions when our findings and their findings were completely different although we started out with the reports they had submitted."

"Indeed," I added on to what Saikat just explained, "we do initially form our opinions on such reports but if our investigations lead us to inferences different from what such reports suggest, we place credence on our findings and do not allow ourselves to run astray simply because others have inferred differently."

"Very interesting," Neha smiled, "okay, now tell me about your research."

"Just as the scope of our activities is difficult to explain, the nature of the research we are involved in is hard to explicate. I will nonetheless try. You might have read in many of my writings, and as Saikat explained a while ago, that what we deem as *paranormal* might actually be perfectly *normal*. In other words, it is possible that we are unable to appreciate something very normal because the level of science of our times is simply inept to explain them. And that is why we might be calling these things *paranormal*. It is also possible that in the years to come what we now think as *paranormal* would be treated as normal as our science would be developed enough to explain them. You would therefore appreciate that one of our primary research areas is to look for connecting links between the paranormal happenings and strings of scientific knowledge presently available to us. An important corollary to finding connecting links is to expand upon the science known to us. Naturally, we try to explore as many scientific possibilities as possible pertinent to the case in hand. Another major area of our research is the gamut of consciousness. This is a very large area as there are hundreds of theories on what consciousness is and how it came into being. Traditional science would have us believe that consciousness results from mere physical and chemical activities happening inside animates. In other words, consciousness is described as the result of interplay of apparently unconscious entities. On the other hand, spiritual science tells us that consciousness is the primal cause of everything one can perceive. Even the physical and chemical reactions inside animates result from the primal consciousness. Putting it more plainly – we repeatedly endeavor to find out if consciousness can exist independent of the body. If it can, the problem of whether or not there is life after death virtually stands solved. If it can be definitely shown that consciousness does not need a body, then the ancient assertions contained in the rich spiritual texts of Hinduism, and for that matter in the books of some other faiths, would stand substantiated."

"But in a number of articles you have mentioned about your out-of-the-body experience. So you don't need any proof to know that consciousness can exist independent of the body. Why do you need to do such research then?"

"Yes, I know that consciousness can exist independent of the body. But this truth has not been established scientifically. The word *scientifically* I am using over here does not refer to science as we understand it today. Rather I am referring to a much wider science that works hand-in-hand with the kinds of subjects we are dealing with. It is in the context of this wider science that we wish to establish that consciousness is completely independent of the body." I looked up at Neha to be sure that I had not delved too deep into ideas of philosophy.

"I am getting the hang of it, go on." She smiled apparently reading my mind.

"Our research does not end with the establishment of this possible empirical truth about consciousness. We wish to go further than that. This empirical truth could just act as a launcher for pushing us towards greater truths."

"What greater truths?"

"Greater truths about matter and energy. There are many questions that have remained unanswered for eons together. BAPRI is and will be making efforts to find answers to these questions."

"You mean questions that are confounding the physicists?"

"Not only the questions that are confounding the physicists but questions that have puzzled the best of brains of all times. Questions which have been answered time and again and yet we feel that we need to find better and still better answers to them. Have you read *My Paranormal Files: The Bureau*? That is my first book in the *My Paranormal Files* series."

"Oh yes," Neha smiled, "I have read it. I know why you are asking

– you have mentioned some of the questions that are of crucial importance to the evolution of humankind as a whole in that book, isn't it?"

"Well, I have made my own humble efforts. To my mind a major share of human endeavors should be devoted to finding answers to questions that have been befuddling humankind since time immemorial. There are hordes of questions that remain unanswered – *what is consciousness? Do we really exist? If yes, who are we? What are we supposed to do? Is there something such as God? If yes, what is His purpose of being? Why did He after all create the physical universe and the sufferings in it? And of course, who created God? Or is it that He is uncreated or self-created? And if indeed He is uncreated or self-created, wouldn't that be in violation of the principle that for every effect there is a cause? And if there could be an effect without a cause, why do we need the concept of a creator to explain the existence of the universe around us? Why can't we simply explore the possibility of this universe being an effect without a cause?* Well, the list of questions is endless."

"But don't you think, Biswajit, that such questions fall within the ambit of a larger discipline called *philosophy*?" Neha asked after pondering over my words for a while.

"No doubt, these are philosophical questions, so what?" I replied.

"As far as I understand you are conducting an advanced research into the paranormal phenomena. If that is true, should these larger issues which fall within the domain of philosophy concern you?"

"Absolutely," I asserted, "Nothing is beyond philosophy. Investigation into the paranormal and the unusual is intrinsic to philosophical research. I cannot imagine conducting these investigations in a manner so as to keep them divorced from the larger philosophical issues. Advanced research on paranormal for me is like an attempt to dig deeper into these larger issues. You could think of my interest in the paranormal as the starting point of my quest for the truth. Dealing with the *paranormal* is not an end in itself in the context of my work. I intuitively deem the *paranormal* as a key to unlock the secrets of self, God and existence."

"Wouldn't the path of Yoga be better to achieve such ends?"

"Sri Aurobindo had observed that all life is Yoga. So what I am doing is also not beyond the ambit of Yoga. In the context of Yoga, meditation, and other activities that hard-core spiritualists practice, I must say that I haven't received any inner call so far to pursue any such path in my quest for the Truth. Whatever little I have understood of my inner voices has led me to believe that my quest to unearth the truths behind the unusual phenomena is only a component of my larger quest for unfolding the secrets of existence or what you may call Absolute Truth." I spoke with my gaze down.

For a long time thereafter none of us spoke before Saikat broke the ice, "Perhaps that's the best way Biswajit could have explained what we are trying to do. So Neha, what is your take on BAPRI?"

"Unique and most interesting," Neha smiled.

"I am so glad you say that," Saikat said with a glow on his face.

There followed a small pause before Neha said, "I have come to the right place. Only you can help her."

"What do you mean, Neha?" I asked.

"Why do you think I am here, Biswajit?"

"I believe to meet us."

"That is for sure one reason but there is another one as well."

"I somehow sense a mystery," a twinkle played through Saikat's eyes.

"A mystery it is," Neha smiled in response.

2 A GIRL IN TROUBLE

"You mean you have brought us a case," I said.

"You are right, Biswajit, I have a case for you," Neha continued to smile.

"I can hardly wait to know what it is," Saikat responded.

"I have come here to seek your help for a very sweet girl. Both of you know her," She gave the two of us a serious look.

"Whom are you talking about?" I asked.

"I am talking about Vaishali, my assistant … or rather I should say my ex-assistant."

"You mean the girl we met in your office?" There were traces of excitement in Saikat's voice.

"That's right," nodded Neha, "The girl you met in my office the evening I tried to help Biswajit communicate with Prerna's spirit and failed. I have no doubts that Vaishali has some terrible problem. As far as I can sense, the problem is of unusual nature. Let me be rather plain, I believe she is in the midst of something paranormal. She is no longer working with me. Although we have had a beautiful relationship, as beautiful as that between two loving sisters, she somehow chose not to discuss her problem with me. Despite my repeatedly asking her, she preferred to keep things to herself. I can still vividly remember her panic-stricken eyes the day she finally left for her village. What an expression that was! I have never seen anybody that much frightened in my life. Her voice sounded as though somebody had grabbed her throat with all the force on earth. Her fear would not let her stand or walk steadily. With a lot of difficulty she carried her luggage down the stairs to the taxi. Before getting into the taxi she gave me one last look of frustration and utter helplessness as I watched from my balcony. As the taxi sped away with her, I looked on in complete realization of the fact that I had lost a highly knowledgeable and an efficient assistant and a terrific friend."

"You must have formed some idea" Saikat said after some thought, "as to what was her problem although she never told you."

"I am not sure if I have a good idea," she moved her head.

"If you don't have a good idea then how could you come to believe that she is in the midst of something paranormal?" Later I realized that I spoke those words rather too fast almost sounding rude. Maybe the smell of paranormal mystery had got the better of my command over my mannerisms for a moment.

"I have a very strong intuition, Biswajit. My vast experiences with the paranormal have made me so sensitive to unusual phenomena that I can intuit their presence even if they are far beyond the extent of my subtlest of senses."

"No doubt, you can do that", Saikat remarked, "but other than deducing intuitively, did you not notice anything unusual when she was around?"

"Nothing unusual happened in our vicinity but …"

"But what?" I could sense my curiosity rising constantly.

"I am not too sure if her presence can in any way be connected to that affair," Neha grew more pensive.

"What are you trying to say?" Saikat asked.

"You both know about the affair of the White Lady, don't you?" There was a sudden rush of excitement in her voice.

"You mean the incident of the sculpture shedding tears of human blood?" I said.

"Yes, that's the incident I am talking about. I felt a strange, though unlikely, connection between Vaishali and the White Lady."

"A connection between Vaishali and the White Lady ….." Saikat repeated her words in a puzzled voice.

"I will tell you the whole story," Neha continued, "everything was moving smoothly till Vaishali received a letter in our office one day. Minutes after she received the letter, she told me that she had to immediately leave for her village *Prithaka* as something urgent had come up there. When I asked her what was wrong, she would simply not give me a clear reply. Soon afterwards she left for her village. She returned after a month but now she was no longer the same Vaishali. Her sweet smile had completely disappeared from over her lips. A chronic fear reflected from her eyes all the time. She would speak very little and sometimes would also forget her responsibilities. In fact, some of the clients expressed a lot of displeasure at the way she spoke to them. At times, she also messed up with the works she was required to do in connection with the séances. I can remember at least four séances that went wrong because of the procedural mistakes she made. Despite all this happening, I never reproached her. I knew some serious issue kept her mind occupied all the time and it was very hard for her to concentrate on the work she was supposed to do. I asked her indirectly many times as to what was bothering her. But as before, she never gave a clear reply. That was not all – all along after her return from the village, I could sense something happening beyond what was apparent. As I told you before, my intuitive faculties suggested that her problem was not merely material in nature. It certainly had connections with the unusual. I also noticed a strange connection between her and the White Lady affair. The White Lady began to shed tears from the day she returned from *Prithaka*. And it stopped shedding tears from the day she left me for good. Now, this could be a mere coincidence. However, I felt I should tell you this as little details, regardless of how unimportant they appear, could sometimes be of great help in unfolding paranormal mysteries. I am not connecting her to the White Lady affair merely because the sculpture shed blood tears only so long as she stayed in the city after her return from *Prithaka*, but also because I often noticed her glued to the television news reports on the White Lady and the analyses thereof with strange facial expressions as though pitying the intelligence of those presenting the news reports and discussing the issue. You two might feel that my attempts at connecting Vaishali to the White Lady are quite obscure, and to be very honest I am not sure if I am doing the right thing by suggesting a possible link between that sweet girl and the horrifying event of that sculpture shedding blood tears … but it would be pretty foolhardy on my part to hide my thoughts on the issue from you, now that I want you to help Vaishali. That's all I have to say."

I went over all that Neha had said about her ex-assistant in my mind and so did Saikat as was evident from his expressions. Meanwhile, Neha appeared to relive some of the moments she had spent with Vaishali, for whom she had a heart full of sisterly love. Our conversation resumed only after the three of us were finished with our respective mental ventures.

"So what do you say," Neha said, "will you take up this case or not?"

"I guess we will," I responded and looked at Saikat.

Saikat nodded.

"Great," Neha smiled, "that's what I wanted to hear. But please understand that I want you to take up this case in a professional manner. You must not feel impelled to investigate into this issue without claiming your professional charges only because I happen to be a close friend of yours."

"But you did not charge us for the séance," Saikat smiled back.

"I would have charged you had the objective of the séance been met."

"Neha, I am sure you understand," I said, "that for people like us the work itself is the greatest reward. However, I completely appreciate your idea that profession should not be mixed up with friendship. If we do succeed in doing what you expect us to do, then you could give us what you think is worthy of our efforts."

"I am glad you say that, Biswajit," Neha smiled again, "so when do you want to begin the work?"

"Quite clearly the case that you have brought us needs urgent attention because if Vaishali is truly in the midst of something paranormal, then she might get badly harmed if we don't act upon this case immediately. So we will be in action right away," I replied.

"I completely endorse what Biswajit is saying," Saikat said.

"It is great to see the two of you wanting to act promptly," Neha responded, "so when do you wish to start for *Prithaka*?"

"The sooner the better," I said, "you could book our tickets for this week itself, if possible."

"Not our tickets," spoke Saikat, "book only Biswajit's ticket. I would not be able to join him as there are some other important cases pending over here. If both of us go to *Prithaka*, then these cases will suffer. In many of these cases, the clients have paid our entire fees in advance. They might not be very happy if none of us is available in the city to help them. I have a feeling that Vaishali's case will take a long time to solve. Therefore, it is not advisable that we both go to *Prithaka*."

"I guess Saikat is right," I remarked.

"But will you be able to manage it all alone, Biswajit? I can sense that Vaishali's case is not an easy one to handle. What if you land in trouble?" Neha said.

"I think I can handle it," I said, "in any case I am not supposed to be afraid of trouble now that I am dealing with the paranormal. Don't worry, Neha, I will be fine. You could book my ticket to *Prithaka*."

"*Prithaka*, as far as I know is quite a remote village in the northern part of the country. So it is not connected by any train or road service. The nearest station to *Prithaka* is *Shyamalpur*." Neha explained.

"But *Shyamalpur* is very far off … it is pretty close to the Himalayas, I believe."

"That's right, Biswajit, *Shyamalpur* is indeed that far, and *Prithaka* is still further and that too uphill. So you can imagine how remote a village *Prithaka* is. You could also gauge the degree of its remoteness from the fact that there is no electricity over there," Neha explained.

"No electricity," I murmured.

"Yes Biswajit, no electricity … after reaching *Prithaka*, you might feel you have gone centuries behind in time … the days when there was no electricity, and candles and lanterns used to be the only sources of light in the dark."

"So you are virtually sending me back in time?"

"You could say that," Neha smiled, "and I am sure you understand what challenges lie ahead of you."

"Well yes, I do understand," I nodded.

"Then I will ask my travel agent to book your train ticket to *Shyamalpur*."

"You could do that but I have some queries for you."

"Yes, I know there are some important issues to be explained," Neha nodded, "go ahead and ask your questions."

"There's hardly anything I know about Vaishali at the moment." I said.

"Indeed." Neha nodded again.

"Who are there in her family?"

"As far as I know, presently she does not have a family. Her father died when she was very young. And her mother died a few years back … she was in college at that time, I believe."

"You mean she is all alone?"

"Absolutely," replied Neha.

"So she lost both her parents before she could stand on her feet," I remarked.

"Well, she really had no need to stand on her feet."

"You mean she had a good monetary backing to fall back upon?"

"I think so, her mother left behind a good amount of money for her."

"She didn't have to struggle for a living ... at least on this count she has been lucky."

"She didn't have to struggle for a living but if my intuition is correct, she did have much more difficult struggles to deal with."

"Like what?"

"Like," she replied after a brief pause for thoughts, "dealing with her sensitivity to the paranormal."

"Are you suggesting that she had been in the grip of the paranormal even before the present problem started?"

"I am not sure. That is what I intuited.

I took some time to register her ideas before our conversation resumed.

"Did she finish her college education?" I asked.

"Yes, she did very well in her studies. She had graduated in psychology before she joined me."

"She studied psychology, that's quite interesting."

"Yes, she did," Neha said, "when she met me for the first time, she told me that she had all along been interested in subjects such as telekinesis, telepathy, yogic levitation, teleportation and the like. To understand such phenomena one needs to have a comprehensive understanding of the cognitive mechanisms of the human mind. And that was the primary reason why she took up psychology. She also told me that she was more interested in what is often branded as parapsychology rather than psychology. Vaishali was not happy that parapsychology is still not one of the mainstream subjects in our universities. When she approached me for a job, I could make out from her words that she possessed very good knowledge of the paranormal. That is why I took her as my assistant. It was only after I had worked with her for a week or so that I could sense her being receptive to the paranormal."

"If she is so well off, why did she have to look for a job?"

"Maybe because of her interest in parapsychology. Perhaps she thought she would learn more about the subjects of her interest if she worked with me."

"Does she have any siblings?"

"No."

"Does she own a house in her village *Prithaka*?"

"Yes, she does have a house in *Prithaka* by the name of *Latika Griha*. Her father had built that house long before she was born and named it after her mother Latika." Neha said as she cleaned her throat.

"*Latika Griha*," I said reflectively, "That translates down to *Latika's house*, isn't it?"

"Yes, that's right. In fact, every house at *Prithaka* is identified by a name … the district authorities haven't allotted numbers to those houses or the plots on which they have been built."

"Who stays in *Latika Griha* now?"

"I guess she is the only one who stays there. The house had been lying empty and unused till she returned to her village," Neha continued to answer my questions patiently.

"Okay," I said with my gaze at the ceiling and going over the answers Neha had given me so far in my mind.

"Any other questions?" Neha said after I had stretched my pause for thoughts a bit too long.

"Yes," I nodded with my eyes still on the ceiling, "Who do you think sent her the letter that apparently started her distress?"

"She never told me, Biswajit. It is for you to find it out."

"Now tell me," I said after another pause for thoughts, "would you want me to help her by staying in the backdrop and without letting her know that I am looking into her case, or by being in open and constant touch with her?"

"I believe you should be in open and constant touch with her. As far as I can understand, her problem is a pretty complicated one and needs constant support of someone like you. That is why there is no need to observe any secrecy. I rather advise that you stay in her house itself in *Prithaka* as she could be in need of your help anytime."

"How about staying in a nearby inn?"

"Given the remoteness of *Prithaka*, I doubt if there are any inns over there. And in any case staying in an inn could defeat the very purpose of your going there. Her problem, as I have already explained, is of a difficult nature and she might need professional intervention at any time."

"What if she does not like my professional intervention in her matter? Since she chose not to tell you anything despite your being like a close sister to her, it is understandable that she is not comfortable with any possible intrusion into her privacy in the context of this matter. What makes you feel that she will confide her problem in me?"

"There again I have my gut feeling to fall back upon," Neha responded, "I believe she will welcome your presence."

"What if she doesn't?"

"Then just have your return ticket booked from *Shyamalpur* and come back. In case you need to put up somewhere for a day or two, choose any good inn at *Shyamalpur*."

"Okay, that's fine with me," I said, "but there's another issue – how do I explain my sudden appearance at *Prithaka* to her?"

"I will write a letter to her explaining very clearly that I have engaged you to help her and that she should let you do so by cooperating in every way. I could post the letter to her for advance information or you could carry it personally to her. I guess your carrying it personally would be the better thing to do as I am not too sure how good the postal service is at *Prithaka*."

"What kind of a place are you sending Biswajit to," Saikat said on a lighter note.

Neha smiled in response. "It would not be wrong to say that I am sending Biswajit to one of the most obscure parts of the globe. It is a place with no public service offices, no hospitals, no electricity, no places for public entertainment, and of course no e-mails. The list of what is not there in *Prithaka* is endless. But I am sure Biswajit will not mind all this as long as *Prithaka* holds a good paranormal adventure for him. Am I not right, Biswajit?"

"Well, you couldn't have been more right," I smiled.

"Are you through with your questions?"

"Yes, Neha" I smiled, "I guess I should be on my way to *Prithaka* at the earliest."

3 HINTS OF DESTINY

The journey to *Shyamalpur* was a long and arduous one. As if nature wanted to give an inkling as to what strange things were to follow during my stay at *Prithaka*, the journey itself turned out to be quite weird. There were not too many passengers in the train. Right in front of me sat two men, both with very dull features, often peering at me as though they had been planted to carry out some secret plan against me. In the entire journey lasting for around fourteen hours, they didn't exchange a single word with each other ... at least in my presence they didn't speak. And whenever they stared at me, I felt utterly uncomfortable. Normally I don't react to what people do around me. However, at one point of time during the journey their gazing appeared so invasive that I asked them if they had any problem with my sitting there. In response, they looked at each other and then passed stupid smiles. As if these two strange creatures were not enough for my discomfort, an ugly looking man with a pointed beard boarded the train from a station roughly lying midway along the route. His clothes were dirty and so was his body and despite my ensuring a safe distance between us his sweaty smell was unavoidable. He surely looked like one belonging to what the governmental authorities of this country often refer to as the deprived classes.

But then his mere presence in the first class bogey put to test the usually accepted descriptions and notions of deprivation. How could he afford the ticket, I wondered. The worst part about him was his murmuring of some terribly sounding chants. The chanting almost sounded like an unending siren of a factory.

My horrific odyssey ended with the arrival of *Shyamalpur*. How relieved I was after getting down from the train! The relief, however, was short-lived for I realized soon that the place I was standing in wasn't a friendly one. It was close to nine in the evening but there was hardly any sign of life in the railway station of *Shyamalpur*. I seemed to be the only hope for humanity on the forlorn platform. There were hardly any lights in the station. With a great amount of difficulty I used what felt like a very fragile metallic bridge connecting the railway station to the outer world. I wondered as I walked out of the exit gate if I would get any transport to *Prithaka*. I was relieved to see a couple of horse carriages lined up outside the station. One of the drivers of the carriages walked up to me.

"Should I take you to an inn, Sir?" The driver said.

"I want to go to *Prithaka*," I responded.

"*Prithaka* is up on that hill," he pointed at one of the hills visible at some distance, "and the path to it is a twisty one. Would you like to go there right now or tomorrow in the morning?"

"I wish to go there now," I said with my eyes on the hills. Their silhouettes against the dark sky made a glorious vista! Some of the hilltops shined even in the very dim light the night offered. Apparently, those hilltops were snowcapped.

"It is a long way, Sir," the driver said pointing at the hill again.

"You mean it will be difficult for you to drive?"

"It is always difficult to manage these horses on the twisty ways in the darkness."

"That means I have no choice but to spend the night in an inn at *Shyamalpur*?"

"I didn't mean that, Sir."

"Then what did you mean?"

"Sir," the driver spoke with some hesitation, "at night we charge double of what we charge during the day."

"That's not a problem."

Very soon I was on the twisty road to *Prithaka*. It was real twisty! The deft driver maneuvered his horses skillfully through the hills. The beauty of the hills in the dark night was unmistakable! The more I moved up the hill, the more beautiful the hills looked. The hills had a thick cover of vegetation and some of the trees were exceptionally tall. Some looked like ghosts waving their arms to catch my attention and some simply danced to the rhythms of the winds. There was one which was shining brightly and I wondered how. I could not help asking the driver about this strange tree.

"How is that tree shining in such darkness?" I said.

"Sir, that is a *ghost tree*. *Ghost trees* always shine no matter how poor the light conditions are."

"*Ghost tree*! That's a strange name for a tree."

"These trees are very common in this place, Sir."

"Very strange trees indeed."

"There are many things about the hills and the forest covers that are very strange, Sir."

"Hmmm," I responded nodding.

"But Sir, there are things stranger than these hills and these forests," his tone suddenly grew serious.

"What are you talking about?"

"The place you are going to, for instance, is much stranger than the strangest things of the hills and the forests."

"Why do you say so?" I tried not to allow my curiosity to show up in my speech.

"*Prithaka* is full of deadly ghosts."

"Don't people stay there?"

"People do stay there, Sir … but very few. After all it is not a very friendly place to stay in. It is cut off from the main township and it is too high up on the hills. That's why not many people wish to buy property in *Prithaka*. On the top of that, there is that problem …"

"Which problem?"

"I just told you, Sir," replied the driver, "*Prithaka* is full of deadly ghosts."

"These ghosts are very harmful, you mean?"

"You city folks might not believe in ghosts but the truth is they exist and can cause a lot of harm."

"What about the inhabitants of *Prithaka*? Don't these deadly ghosts harm them?"

"Most of these inhabitants know how to put up with ghosts," he said, "some of them also know how to control these spirits."

"Where do you stay?" I asked.

"I stay in a village close to Shyamalpur, Sir."

"Do you have to carry passengers to *Prithaka* very often?"

"Very often, Sir," the driver replied, "many inhabitants of *Prithaka* have their offices and businesses in *Shyamalpur*. There is no school over there. So all children of *Prithaka* study in various schools in *Shyamalpur*. And of course people from the village also visit *Shyamalpur* for purchase of goods including food items. Therefore, we have to carry passengers from and to *Prithaka* very often … almost on a daily basis."

"Doesn't it make you jittery going to *Prithaka*, whenever you have to go there?"

"Not really," he said, "we horse cart drivers are used to going there. And in any case, poor people like us cannot afford to be afraid. If out of fear we stop taking passengers, then we shall not be able to survive."

Meanwhile I noticed that the twisty path had given way to a smoother and straighter road sandwiched by very thick forests. As we moved along, the density of trees on both sides waned, and soon I found myself in the midst of what looked like a desolate village. Although there was little light, I could still sketch a good picture of the village in my mind. Distant highlands simply cast a spell on me. The tiny houses visible on them brought images of the beautiful English countryside to my mind. I checked the time on my mobile phone, it was close to ten-thirty! Strange that more than an hour had passed since I had taken the cart! The conversation with the driver was so engrossing that I almost lost sense of time. The village was not fully in the grip of sleep as was evident from light emanating from some of these houses. The deeper we moved into the village, the more attractive it looked. And then came the most beautiful part of the village. It was a rivulet! From the position I was in, it looked like a swerving streak of silver. *Kal kal kal kal* sounds of its movements added to its beatific appearance. Indeed, pristine nature could be beautiful even in the night! The cart moved on and by the time we were in the heart of the village with beautiful highlands and thin and thick forest stretches surrounding us, I was almost in a meditative state.

"Which house do you want to go to, Sir?" The driver's words pulled me back from my musings.

"*Latika Griha*," I replied.

"What? What did you say, Sir?" A chill could be sensed in his voice.

"I said *Latika Griha*."

"*Latika Griha*," he repeated and drove on.

"Why do you sound jittery?" I asked.

"Sir …" He hesitated.

"Come on now, tell me."

"Sir, do you know to whom that house belongs?"

"A young girl stays there now, I guess."

"She is just the daughter of the one I am referring to," he responded.

"Are you talking about her mother?"

"Yes, her mother's name was Latika. Do you know who she was?"

"No."

"She was the most wicked witch in this part of the country," the driver said, "God knows how many people she harmed in her life. She was known to command hundreds of spirits, most of them evil. She died some years ago but it is said that her spirits are still roving around everywhere. It is not my business to tell you this, Sir, but I still deem it to be a duty to warn you from going there. Going there could be suicidal."

"Thanks for your advice but I have some professional commitments."

"Excuse me for saying this Sir, but is your work more important than your life?"

"Are you suggesting that the girl is as evil as her mother was?"

"All I am saying is that it is not a good idea to associate oneself with anything or anyone connected to Latika. In any case, there is a buzz around that Latika's daughter is also following her footsteps."

"You mean she is also a witch?" I asked.

"I think so. It is an open secret that she is learning witchcraft. Many have seen her sitting atop the *Mahachoti hill*, the highest hillock of this region and also known to be infested with spirits. As far as I know, the people in *Prithaka* have, for all practical reasons, ostracized her socially for her questionable activities. If I had known that you would be going to *Latika Griha*, I would have refused to bring you here. I would never want to be a party to something as suicidal as this. Think over again, Sir." The terror in his voice had intensified.

"Look, good man, I heartily thank you for your kind concern but I have not come this far to go back."

"What can I say, Sir? My job was to advise you and I have done so. The decision is all yours," he said with clear shades of disappointment.

Minutes later I was before *Latika Griha*. The driver was in an utter hurry and moments after he received his payment, he sped his cart away from my sight.

4 I MEET MY BEAUTIFUL HOSTESS

Latika Griha was shining like an edifice made of special stones. It was a two-storey building built in Gothic style surrounded by a bushy fence. The two ends of the fence met at a small metallic gate which led up to the main entrance. As I moved closer to the gate, I had a better glimpse of the building. Its shine appeared all the more pronounced. The outer wall that faced me carried skillfully crafted figures and in the light of a small lantern hanging roughly in the centre of the wall, they appeared to be endowed with ethereal qualities. I pushed the gate open and treaded up to the entrance. Right from the time I started my journey from our residence-cum-office, the thought as to how Vaishali would react on seeing me had been hovering in my mind. The thought now turned most intense. However, I was confident that even if she were not to allow me to investigate into the problem that plagued her, she would be courteous enough to accommodate me for the night at least so that I could go back to *Shyamalpur* the next day to make further arrangements for my return journey. Finally I was there – at the threshold of what would turn out to be one of the greatest paranormal adventures of my life! I raised the small handle meant for the purpose of knocking and struck it several times against the wooden entrance. A couple of minutes passed without any response. I raised the handle again and knocked the door harder. Moments later I heard some movements inside. The movements got louder and soon I could hear someone unbolting the door. The large door opened creakily and I was now face-to-face with Vaishali. She had changed all together. In the light of the small lantern she was holding, I could make out that her sweet looks had indeed made way for a troubled disposition, just as Neha had described. She was undoubtedly beautiful still but an element of what can be best described as aggression and uncertainty made itself visible in her beauty. Her hair was unkempt and fell over her shoulders. Her somewhat carelessly worn loose gown looked too large for her frame. Her dark eyes carried a piercing look and her sharp nose swelled up often as she tried to make sense of the goings-on. Vaishali's thin lips showed a tremble or two before a faint smile appeared on them.

"Mr. Banerjee, I believe," Vaishali's smile widened.

"Yes, indeed," I smiled back and nodded, "I must have taken you by surprise."

"No Mr. Banerjee, I knew you would come."

"What … really," I could not hide my puzzlement, "but how?"

"Do you wish to discuss everything standing outside?" Her magical smile reappeared.

 I smiled too and went in. She closed the door behind me and then led me to the living room. It was a small room illuminated by fixed wall lanterns on opposite walls. It had four large chairs with a round table at the centre. The wall that I faced now had a large window. Its curtains played to the eccentricities of the wind.

"Please sit down, Mr. Banerjee," she said, "you must be very tired. I shall make you some tea."

"Tea will be great, Vaishali," I responded, "but I really feel bad about troubling you at this hour."

"*This hour*," she laughed, "for me all hours are the same, Mr. Banerjee … there is no *this hour* or *that hour*. I keep making and sipping tea all through the day, sometimes even in the middle of the night. So don't worry – making some tea now is no problem at all."

I kept my luggage close to a wall and sat with the window to my left. The hilly winds brushing past me were truly comforting. Shortly, Vaishali was back with tea. She placed the tray with two cups of tea and a plate carrying biscuits arranged in a circular fashion on the table and took the chair placed across me.

"Since we shall be having dinner soon, it will not be a good idea to stuff ourselves with heavy snacks. That is why all that I am offering you now with tea is biscuits," Vaishali said as she tenderly pushed the biscuits and a teacup towards me, "please feel at home, Mr. Banerjee."

"Biscuits are fine," I picked up a biscuit and the teacup, "in fact, they would be more than enough."

"So Neha Madam thought that you could help me."

"Well, yes, you are right," I nodded and took out Neha's letter, "she has written this for you."

She took the letter from my hand and got up from the chair. "Wait a minute," Vaishali said and walked away from the living room. She was back soon with the same cuboidal lantern. She placed it on the table and read the letter.

"Very sweet on her part to be so concerned about me," she said smilingly, "she has always been like an elder sister."

"O yes, she loves you a lot," I responded.

"No doubt she does but she failed to appreciate the state I am in."

"She never claimed that she understands your problem," I said after a brief period of silence.

"Yet she has sent you to me," a smile of despondence came over her lips.

These were uncomfortable moments for me. She had been very polite and welcoming so far and yet her words and expressions somehow conveyed that I was of little or no use to her.

"Please don't feel bad about my words, Mr. Banerjee," she continued, "I just spoke my mind. I appreciate her concern and all the trouble you have taken to come to this remote village with the intent to help me but the truth is nobody can help me."

"Well, Vaishali," I chose my words with care, "I shall certainly not intervene in this matter if you don't want me to. And in case you feel my presence could accentuate your problem, I shall leave without the slightest complaint. All I want is your well-being."

We finished our tea without exchanging any more words. Then she got up from the chair and said, "Come with me. I will show you your room. I hope you will not mind staying in the upper storey."

"Certainly not," I got up from my chair and picked up my luggage.

She guided me through the winding staircase to my room. Vaishali pushed open the door and raised her lantern to help me enter. The room was a spacious one made somewhat in the pattern of the living room. There was a large window at some distance from the bed and its translucent curtains played the same dancing games with the hilly winds. Two lanterns, one fixed on the wall right next to the side of the bed with fluffy pillows and the other fixed on the opposite wall, provided a good amount of light. Close to the wall with the window were a table and a chair. A small lantern and a matchbox were placed towards one side of the table meant to be used for study purposes. Indeed, just as Neha had said, I felt like being in a daintily arranged room of the bygone eras. Vaishali opened the door of the small washroom attached to my room. It was dark inside. She picked up a matchbox from what looked like a small washroom shelf, took out a matchstick and lit it up. I could now see a mirror and a couple of shelves on the wall to our right. There was also a beautiful sink under the mirror. There was, however, no water tap. That was understandable for there was no electricity in *Prithaka* and therefore no scope for any water supply. A metallic rod stood against the same wall. Vaishali drew it towards her. There was a wick at the end of the rod. She lit it up with the matchstick and then raised the rod up towards a lantern fixed a couple of feet over the mirror. The light from the lantern spread uniformly to all sides. Now I knew how she lit up the lanterns fixed at such formidable heights on the walls of her house.

"You might not find the settings very comfortable. There's no electricity. The people at *Prithaka* are still living in medieval settings," She looked at me.

"I guess I can manage."

"You have to use the water from those buckets," Vaishali pointed at the buckets in one corner of the washroom, "all of them contain fresh water. I filled them up this morning itself."

"It must be a lot of hard work filling these buckets and climbing up the stairs with them."

"I have been doing such things since my childhood … not a big deal for me."

"From where do you get fresh water? From the rivulet?

"Yes," she nodded, "every household in the village has a channel cut out from the rivulet which brings its water to a small reservoir, usually built in the rear of the house. There is a covering which can be adjusted to allow or stop the flow of water. Once the water is collected in the reservoir, it is cleaned, first by filtration and then by heating it with a surrounding stove fuelled by coal. Some of us also use chemicals to treat the water to ensure complete hygiene. Well, this is indigenous technology at work, you see!"

"That means a large network of pipelines is operating in the village."

"No, Mr. Banerjee … there are not many households in *Prithaka*."

"How many are there?"

"Around fifty, that's all."

"Interesting," I remarked.

"So, there are no reasons to worry, Mr. Banerjee," she laughed, "the water we use at *Prithaka* is completely fresh and hygienic."

"I am not worried about that at all," I laughed too, "I am pretty immune to infections, I assure you."

"Okay then, after freshening up you could come downstairs. Meanwhile, I shall arrange the dinner."

"Will you have to cook some food now?" I asked.

"I don't think so, there is enough food for the two of us," she replied, "you get ready quickly and come downstairs."

"Okay, thank you so much, Vaishali."

"Just a piece of advice for you – the hilly climate is very unpredictable. I suggest you don't take a bath now lest you should catch cold, just a mere wash would be fine, I believe," she smiled again.

"Thanks for your concern, I will do as you say."

5 POSSIBLE SIGNS OF EVIL

The dinner table had been very neatly arranged and the food was very good. There were four vegetable curries and dal to go along with very carefully prepared fried rice. I enjoyed the food but not the conversation as her manners had taken a u-turn. The sweetness of her approach was completely gone!

"The food is excellent," I said.

She just nodded with an impassive look.

"Did you really have an intuition that I would come?"

"What do you mean?" She responded.

"You have prepared so much of food, it appears as though you knew that I would be here at dinner with you today?"

"Mr. Banerjee," Vaishali replied with shades of sternness, "didn't I tell you at the door that I knew you would come?"

"Yes, you did but …" I found myself completely unprepared for a coherent reply.

"But what, Mr. Banerjee? You didn't believe me?" these words were even sterner.

"No ... I didn't mean that ..." Yet again I fumbled with my expressions.

"I knew very well that you would be here. That is why I changed the water of the buckets in the washroom upstairs and that is why I prepared so much of food."

"Okay," I nodded.

The next few minutes passed without a word exchanged. The heaviness of the air around was beginning to make itself feel when she said, "Would you like to have anything more?"

"No Vaishali," I moved my head.

"Fine then, I am very tired and need to sleep. That is my bedroom," she pointed at a room connected to the dining space through a very small passage, "in case you need anything, just let me know. I will take your leave now. Don't bother about the utensils, leave them on the table itself after you finish eating. I will clean them in the morning. Good night, Mr. Banerjee, we will talk in the morning.

"Good night," I said feeling low.

"One more thing," she said as she moved towards her room, "let me tell you how to put off the wall lanterns. You saw me using the rod with a wick in your washroom, didn't you?"

I nodded.

"The other side of the rod has a cup like structure. All you have to do is to hold the cup over the flame and the lantern will be put off. Do you understand?" Shades of sternness became all the more prominent in her voice.

"Yes," I nodded again.

"There are separate rods for the room and the washroom, the one for the room is longer," she said as she pushed open the door of her bedroom.

"I understand."

I finished whatever crumbs were left on my dish and went upstairs. It was clear that she did not want my involvement in the matter and the best thing I could do was to leave at the earliest opportunity the next morning.

I put off the lanterns and got into the bed. I had been through a very tiring journey and yet sleep eluded me. The sudden change in Vaishali's behavior was too difficult to digest. What could have made her angry with my presence so suddenly? Till sometime back things seemed to be all right, her words had never suggested that I was welcome to investigate into her problem but they were never harsh enough to explicitly convey that I was completely unwanted. What she said and the way she said it at the dinner table flummoxed me to the limits. But then, was I right in inferring that I was unwanted? Could the thought of my leaving *Prithaka* be too premature? I told myself not to act impulsively. Maybe I was simply pondering over what was visible at the surface. It was possible that something terrible was happening in the depths of the matter that I was unable to fathom. Could it be that some force or some entity compelled her to speak so rudely to me? It was possible that the force did not want her to be helped in any way and was simply trying to cut off all possible support from her. Countless overlapping thoughts hammered my mind on all sides till I was capable of thinking no more. Soon sleep had the better of me.

Suddenly a shrill cry broke my sleep. I sat down wondering as to what I had heard. Did I really hear something or was the cry a construct of my tired mind? I looked out of the window. The signs of dawn appeared too far away. My mobile phone still had some charge left. I pressed its *home button* and saw the time. It was 1.59 a.m. I got up and moved over to the window. The winds were still playing a wild game with its curtains. It was really dark outside. I looked up and could spot some common constellations on the clear sky. I had never seen stars so bright in my life. This part of the country which was nearly divorced from the so-called developed areas could be the perfect home for a positional astronomer. I remembered my good old days in college when I was an active member of the Amateur Astronomers' Club of the city. We used to hold so many camps for star gazing but hardly any turned out to be satisfactory for the obvious reason of the city being too developed. The glaze of the city accentuated by its pollution used to be our greatest enemy. I wondered how my friends and I would have felt if we had a chance to hold a star gazing camp in *Prithaka* at that time. In a while when my pupils were more adjusted to the light conditions outside I had a clearer impression of the landscape. Beyond the fields that extended up to a little distance from the house there were hills all around. Evidently, the forest cover over them was dense. The highest of these hills appeared very daunting. It was too high for the hills surrounding it and its top looked almost like a pointed arrow. Was it the highest peak in *Prithaka*, I wondered. Then came the cry again! Unmistakably, it was the same cry that had broken my sleep. It was shrill and full of pain! And I hated to infer so but it was strongly human! Who could it be? Some animal from the woods? Or some human in the vicinity? Then it came again and yet again. No doubt, it sounded human. Saikat Mukherjee had once told me that there are many animals and birds in some parts of the Himalayan woods that shriek like humans. Could it be one such animal or bird? The possibility that I had the least intention of exploring was if Vaishali could be the source of the shriek. I had to reckon this possibility anyway as the cry pierced the air again. This time the cry was more intense as though the pain of the being had become worse. No, it couldn't be her, I reasoned. Such a soul-tearing cry could not emanate from Vaishali's throat regardless of how bad a shape she was in. I could describe what happened next as one of the most chilling experiences of my life. A white figure, flashy and distinct, ran past the place adjoining the house at a lightning speed. It was a luminous humanoid! What was it? Just a flash from some unseen source which my brain interpreted as resembling a human? No, that was very unlikely, I reasoned. It couldn't have been a mere flash of light. But then, if it was truly a humanoid, what was it? A ghost? Some demoniac being? I felt my hair standing up. The last time fear gripped me so heavily was when I saw the whistling spirit in the Tailabi Hills with Prerna by my side. I walked back to the bed completely unsettled. I also wondered if it could be a warning from the other side. It was then that the cry came again – louder and more distinct. I had no doubt in my mind now that it was a human cry. Maybe it came from the flashy humanoid figure I just witnessed. As I felt fear gripping me, a very uncomfortable thought crossed my mind. Could it be Vaishali trying to frighten me ... was it all her doing? I hated to think that she was after my life but I could hardly ignore that possibility. I sat down on the bed panting heavily. The conditions were quite wintry, yet I could feel the flow of sweat over my face. Then the thoughts of Swapanda came to my mind. He had once during the course of a conversation mentioned that fear is never good for a person placed in circumstances such as those I found myself in. Fear could feed the unseen forces allowing them to attack with greater ferocity. I had read a number of narratives on ghost and poltergeist activities wherein the evil forces had assumed greater power because their victims had given in to their fears. So it was important for me not to be afraid. I pushed myself to face the situation head-on. It wasn't easy to keep calm for the forces around me appeared very powerful and hell-bent upon harming me. Yet, I had little choice but to be composed and in charge of myself. I chanted the holy name of Lord Krishna and it helped me. In a while I felt better and my breathing became normal. I don't know how long I sat there with a blank gaze and never quite understood as to when I fell asleep.

I was woken up by the slanting rays of sun caressing my face. I got up and found a paper lying on my side. It was a note from Vaishali. It read: *I have changed the water in the buckets; the breakfast is ready on the dining table. After you are done, you could come over to the side of the rivulet, if you want. I will be there till noon. From the steel gate walk to your left, first you would see a streak of thick trees. Once you cross these trees, you will get a clear view of the rivulet. You would find me sitting on one of the prominent rocks jutting out from the edge of the rivulet – Vaishali.*

It was strange indeed that she entered my room in the morning and apparently did a number of things including filling the buckets with fresh water and leaving the note on my bed, while I slept all the while! I looked around and found that she had also arranged my things properly on a large wooden rack placed a little away from the study table. My neatly folded clothes placed on hangers were dangling from a wall cupboard with a glass cover. Some of my notebooks had been beautifully arranged on the study table. My glasses were lying on a small round table towards the right of my bed. O my God! She did all this while I was sleeping! It was embarrassing to think that she might have seen me sleeping in a reckless way on the bed. I didn't know what to think of her! Her gesture was appreciable and yet I couldn't help reckon all this as an intrusion into my privacy. I was angry with myself for not bolting the door at night. But then bolting the door would also perhaps not be the right thing to do. Who could tell whether or not a bolted door would infuriate her. Making any judgments about her mood after what I saw of her last night would be unintelligent. I also wondered as to how her movements could have been so smooth and quiet so as not to cause my sleep to break. After having wrestled with my thoughts for a while I realized that it was no point spending time over what happened in the morning, and that it was more important to mentally ready myself for the possible challenges of the day. It was time to move on …

6 THE EXTENDED BUT BLUNTED PEAK

When I left the house I wondered if I was expected to lock the entrance door from outside. But then I had the least idea as to where to look for the lock and the key. And most certainly it would not be the right thing to fiddle with Vaishali's things without her knowledge. So the best I could do was to shut the door tight from outside and that's what I did.

Vaishali's directions were very good. I had no difficulty in spotting her on the rock jutting out prominently from a place towards the periphery of the rivulet. Her eyes were closed and she looked to be in deep meditation. I chose to sit on a rock a little away from the one she was sitting on. The rivulet's *kal kal kal kal* sounds had a soothing effect on me in no time. Its rhythm was far better than the best of musical symphonies I had ever heard.

"Good morning, Mr. Banerjee," Vaishali's voice brought me out of my growing meditative stupor.

"Good morning, Vaishali," I said softly after opening my eyes.

"Did you take your breakfast?" There was again warmth in her words.

"Yes."

"I hope I left enough for you to eat on the table."

"You left more than enough, Vaishali, it was a rather heavy breakfast."

"And did you sleep well?"

I nodded softly vanquishing my urge to jumpstart a discussion on what I saw and heard last night.

"You really did?"

I looked up at her trying to gauge what she was trying to say. It was impossible to read from her face as to what was going on in her mind.

"I slept," that is the best I could think of as a response.

Quite a few minutes passed thereafter without any exchange of words. The sounds of the rivulet and the birds around appeared all the more pronounced during this interval.

"I come here every morning," Vaishali finally said with her eyes on the rivulet.

"This place is really beautiful."

She didn't respond.

"What is this rivulet called?" I spoke again after a while.

"*Tarangini.*"

"*Tarangini*, that's a lovely name."

"*Tarangini* is the most renowned musical work of Narayana Teertha, one of the best Carnatic music composers of the 17th century. No other name would have suited this rivulet. This is nothing but a material expression of a soulful musical composition." A poetic expression adorned her face.

"I completely agree with you. This is nature at its very best!"

"But Mr. Banerjee," she looked at me, "all this beauty is nothing but a veil."

"A veil? I am sorry I don't quite understand that."

"Maybe you will understand if you decide to stay on."

"Do you want me to stay on?" I asked candidly.

"I don't know what to say, Mr. Banerjee," she turned her gaze towards the rivulet again.

"I would certainly not want to stay on if my presence could cause any problem for you."

"Your presence could only cause a problem to yourself, Mr. Banerjee," shades of sternness returned to her voice.

"Your words are quite puzzling, Vaishali," I chose to be candid.

At this she had a hearty laugh. Her shining hair covered a part of her face as she laughed carelessly. Despite the elements of hostility I felt in her tone, I could not help appreciate her radiant beauty.

"So you find my words funny," I said.

"No, Mr. Banerjee, I am not laughing at your words," she said with spills of laugher still in her voice, "I am laughing at myself."

"At yourself?"

"Yes, Mr. Banerjee," she looked at me again.

"Why?"

"My life has become a joke, Mr. Banerjee … I don't know what to do with it. That's why you might sometimes find my words very strange and incomprehensible. Simply ignore my words if you don't like them and never take them to your heart."

"Why do you say your life has become a joke?"

"I wish I could answer that question."

"Answer this question at least – do you want me to intervene in your matter or not?"

"You mean if I want your help or not?" She smiled.

"Yes."

"Well, who doesn't want help, Mr. Banerjee?"

"Does that mean you want me to resolve your problem?"

"Are you aware what my problem is?"

"No, how can I know if you don't tell me."

"Mr. Banerjee …" She looked for words.

"Is it a problem you cannot discuss?"

"Something like that," she nodded.

"So my staying here is of little use," I said in a dejected tone.

She did not answer and turned her gaze towards the rivulet again. For a long time thereafter we sat there listening to the rivulet. Vaishali closed her eyes, so did I. The rhythm of the river worked as the perfect lullaby and I fell asleep. A strange dream followed. I saw elves and fairies flying over *Tarangini*. I turned around and found elves and fairies in all directions. I also had a glimpse of the highest and the steepest hill of the region that I had spotted from my bedroom window the night before. There was something different about its peak. Every time I wanted to find out as to what was different about it, the elves and fairies blocked my vision. I turned towards the rock on which Vaishali was sitting. Vaishali wasn't there anymore. I thought I would get a better view of the hill if I climbed that rock. I did so and looked at the tip again. Surely, something was different about the tip. Yet again, the elves and fairies crossed my line of vision. 'Move away, move away,' I shouted. It worked. They moved away and now I could see the tip of the hill without disturbance. I soon discovered as to what was different about it. Its penetrative appearance had changed. Last night the tip appeared just like the head of an arrow. Now, it looked as though something had been put over the head so as to give it an extended but duller appearance. What was it? I concentrated harder and realized it was a human standing on it. The more I concentrated the greater was the clarity of my vision. It was almost like zooming in on the tip. Then I knew who was standing there. It was Vaishali. I wondered why? 'Vaishali, what are you doing there?' I said. Despite the miles that separated us she seemed to have heard me. And then she opened her lips and said, 'This is my destiny, Biswajit.' I could hear her clearly. It was as if she had whispered the words into my ears. 'What is your destiny, Vaishali?' I asked. She smiled. It was however not the sweet smile that brightens her face up. It looked just the opposite of that. The more I focused on her smile, the more I wanted to cry. And then I realized that it was not her smile at all. It was death smiling through her lips. Before I could say another word, she bent down and let herself fall freely into the terrible depths of nothingness. It was all over. I screamed in horror.

"Are you okay, Mr. Banerjee?" Vaishali's words seemed to flow in from a great distance.

Then I felt a jerk inside me and woke up to find her standing before me with a concerned look.

"You seem to have had a bad dream," the comfort her beatific smile brought to my eyes is indescribable.

I struggled to get command of my senses as she placed a hand tenderly on my head and said, "You have been sleeping for quite a while, Mr Banerjee. I didn't wake you up as you might not have got adequate rest last night."

So it was the second time she saw me sleeping in the morning. It felt embarrassing again. However, beyond these mortal feelings lay the pleasure of seeing her all right.

"It must have been a terrible dream," she said, "as you slept you looked more and more uncomfortable, and then you shrieked."

"O yes," I nodded as I stood up, "it was a very bad dream."

She looked up at the sky and said, "The sun is almost on our heads, it is time to go back. Come …"

I followed her back to *Latika Griha*. As she opened the metallic gate, my eyes fell on the unlocked door.

"I could not lock the door as I had no idea where the lock and key were," I remarked.

"Don't worry about that," Vaishali responded, "thieves don't come here."

"There are no thieves here?"

"That's not what I said," she smiled, "I said thieves don't come here."

"Why?"

"Because they are afraid of me," she pushed the entrance door open.

"Why?"

"If you are staying on, then you will know why."

I did not drag the discussion any further. It was of little use. Expecting direct answers from her would be foolhardy. Maybe she played with words under some compulsion. Anyhow, after whatever transpired between us, I could sense that I was not too unwelcome in her place. And even if I was, I now somehow felt morally obligated to help her deal with her problem regardless of whether she wanted me to help or not. But what was her problem after all? Well, I was still looking for clues to find an answer.

"You could go for a wash if you want," she said, "meanwhile, I will warm and arrange the lunch."

After sometime when I returned to the dining space, I found the food nicely arranged on the table.

"Come, let's have lunch," she smiled and pulled a chair out for me to sit.

As I sat down to eat, I wondered if she would discuss her problem now.

7 HOW DOES SHE KNOW?

"I will have to go out for a while," she put some rice into her mouth, "I will be back by late evening. You would be able to manage alone till I return, wouldn't you?"

"I guess so but what should I do if …"

"If …"

"… if someone comes over?" I finished my question with food in my mouth.

"But who will come over?"

"Anyone, there could be a visitor, couldn't there be one?"

"Rest assured, no one will come here," she replied.

The horse cart driver had told me that she had been ostracized by the inhabitants of *Prithaka* but she had thus far not spoken about it. This was the first time that her words hinted, though in quite an unclear fashion, that she was in a state of social isolation. I intuited an opportunity to grab a lead into what Vaishali was living through. I felt if I asked the right questions and persisted enough with them, she could open up some of the secrets that she had been so teasingly guarding from me.

"How can you be so sure, what if someone just pays a visit?" I tried giving shape to my plan.

"Mr. Banerjee," my question triggered another of her swings in mood, "when I am saying no one is going to come, why can't you simply go with my words?"

Apparently, my plan was working.

"Vaishali, all I am asking is how do you know that nobody will come?" I persisted as I had thought.

"Can't you be satisfied with what I am saying?" She raised her voice.

"Come on Vaishali," I tried sounding upset, "ever since my arrival at your place you have been talking in riddles. Why don't you simply ask me to go away if you don't want me here?"

"I have never said that I don't want you here."

"But you have been saying it indirectly."

"Never," she softened her tone, "I never made any such suggestion, directly or indirectly."

"Maybe you never made such a suggestion consciously but … but I somehow drew such an impression."

"Which of my words made you feel so?" Vaishali appeared very eager to know.

"All those words that sound like riddles," I said.

After what looked like quite a cogitation she said, "This will not work, Mr. Banerjee."

"What will not work, Vaishali?"

"What you are trying to do will not work."

"What am I trying to do? I am simply saying that I sometimes feel unwelcome when I hear your riddle-like words," I had a sense that she had fathomed my plan and I was right as her words would eventually prove.

"Never try to do this again, Mr. Banerjee," She was firm and meant business.

"What are you talking about?" I turned more defensive of myself.

"You are trying to extract information from me but you will not be successful. For a moment I did feel you are seriously disappointed with me but then ... I could make out that you are purely play-acting to gather more information about me."

I made no effort to defend myself for I saw no use in putting up a defense. No matter what I said she would never be convinced that I wasn't trying to trick her into telling me things. My words could only fuel her anger.

"Please understand Mr. Banerjee," she continued, "you can never extract any information in this way. You can't simply lay a trap like this for me. This is really unbecoming of a man like you. You might be an intelligent man but that doesn't give you the license to treat others like morons."

Her words were surely harsh but I felt she really had reasons to be harsh for I had indeed tried to trick her. I wasn't happy with the way she protested but I wasn't happy with myself either. I should have thought twice before acting on my plan. Perhaps it was too naïve a plan. Or was it, I wondered. Maybe it wasn't. It was possible that she perceived the truth because she was exceptionally intelligent. Or did some ethereal being tell her about what I was trying to do? The way she suddenly discovered that my intent was to gather information was weird beyond limits and the possibility that someone or something conveyed the reality to her could not be ruled out.

"I will expect you not to do such a thing again, Mr. Banerjee," she got up from the chair, "if I see a repeat of this I shall take that as breach of trust."

She picked up a few items from a wooden shelf, I didn't notice what, and said, "I am leaving. If you feel hungry you could open that cabinet and take whatever snacks you like. And the bottles over there on that little stand are all full of drinking water. I will be late."

All those hours that I spent alone after she left would have been very difficult to bear if I had not put them to the right use. After having failed to arrive at a distinct premise as to how she could so suddenly know what I was up to, I went upstairs to my room. I took out a diary and began to write down in essential details the things that I had experienced so far. The strange men in the train, the words of the horse cart driver, how Vaishali received me on my arrival last night, her sudden change in mood, the haunting human shriek and the whitish humanoid that I saw running outside the house, our talks in the morning that day in the vicinity of the beautiful *Tarangini*, the strange way in which she knew about my plan – I wrote everything lest I should lose track of an important detail which might be necessary to unearth a lead in this matter, in case circumstances would have me investigate it.

I was so much engrossed in writing that it was only while writing the last few lines that I realized that the light conditions had dimmed considerably. I put the diary back into my bag and moved over to the window. The fields, hills and the forests wore a new look in the dusky conditions. Evidently, *Latika Griha* was the last house on this side of the village. As it got darker I wondered if it would be right on my part to light up the lanterns of the house. It was difficult to tell what Vaishali's reaction would be if I did such a thing. So I decided to light up only the lanterns of my bedroom and the washroom.

I hadn't brought with me any reading materials. There was thus nothing more substantive to do than to watch the changing colors of the contours outside. For a while I mused over where Vaishali could have gone. From the look of things I had little reasons not to believe that she was in a state of social ostracization. So there was little chance that she had gone to meet someone at *Prithaka*. Could it be that she had gone to *Shyamalpur* to purchase things for the ensuing week? Or had she gone to practice the occult in some obscure corner of the village? Whatever the truth was, I was far removed from it with little hope to bridge the distance in the near future. What if that distance never got bridged? If Vaishali didn't cooperate with me, and she certainly didn't look inclined to do so, then I could do little to help her.

The thought that she might not be herself and under the influence of some intangible being or phenomenon kept floating in and out of my psyche. I reasoned that this possibility was actually very strong. If she was indeed under some influence then my job would be extremely hard to do, if not impossible. The source of that influence, whatever it was, would never let even the most nebulous of clues to come to me. I could only hope it was she, and nobody else, who was in charge of her own self.

Another strong possibility was that she was only at times coming under the influence of the ethereal being. Her alternating between the soft and harsh tempers had a simple yet plausible explanation – she was soft when she was herself and harsh when the ethereal entity took charge of her.

In a while when I was out of my circle of thoughts, I found that darkness had engulfed *Prithaka*. The eeriness of the fields, hills and forests felt all the more pronounced. Then I heard some movements downstairs. Who was it? Vaishali?

8 MOVEMENTS IN THE DINING SPACE

I quickly moved out of my room and walked down the stairs. The movements had grown louder. "Is it you, Vaishali?" I said. There was no response but the movements appeared to have stopped. It was very dark and I could hardly see anything. I should have been prudent enough to carry the small lantern with me, I thought. Slowly I moved forward towards the dining space for it was there that the movements seemed to have happened. "Is it you, Vaishali?" I said again. Yet again there was no response. And then the entrance door opened creakily and someone entered the house. "Who? Who's it?" I virtually screamed in terror. The one who had entered got startled for a while before speaking in a voice loaded with heavy breathing, "It's me, Mr. Banerjee … Vaishali."

"Vaishali," I responded.

"Yes," she said, "are you okay?"

"I heard some movements," I said rather incoherently.

"Movements, what movements?"

"I don't know. I was in my room and came downstairs when I heard some sounds. First I thought you had returned but now I see that the movements were not yours," I regained some amount of composure.

"Don't worry," she responded in a friendly tone, "you just sit in the living room for some time. I need a while to light up the lanterns. Thereafter we can talk about it."

"Okay," I walked towards the living room.

"Be careful, don't trip over," the warmth in her voice was unmistakable.

From her words I could sense that she had some idea as to what was going on. I sat down on the same chair in the living room and watched again the game that the hilly winds played with the curtains. That day, however, the winds were not very strong. Yet the chill they brought with them was enough to soothe my nerves. I got up and moved close to the window to take more of the winds on my face. The night had painted the village here and there with tinges of dark blue. The very aura of *Prithaka* had begun to have a strong impact on my mind and soul. The solitude that the apparently forlorn terrains of *Prithaka* offered was widely different from the solitude that a spiritualist seeks. I reasoned that all solitudes are not the same. Some solitudes, like the one that permeated the air of *Prithaka*, could be very scary and disheartening. The solitude of *Prithaka* seemed to have a life of its own. It was breathing with the intent of fusing with the consciousness of the being it finds within its folds so that it could eventually suck up all originality of the being leaving behind a personality devoid of all its innate and acquired traits. Only one with a very high degree of willpower and mental strength could sustain the onslaughts of this solitude. Did I have such willpower and mental strength? Well, only time would tell. All I needed to do now, and there was hardly any scope for doing anything else, was to wait hoping that *Prithaka* would at some point of time, either consciously or unconsciously, allow me a peek into its secrets. The thought continuum ended as I heard the creaky noise of the entrance door again. I turned my glance left and saw Vaishali standing with a long metallic rod with a burning wick through the window. She raised the rod and the surroundings brightened up a little as the lantern on the outer wall began to glow.

I walked back to the chair and sat down. Soon Vaishali was in my room with the rod. She lit up the two wall lanterns of the living room.

"It will just take me another minute," she smiled, "just a couple of more lanterns are left."

She took a lot more time than she said to be back again in the room. I thought she would sit down and have a talk with me. Instead, she just smiled again and said, "The dinner is ready. I am afraid I haven't been able to make too many things tonight."

"The dinner is already ready?" I remarked.

"Yes, it is."

"I must say you are very prompt with things," I said as I got up from the chair, "you just returned a short while ago and you have already finished lighting up the lanterns and preparing the dinner."

"It was not a short while ago that I returned, Mr. Banerjee," Vaishali had a bit of laugh, "it has been more than an hour now. That's enough time for lighting up the lanterns and cooking the few items that I have kept for dinner today."

"Really, has it really been more than an hour?" I wondered as to how time passed so quickly.

"Yes, Mr. Banerjee," she responded, "what is wrong? You are speaking as though you have lost your sense of time."

I wondered if her words actually spelt the truth. Could it be that I had really lost sense of time in the grip of *Prithaka's* peculiarities? Then I reasoned that my thoughts might have pushed me away from sensing the passage of time. I followed her to the dining space. There were just three items for dinner that evening – rice, dal and cabbage curry. She was in a good mood as we ate.

"What movements were you talking about, Mr. Banerjee?" It was good to see her coming straight to the point.

"Apparently there were some movements over here."

"You mean there were movements here … in the dining space?"

"Well, that's what I could infer from the sounds," I replied.

"Were the sounds very loud?"

"Loud enough for me to hear from upstairs, when I came down I found them to be much louder."

"What kind of sounds were they?" She asked.

"It felt as though someone was inside the house."

"Did you hear footsteps?"

"No, not footsteps but … they were like sounds of someone moving around in the house."

"Might have been a cat that entered through the kitchen window," she observed.

"A cat … well may be," I responded.

"It could also be the sounds of this building. This is a very old house, you see … the beams and the wooden frameworks sometimes vibrate in a manner so as to cause strange sounds."

"Well, could be anything ..."

"You must have been very frightened, Mr. Banerjee?"

"I surely was frightened."

"So paranormal investigators can also get frightened at times," Vaishali laughed.

"Of course," I nodded and smiled, "paranormal investigators are humans after all."

"Take it easy, there is nothing to be worried about."

After a brief period of silence she asked, "Is the dinner okay, Mr. Banerjee?"

"It is very good actually."

"I would have made some more items but then we would really get late for dinner."

"What you have made is more than enough, Vaishali," I said, "the dinner is really good."

"You mean it?"

"Of course, I do. I have already begun to regard you as a great cook."

"Thank you so much, very sweet on your part to say that, Mr. Banerjee," the beatific smile returned to her lips, "you are indeed a very kind man."

"But I spoke the truth ... I am not being kind at all with my words. Trust me, it's a true compliment."

"I know. I am not calling you kind because you have given me a compliment; I am calling you kind for a good number of other reasons."

"Like what?"

"Well Mr. Banerjee, I have heard a lot about you from Neha Ma'am. She has the highest of regards for you. She often talked about how you were of immense help to her during her days of crisis. Besides, I have read scores of articles and essays written by you for various forums. I could always sense the soft-hearted man in you from the tenor of your language. And the biggest proof of your being a kind man is your being here. You have taken so much pain to come to this remote village with hardly any amenities simply to help a girl whom you hardly know," her eyes sparkled.

"I feel you are rather being kind to me by calling me a kind man," I laughed, "the truth is I never did anything to help Neha during her days of crisis. All I did was to listen to her problem patiently. Neha is big-hearted to reckon that as a help. In fact, my primary purpose of listening to her accounts was to satisfy my curiosities about the paranormal and to gather materials for my first book. And as regards my being here – well, I certainly want to help you but then there is also this purpose of understanding more of the paranormal. I am sure our association will fuel my research into the unknown. So one of my primary interests stands to be served. Now you can see it is not so kind, as you think, on my part to be here."

"I wouldn't change my impression about you regardless of what you say."

After we were done with the dinner she said, "Are you in a hurry to sleep, Mr. Banerjee?"

"Not at all," I replied.

"In that case would you like to go for a small walk with me?"

"Sure."

"Fine then, let me do the dishes first. It will take just about ten minutes. Then we can go for a walk."

"That suits me perfectly but would you want me to help you with the dishes?"

"No, no, thank you so much … you are my guest and I wouldn't let you do the dishes, for sure," her sweet disposition could conquer the hardest of hearts.

9 THE ROBED FIGURE

We walked towards the rivulet again. Vaishali's tresses cavorted about her shoulders under the influence of the winds. The interplay of the dim moonlight and the shadows it cast made her sharp features appear even more stunning.

"Mr. Banerjee," she said, "first, let me apologize for being so rude to you at noon. It was really uncouth on my part to have spoken that way."

"Never mind, Vaishali," I responded, "I understand that you might have been under some stress."

"Stress or no stress … there is no way I can justify what I did at noon."

"Forget about it, I haven't taken anything to my heart."

"See," her smile appeared even more attractive in the dim light conditions, "I have reasons to call you a kind man."

"Where are we headed now?" I asked.

"It is a beautiful rock in the shape of a peacock. People at *Prithaka* call it *Mayur Paththar* which translates down to *Peacock*

Rock. The sight of *Tarangini* from *Mayur Paththar* is breathtaking. And in a dimly moonlit night like this one, *Tarangini* appears even more beautiful."

"That's very interesting."

We turned left from near the point where the streak of trees eclipsing *Tarangini* starts. Soon we were on a sandy road winding around a small hillock. Close to the summit of the hillock lay the *Peacock Rock*. Even in the poor light conditions I could read the distinct similarity between the rock and a peacock with its feathers fully open. Climbing the rock posed no difficulty to Vaishali. I, however, slipped once before managing to reach its top with a little support from Vaishali.

"Are you hurt?" Vaishali said.

"No, I am all right. And to speak the truth I don't mind being a little hurt to be in a beautiful place such as this one," I replied.

"You haven't seen the beauty yet," she raised her hand and pointed at the rivulet.

She was right. The silvery flow of the rivulet could beat the imagination of countless poets put together. The elegant movements and curves of *Tarangini* were truly divine! The rivulet seemed to have a light of its own and at that moment I could vouch that the shine of the waters would not be affected even if the moon were removed from the sky. I couldn't take my gaze away from *Tarangini* and the more I watched its supernal glow, the more I felt that it was a living entity. Perhaps it had the soul of a demigoddess as its driver. The demigoddess looked all ready to bare its bosom as if inviting me for an embrace. It was an invitation to let my soul out to it.

"Divine, isn't it?" Vaishali said.

Her words brought me out of one meditative stupor and put me into another. I looked at her and wondered as to who was more beautiful – the luminous demigoddess of *Tarangini* or the hypnotic girl sitting next to me? It was possible that the demigoddess of *Tarangini* had borrowed her supernal glow from this enchantress whose charm had captivated my soul. If the rivulet was divine, this girl was the core of divinity. And then again her lips parted to accommodate the beatific smile that could turn the roughest of brutes into a poet. Who was she? A human or an angel? I don't know for how long I looked on as if I was under an unbreakable spell. She perhaps waited for a verbal response but I couldn't speak. And how could I have spoken? The sweetness of her being had driven my verbal powers far away from my command. Only she could break the spell. And she did it by speaking again.

"What are you looking at?" The glow of her eyes suggested that she was aware of my soul being a captive to her bewitching beauty.

"Nothing," I answered cumbersomely in a bid to gather control over my senses.

"Isn't the rivulet divine?"

"Absolutely," I nodded.

"Sometimes I feel like mingling with it."

"I can understand that feeling. I remember having read in a Bengali poem that, amongst other things, conveyed the idea that a true lover of beauty always looks for symbols of cosmic beauty, and if such a person finds an object of cosmic beauty, he or she feels like becoming one with it. And this rivulet, without a trace of doubt is replete with cosmic beauty. It is rather cosmic beauty personified. My subtler senses suggest that such beauty cannot be devoid of life."

"Do you really feel it is living?"

"Of course I do … I can almost feel its breaths."

"I feel exactly the same for it."

I gazed at *Tarangini* again. Its silvery flow was still beautiful but I could no longer sense the demigoddess in it. That was understandable of course – the demigoddess was too bleak an entity to register in my senses anymore in the presence of the one whose beauty could with utter ease beat any symbol of cosmic beauty. I resisted myself from telling my feelings but I had little doubts that she knew what thoughts had gripped my mind.

"I come to this place very often and watch the flow of *Tarangini*. Sometimes I spend hours talking to it."

"So she is like a friend to you?"

"Of course she is a friend to me. In fact, *Tarangini* is my only friend in this village."

I did not respond waiting for her to tell me more and she did.

"I don't know if you are aware or not that I have been socially ostracized by the inhabitants of *Prithaka*."

"I have some idea. The horse cart driver who brought me here did speak about your isolation from the rest." I said.

"Then he also must have told you as to why I have been put in isolation." A deep seated pain cast its impressions on her face.

"Yes, he did."

"What did he say?" She asked after a short while as the pain made its presence more prominent.

"As far as I could gather from his talks, people think that you practice some kind of magic."

"You don't need to be so careful with your words. I am sure what he told you was different."

"You are right … he called you a witch," I preferred being more candid this time.

"Yes, I know," she put her gaze down and nodded, "most people in *Prithaka* would say the same about me. They all think I am a witch."

"Does that upset you, Vaishali?"

"It does sometimes … I am a human being after all."

"It will be too simple for me to say that you must not bother about what people think about you but it is easier said than done."

"The name of this village perfectly describes my state," traces of tears shone in her eyes, "in Sanskrit *Prithaka* means *separate* or *isolated*. I am completely isolated from the rest just like an island."

"Sometimes we have little choice but to brave the circumstances we find ourselves in," I pressed her hand.

She moved her hand immediately and wiped her tears. I sat there without a clue as to what would be an appropriate response from my side. After a short while she spoke again.

"What do you think about me, Mr. Banerjee?" she asked turning her gaze at me.

I was completely unprepared for this sharp question. My verbal abilities cheated me yet again as I gave her a blank look.

"You didn't answer my question," the pain in her gaze had turned into what looked like the fire to meet the challenges head-on, "what do you think about me? Do you also think I am a witch?"

"I can only think of you as a wonderful soul. I have a great deal of respect and admiration for you." That is the best I could come up with at that moment.

"That doesn't answer my question, Mr. Banerjee. Are you also of the view that I am a witch?"

I was in a big dilemma. I certainly hadn't formed a definite opinion about her in the little time that I had spent with her at *Prithaka*. The sequence of events around me after my arrival at *Latika Griha* could by no stretch of imagination be deemed as normal. Some of my experiences rather pointed to her possible dealings with the ethereal and I didn't want to tell her a lie.

"You want me to speak the truth, Vaishali?" I said putting some force in my voice.

"Yes, I do."

"Then listen – I am yet to form an opinion about you."

Her reaction came after a few moments in the form of a wry smile.

"I am sorry, Vaishali, but I preferred to speak the truth."

"Let's go," she said and in one smooth jump she was at the base of the *Mayur Paththar*.

Jumping like that was quite beyond my capacities, I reckoned. So I got down rather cumbersomely by using the depressions on the rock as footrests. The walk back to *Latika Griha* was a difficult one – not because of the distance or the unfriendly terrains but due to the heavy atmosphere that now separated Vaishali from me. It was strange indeed that despite being so intelligent and knowledgeable, she was annoyed with me for my having spoken the truth. I wondered if I should have told a lie. But then that was fraught with dangers. What if some ethereal being, or whatever other medium she used, told her that I was lying just as it might have done when I used the little trick to extract information from her? And the possibility of that happening felt quite strong. I was convinced that I had done the right thing by telling her what I really felt. As we walked, at one instant I thought that I should start a conversation but the very next moment it struck me that the best course was to let the heavy atmosphere melt away naturally. Shortly, we were at the entrance of *Latika Griha*. She opened the door for me to enter first.

"Good night, Mr. Banerjee," she followed me and bolted the door, "have a good sleep."

"Good night, Vaishali," I smiled, "you too take good rest."

She walked straight to her room doing little to hide her dissatisfaction.

I walked up the stairs to my room and put off the wall lanterns. As I got into the bed I made an autosuggestion to my mind that I should get up very early the next morning. I wasn't sure that the autosuggestion would work but that was the best I could do for neither was I carrying an alarm clock nor was any charge left in my mobile phone. The comfort of the soft bed soon drove me into a deep sleep. Or was it deep for it broke as suddenly as it had come? I wondered if I had woken up because of the autosuggestion. A look outside suggested that dawn was nowhere in the sight. I got up and don't quite know as to why I walked up to the window again. The highest hill and its forest covers wore an intimidating look. But why? Maybe something about it was different. The horrors of the dream I had seen sitting close to *Tarangini* invaded my psyche and the relief that descended at the realization that the peak of the hill didn't have the extended appearance as it had in the dream settled some of my excited nerves. The feeling, however, that something about the hill was different persisted. What was different about its appearance anyway? Was it the color ... or the steepness ... or the cushion of the trees around it ... or all the facets put together? Perhaps, nothing was so different about it, I reasoned. Perhaps, it was only my mind playing games again. What I sensed next flattened this reason. The difference about the hill was a slow and almost imperceptible movement on it. It appeared as though something was moving towards the summit along the steep edge to my right. The more I concentrated on it the more convinced I was that the movement was really happening and wasn't a trick of my mind. With time the movement became more distinct. Then I saw a tiny light. Apparently, the one who was moving up the hill was carrying that light. Soon I could see the light no longer. Shortly thereafter the movement ceased too or maybe I lost track of it. Everything about the hill was back to normal. What was it that I saw? Why would someone move up the hill at that hour? I had no clues whatsoever. I looked at the hill again. Its pre-domineering presence penetrated the skies as if throwing a challenge to one and all to match its majesty. Then it struck me like a flash that the movement on the hill was not even a fraction as strange as my very perception of it. How could I note the movement that was happening so far away? One reason could have been that the movement was pretty large and from the point I was in, it appeared to be a miniscule one. But my gut feeling suggested that the movement wasn't a large one. It couldn't have been, for instance, a large group with lights moving up the hill because the look of such a passage would have been very different. I could, however, only speculate for there was no way to make any concrete inferences. I turned around without the knowledge that a shock would confront me! There was someone standing at a cubit's distance from me! Clad in a dark robe, the figure looked no less than a ghost with an airy aura the likes of which we often get to see in movies and comic books. I shuddered and moved back with a shriek as the figure moved out of the room in a flash. Although it was completely covered, I could make out that it had traversed backward on its way out of the room. Let me repeat it was a movement in a flash! It was as if its feet were on a jet. A human couldn't have moved like that. The worst part about the figure was that it appeared evil! I wondered what harm it had come to cause me. Or was it there to harm me at all? I couldn't be sure for if it was there to cause harm, why did it move away without causing the slightest hurt? It wouldn't be right anymore to sit silent and wait for cues to arrive at their own pace. It was time to talk directly about what I had seen and felt happening around me to Vaishali. As a paranormal investigator and researcher it was a part of my job to brave life threatening situations but to meekly accept them without making a forceful effort to unearth the causes and reasons behind them would be foolhardy. I decided to wake Vaishali up from sleep and talk to her right away.

10 THE WALL CLOCK

I lit the lantern on my study table and held it in my hand. Carefully I moved out of the room ignoring the strange shadows of things that the light of the lantern cast around me. As I moved I had this terrible fear of running into that figure again. But there was little choice. Something very terrible was happening all around me or so I sensed and talking to Vaishali about all this could not wait any longer. It was with great difficulty that I walked down the stairs. Suddenly there was this feeling that somebody touched the heel of my left foot! I almost tripped out of fear as I paced up my steps. Thankfully, I managed to reach the ground floor without hurting myself. I rushed to Vaishali's room. It was too dark and the light was too dim to provide a reasonable impression of the passages that led to Vaishali's room. My intuitive senses pulled me through and very soon I found myself facing the door of her room. I knocked it lightly. There was no response. I knocked it again and there was no response again. When I was about to knock it for the third time, somebody called my name from behind.

"Mr. Biswajit Banerjee," it was a deep voice.

I turned around in a daze and saw Vaishali standing with a strange smile. It wasn't evil but felt unacceptable. The next few moments were difficult as I came to terms with her sudden and unexpected appearance behind me.

"You seem to be disturbed, Mr. Banerjee," she spoke again with the smile still on her lips.

"Yes, I am," I reacted wondering as to how and why her smile had turned so strange.

"What happened to you?"

"Lots of things, lots of strange things."

"Relax Mr. Banerjee," she tenderly placed a hand on my shoulder, "it seems you have had a bad dream."

"No Vaishali," I lent force to my voice, "it is no dream I am talking about."

"Relax, relax," her smile widened and so did its strangeness, "it will do you no good if you remain so excited."

"Vaishali, you need to tell me."

"Tell you what?"

"Tell me what's happening over here."

"But what is happening over here, Mr. Banerjee?"

"Vaishali, please," I raised my voice again, "you know very well what I am talking about."

"Not really," finally her smile ceased to my great relief, "but I can sense you have gone through something terrible."

"I have gone through many terrible things, Vaishali and I have no clues as to what they are. And I am constrained to say that you have done little for me to make sense of them."

"You sound too excited, Mr. Banerjee. Perhaps you should cool down first before we talk."

"I am cool enough to talk, Vaishali. Let us talk right now."

"Do you know what the time now is?"

"How would I know? I am not carrying a watch. And my mobile phone has no charge left. If I had known that clocks would be a rarity in *Prithaka*, I would have certainly carried a watch," I spoke in a rather mocking tone.

"What is wrong with you Mr. Banerjee? There is such a large clock right in front of you and you can't see it."

I looked straight and found no clock.

"I don't see any," I reacted.

"It is right there on the wall to your right," Vaishali stressed.

"I don't see any," I looked to my right.

"You don't see any because there isn't enough light falling on the wall. Why don't you just raise the lantern?"

I raised the lantern and saw a huge wall clock with a massive pendulum. To say that it was extremely strange to spot such a prominent clock on that wall would be a gross understatement. My bafflement knew no limits. I was fully sure that it wasn't there before. From where did it emerge? Was it a stroke of evil magic on the part of Vaishali? Was she really a witch? Or was she under the influence of forces beyond her control? A storm of fear and confusions enslaved my intelligence. I had never before in my life felt so helpless. What was Vaishali, regardless of whether she was herself evil or under the influence of some evil forces, trying to do to me? I wished I had the answer.

"Mr. Banerjee," she said moving a finger on my forehead, "you are sweating. What's wrong? Are you unwell?"

I jerked my forehead away much to her surprise or at least what looked like much to her surprise.

"Mr. Banerjee, are you okay?" She sounded concerned.

"No, I am certainly not okay," I moved my head.

"Please tell me what's wrong. You are my honored guest and I would be really sad to see you inconvenienced in any way."

"V-a-i-s-h-a-l-i," I was losing my voice.

"Tell me Mr. Banerjee, tell me, I will help you, trust me."

I pointed at the clock raising the lantern again. She looked at it and said after turning her gaze back at me, "What's bothering you?"

"T-h-a-t c-l-o-c-k," I spoke with difficulty.

"Please sit down first, Mr. Banerjee," she took the lantern from my hand and moved towards the dining table gesturing me to follow her.

I took a while to gather some of my sapping spirits and then walked up to the dining table. She pulled a chair and helped me sit. After placing the lantern on the table she moved over to a cabinet where she stored water and sundry food items. She took out a bottle of water and then picked up a tumbler from a metallic shelf fixed to the wall in the vicinity of the cabinet.

"Please relax, Mr. Banerjee," Vaishali said as she came back to the table.

She poured water into the tumbler and pushed it towards me.

"Hmmm … there you are," she smiled.

I was relieved to see that the strangeness I spotted in her smile a while ago was no longer there.

She pulled a chair and sat close to me.

"Drink the water, Mr. Banerjee. You will feel better. Everything will be all right," her caring self made its presence felt again.

I picked up the tumbler and gulped the water down.

"Would you like some more water?"

I moved my head.

"I insist you drink a little more, you really don't look well," Vaishali poured some more water into the tumbler.

I drank it and made a conscious effort to get a hold of myself.

"Are you feeling better?"

My breathing appeared to be getting normal and I nodded.

"Good," She patted my hand that was resting on the table, "now tell me what is so wrong."

"Too many things are wrong, Vaishali," finally some clarity returned to my speech.

"Tell me, Mr. Banerjee."

"I have seen and felt so many weird things happening that I don't know from where to start."

"Let me make a suggestion, start with the wall clock over there," she pointed at the wall clock, "you were saying something about it, weren't you?"

"It wasn't there," I said doing little to prevent the element of rudeness from creeping into my tone.

"What was not there? The wall clock?" She spoke with surprise.

"Yes, the wall clock was not there."

"But Mr. Banerjee, that wall clock has been hanging on that wall from a time long before my birth. Maybe you did not spot it earlier."

"As far as I can recall, that wall didn't have any wall clock till last evening."

"I assure you Mr. Banerjee, the wall clock was there. It is possible that you didn't notice," Vaishali responded.

"It is too gross a thing to go unnoticed, I couldn't have missed it."

"Mr. Banerjee," she tried to explain, "All of us have imperfect perceptions. Sometimes we perceive what we think. Sometimes we are so occupied with our thoughts that we fail to notice what is happening around us. There could be countless reasons for misjudgments or errors in perceptions. It is possible for even the best of minds to fail to notice even the most obvious things. Not taking note of the wall clock could just be an error in perception. Why don't you wish to reckon such an error as a possibility?"

"So you are trying to suggest that everything I have felt happening around me at *Prithika* has been an error of my perception?"

"I never suggested that Mr. Banerjee," suddenly a serious look came over her eyes, "I have always admired your intelligence and analytical powers, and I would be the last person to make such a terrible suggestion that all your inferences have been judgmental errors thereby belittling your wisdom. In fact, I am curious to know what experiences you have had. Kindly tell me, Mr.

Banerjee."

"Strange things began even before I reached *Prithika*. Would you like to listen to each one of my experiences?"

"Of course," she nodded, "please tell me everything you have lived through."

I told her everything right from my meeting the strange men in the train to the sighting of the wall clock in good details. She listened to my accounts very intently and after I finished she sat thinking for a while.

"Well, Mr. Banerjee," she said, "I guess I have some explanations for some of your experiences."

"I am glad to hear that, Vaishali."

"I shall certainly tell you what I know but not now … there are some important chores that I need to do now."

"I insist you tell me right now, Vaishali."

"Please Mr. Banerjee," she virtually implored, "it is close to half past three in the morning. I need to change the water in the washrooms, do some cleaning, and prepare some food for the morning. I promise I will tell you all that I know after I finish doing these chores. Just give me a couple of hours. Thereafter, we could walk down to the same rocks at the edge of *Tarangini* and discuss all this. Till that time you could rest in your room. Maybe you could take a small nap."

"I am not willing to go to that room again," I saw no point in hiding my fears.

"Please trust me, Mr. Banerjee, that room is perfectly safe."

"How can you say that, Vaishali? A hideous creature entered that room possibly with the intent to kill me and you are calling it safe!"

"Do you trust me, Mr. Banerjee? Would you believe me if I insist that despite what you experienced in that room, it is a perfectly safe room for you?" Vaishali said with an unmistakable shade of sadness, possibly caused by the harshness of my tone, in her eyes.

"Well…" I wondered if speaking the truth would be right.

"Go on Mr. Banerjee … speak up. Tell me if you trust me or not."

For sure there was no way I could repose my full faith in her although I did want to do so. I refrained from speaking the truth and kept mum.

"I have got your answer, Mr. Banerjee. Your silence makes it all very clear. Perhaps I shouldn't have asked the question in the first place. I should have known that if you are still not sure whether or not I am a witch, you could never have full trust in me," The bottom edges of her eyes glistened up as tears appeared.

"Look Vaishali," I softened my tenor, "I have no intentions to hurt you but you wanted me to speak the truth at that time and that's what I did. Indeed, I am yet to form an opinion about you. You would appreciate that the circumstances around me have been too eerie and there was no way in which I could have concluded on a complete disconnect between you and these circumstances. So, to speak the truth again, I can't be sure if you practice magic or not. But that doesn't mean I don't respect you. Regardless of who you are and what are the reasons why you have been socially ostracized, I have tremendous admiration for you. I am sure you remember that when you asked me as to what I think about you while we were on *Mayur Paththar*, I did say that I can only think of you as a wonderful soul. Trust me, I meant every word of what I said."

"It is a peculiar situation indeed," she said wiping her tears and forcing a smile on her lips, "you have high regard for me and yet can't trust me."

She was actually right! It was so weird a situation! Whereas I could sense her goodness, I was not willing to place my faith in her.

"It is your wish, Mr. Banerjee, if you do not wish to go back to that room, you could wait in the living area till I finish my chores. Thereafter, we could walk down to the edge of *Tarangini*."

That sounded a better idea. I got up from my chair and headed towards the living area.

"Take this," her words arrested my motion.

She offered me the lantern.

"Won't you need it?" I said as I took hold of the lantern.

"Don't worry about me, Mr. Banerjee, even the most obscure corner of this house is at my fingertips. You take some rest, I will join you in a while."

The living area felt safer. The curtains, as usual, were playing to the whims of the winds. The flame of the lantern too played its own little games with whatever of the passing drafts it got in touch with. The shadows of the flying curtains cast by the flickering light lent themselves to myriad imaginations. I spotted the loose end of a sari of a mysterious woman standing on moorland braving the naughty winds, and some linen flying carelessly in a space separating hillocks, and the wings of a dragon in a rather docile mood, and the fluttering robe of a magician's dress while he is acknowledging the applause of his audience after having performed an incredible trick, and ... and ... and ... the images I imagined turned more and more feeble as my stress began to take control of my mind, and very soon my mind was conjuring images in my dreams. The scale of time is very difficult to comprehend. Sometimes in our dreams we live through experiences in what feels like real time which in actual real time would take ages. I relived many of my experiences with many plusses and minuses. Some of the distasteful experiences felt less painful while some pleasurable ones felt even more pleasant. And I relived each one of these re-engineered experiences to the full in the short span of my sleep. Strange are the ways of time and strange are the ways of psyche!

A large bang woke me up. Early morning rays had already made their way through the window. I got up from my chair and looked around. Nothing had apparently changed. The vast expanse visible through the window looked the same and so did the arrangements in the living area. I walked out of there and found Vaishali cleaning the floor in the vicinity of the entrance door with a moist rag.

"I have almost finished, just five minutes more," she said.

"I heard a sound," I said.

"O that was because this bucket toppled over," she pointed at the small bucket of water she was using to clean the floor.

"But it was a pretty big sound," I said, "how could such a small bucket of water cause so big a sound?"

"Well ... Mr. Banerjee," she looked short of words, "I am telling you what actually happened. It seems you doubt everything I say."

"I didn't mean that, Vaishali," I realized being somewhat unfair to her, "please finish off your chores, really need to talk ...

11 A PEAK INTO CONSCIOUSNESS

The sweet breeze carrying with it the coolness of *Tarangini* caressed my spirits. Vaishali, however, looked too stressed for the breeze to have any soothing effect on her.

"What I want to tell you is too difficult to express in words," she explained, "but I will certainly try. Before I say another word it is important that I tell you as to why I am revealing these personal and obscure truths to you. At the *Mayur Pathhar* when you effectively conveyed to me that you were not sure whether or not I am a witch, I didn't say or do anything to clear your doubts. At that time, I saw no point in telling you the truth. In any case, even if I had told you the truth, you wouldn't have believed me. I guess, you will not believe me even now when I explain things to you. But in view of the fact that you are too disturbed because of your experiences at *Prithaka*, and that these experiences could have a telling effect on your psyche if you go back to New Delhi without the slightest idea as to what happened around you, and that I would never want you to suffer for reasons directly or indirectly connected to me, I decided to speak the truth to you even if you choose to disregard it as a pack of lies. As regards why am I so concerned about your well being, I believe you understand that I admire your goodness and highly appreciate your will to help me out of my problems. Besides, as I have already said this before, you are my honored guest and I do not want you inconvenienced in any way. On the top of that you are also a dear friend of the woman I see as my elder sister."

"I must thank you for being so considerate," I nodded.

"The truth I am going to tell you is not the complete truth. That's because I am myself not too sure as to what is the complete truth. There are certain things I know for sure and certain things which I can only speculate about. But I promise to tell you all that I know and believe on the basis of my direct experiences and inferences. Am I making sense, Mr. Banerjee?"

"You are making perfect sense, Vaishali, go on."

"I am sure the horse cart driver also spoke to you about my mother. He must have told you that she was a witch … and that I have also followed her ways and become a witch myself. The truth is, whether you believe or not, neither my mother was a witch nor am I. My mother was deeply into the study of the *occult*. She had in her collection hundreds of books on the *occult*. After having studied the subject for years together she thought of experimenting with the methods she had found in many of the books in her repertoire. She wanted to know if there was anything such as *real magic*. I hope you understand what I am trying to imply by the expression *real magic*. What you see the magicians, the so-called magicians I mean, perform on streets or on stages are nothing but tricks of one kind or the other. No matter how reputed the magician is or how impossible his or her acts appear, all such performances are nothing but cleverly designed activities that defy common reason of the audiences. The best of tricks such as levitation, cutting a living human into two or more pieces, sudden disappearance or appearance of the magician and his or her assistants, mind reading and the ancient Indian rope trick are actually intelligently crafted tricks that defy common intelligence and level of attention. I am not talking about such magic. The magic I am talking about is real in every way, magic that does not use any deception or trickery, magic that is not meant to entertain the audiences but performed more often than not to accomplish a material or spiritual objective, magic that really happens, magic that is as real as the law of gravitation."

"Very interesting indeed," I remarked as she took a pause for a breath.

"My mother kept working on *real magic* and very soon she had become a magician in the true sense of the term. She could control the five elements that make up the universe."

"You mean the five elements of the nature – what we refer to as *panchamahabhuta* in Sanskrit?"

"That's right Mr. Banerjee. The five elements – *Bhumi* or earth, *Jala* or water, *Agni* or fire, *Pavan* or air, and *Aakash* or sky; she mastered the force of gravity and could levitate herself and things around her by controlling the properties of earth, she had water to her command and could walk on deep water masses without the slightest difficulty, fire being subservient to her could not burn or injure her, she could change the directions of winds regardless of how strong they were as her control over air was also unmistakable, and she did also command the respect and obedience of the sky. You might find all this very hard to believe but every word that I spoke about her and her powers is true."

"I don't have problems believing in anything after all that I have seen and felt at *Prithaka*."

"But what exactly are these elements of nature? They are not simply agglomerations of matter and energy as many scientific theories would have us believe. These five elements are much more than matter and energy." Vaishali said without bothering about the mocking tonality of my last words.

"I can perhaps sense what you are trying to suggest," I now spoke in a tone bereft of all derision.

"I have no doubts you can sense it because a number of articles that you published on various forums touch upon the truth I am now going to explain."

"Do you read my articles?"

"I am very fond of reading. I love all kinds of literature – short, long, fiction, non-fiction or creative non-fiction. As regards your articles, I find them very interesting," she replied.

"Thanks, but I am still not sure as to which truth you are going to talk about."

"Well, the truth is this – the five elements of nature and their combinations are broadly categorized into living and non-living by us humans. But what we call non-living are actually not non-living entities as many self-proclaimed rationalists suggest. Every non-living entity has a life of its own. I must tell you at this point of time that I am quite averse to using the expression *life*. I should rather say that every non-living entity, just like every living entity, has consciousness. The word *life* has very little meaning for me because what we call *life* is nothing more than one of the many consequences of consciousness. You could say that *life* is simply a function of consciousness if we are to talk in the mathematical parlance. We call the living beings *living* because what we call *life* is more visible in them. However, we fail to sense the *life* in the so called non-living entities because the processes of *life* in them are nearly invisible. But a trained eye … I mean a man or a woman with higher levels of perception can sense *life* even in a so-called non-living entity. You might have guessed that higher the level of consciousness of an entity, the greater the quality of *life* it will exude. It is thus easy to understand as to why some entities appear living while others non-living. The level of consciousness of what we think of as living beings is much higher than the level of consciousness of what we perceive as non-living entities."

"O yes, that is what our Upanishads suggest. And you are right, I have indeed written on this subject in a number of my articles. In fact, this idea finds mention in my book titled *My Paranormal Files: The Bureau.*"

"I know that," the characteristic sweetness had returned to her smile and she too now seemed to be enjoying the sweet breeze reaching out to us from over the waters of *Tarangini*, "I read that book too."

"You did?"

"Yes."

"By the way that book also mentions you."

"I know," she now laughed, "I find mention in the later chapters as one of the *not so important* characters."

"None of the characters I write about is unimportant, Vaishali," I enjoyed the lightness that was building up in the air between us.

"Maybe I will find a more prominent place in one of your future works."

"I am sure that will happen. In fact, you might figure as the most important character in my very next book."

"O I hope there will not be too many negative shades to it," she looked up at me.

"O come on Vaishali, need I tell you again how much I admire you."

She looked down perhaps in a bid to allow a streak of muddled thoughts pass through her mind and then looked up again and said, "Should we now get back to the principal theme of our discussion, Mr. Banerjee?"

"O yes, certainly."

"Every entity – that rock, these grains of sand, the water of *Tarangini*, those hillocks and every other inanimate in our view and those outside our view are actually conscious beings. Some are more conscious than others. The entities that are more conscious than others can also be called more evolved entities. In other words, the higher the level of consciousness of an entity, the more evolved it will be reckoned. The living beings, it goes without saying, are therefore much more evolved than the non-living entities. And of the living beings, of course, the humans are the most evolved. I am sure you understand that I am not talking about biological evolution alone. I am talking about spiritual evolution, biological evolution being a mere part of it. The entire universe is actually nothing but the process of spiritual evolution of consciousness. Every entity, right from an insignificant and apparently inanimate particle right up to the most intelligent human being on the planet, is going through the process of evolution either consciously or unconsciously. My mother sensed this truth after studying various kinds of occult literature in depth. Her experimentations with the occult further fortified the truths she had sensed in her mind. During her initial days of practice, she successfully contacted many disembodied consciousnesses or what we call spirits or ghosts in common parlance. With time her skills of occult practice improved considerably and she could now contact even the consciousnesses that had never got embodied or that had escaped, for one reason or the other, from inanimate entities. To put it more plainly, she successfully interacted with many spirits that had never quite assumed a body; also, she mingled with hordes of spirits that had escaped from inanimate objects. Am I still making sense, Mr. Banerjee?"

"You are actually making great sense, Vaishali. Sometimes you are giving me the feeling as though you are reading an extract from one of my writings."

She laughed again and continued, "Henceforth, whenever I use the word *spirit*, I would mean some disembodied consciousness or some consciousness that never assumed a body. You know Mr. Banerjee that some spirits are intelligent while others are not. Quite understandably, it is easier to interact with intelligent spirits than to commune with unintelligent ones. From what I have said so far you can also easily deduce the plain fact that the higher the level of evolution of a spirit, the greater would be its intelligence."

"Yes, indeed," I nodded.

"Now, the spirits that had inhabited living bodies are almost always more evolved as compared to those that escaped from non-living entities. And of course, the more intelligent the species a spirit had embodied, the more evolved it is."

"Well yes, that is logical enough – a spirit that had been in a human body would be more evolved than one that had inhabited an ape, for example."

"That's right but it mustn't lead you to believe that a spirit can be born into a species of its choice or that it is free to choose any body within the species it is supposed to be born into. The species and the body within the species it will be born into will depend upon the quality of the spirit. The better the quality, the higher are its chances of getting a good species and a good body within that species. Please appreciate that when I use the expression *species*, I am keeping the inanimate entities within its fold."

"O yes indeed," I responded, "the relationship between a spirit and the species it is supposed to be born into is very interesting. While on one hand the species and the body it is supposed to be born into will depend upon the quality or level of the spirit, on the other hand the level of intelligence a species and the concerned body within it are endowed with will decide the scope of evolution of the reincarnating spirit."

"Absolutely," she continued, "now, communicating with an intelligent spirit is far easier than communicating with an unintelligent spirit. The more intelligent a spirit is, the easier it would be to communicate with it."

"That is the same as saying the more evolved a spirit is, the easier it would be to interact with it," I said.

"Indeed, and that means only an expert occultist can interact with less evolved spirits; it is like this – interacting with an adult who understands your language is far easier than interacting with an infant who does not have the resources of a language to communicate its feelings. However, the parents, who may be likened to expert occultists, can understand the infant as well."

"I guess I am making sense of what you are trying to drive at."

"Mr. Banerjee, the problem with these ideas is that they are very difficult to explain in human language. These are truths that can be understood in their entirety only by experiencing them. Some occultists and magicians go on to suggest that even attempts to explain these truths in human language must not be made as such endeavors make these truths appear far different from what they really are."

"Indeed, indeed," I nodded again.

"And of course, even the best of attempts to verbalize these truths fail to quench the thirst of a curious mind. In fact, such attempts raise more questions than the answers they supply."

"You are right, Vaishali. I couldn't have been more in agreement with you," I said.

12 ELUSIVE ANSWERS

She kept on talking about obscure ideas as seconds built up minutes and minutes built up hours. My wait for her to explain the paranormal events seemed endless.

"These ideas are difficult to comprehend, Mr. Banerjee, aren't they? She looked at me.

"O yes, they are," I responded.

"Thank you Mr. Banerjee," she said after a lengthy pause for thoughts, "I think we should go back now. It is close to noon."

She got up. Her sudden closure of the discussion did not impress me in the least. I failed to understand her motive. Was that all she wanted to tell me? Or did she intend to explain everything in parts in order to buy time so that *Prithaka* could unleash more of its horrors on me. I also felt now that she could have very well avoided all her philosophical discourse on consciousness and come straight to the point as to what were I to make of all those unusual occurrences I have had to put up with ever since I stepped into *Latika Griha*. No doubt, I found her talks very interesting and had a big role in allowing her to linger her discourse on consciousness but little did I know that she would abruptly end the discussion.

Maybe she had tricked me into a discussion of my choice simply to avoid talking about the horrors of *Prithaka*.

"But Vaishali," I didn't mince words, "you have hardly come to the point. Nothing that you have told me explains the paranormal phenomena that have gripped me at *Prithaka*."

"Mr. Banerjee," she didn't mince words either and undertones of sternness sharply crept into her voice, "Every word I have spoken so far has been with a view to explain these paranormal phenomena. These phenomena are not easy to explain or understand. They are not things which can be defined mathematically. What did you expect from me? To tell you everything about these phenomena in a flash? Come on Mr. Banerjee. You should have understood that I am building a solid base so that you could have a deep understanding of the phenomena but it seems you are rather interested in surface knowledge of things. Your words are very disappointing, Mr. Banerjee."

"I didn't intend to disappoint you, Vaishali. And I must say what we have discussed is very interesting but … but I haven't found my answers yet. Do you think it is too much on my part to ask for an explanation of the events that are so horrific? Events that felt so life-threatening?

"Mr. Banerjee, that is enough," she raised her voice almost to the level of yelling, "I have been listening to your baseless ideas for a long time now. Please understand that your life is not under threat. At least it is not under threat as long as I am alive. I have been trying to impress upon you repeatedly that nothing that you have seen or felt happening over here is life-threatening. You were unwilling to go back to your room despite my repeated assurances that nothing is going to happen to you. Now, you are insisting that I finish discussing the entire gamut of the occult and the unusual in just one sitting because somewhere in your mind you are unsure about my commitment to your safety. You might have felt that I am leaving the discussion in the middle because I don't have any true desire of explaining the things to you in their entirety while the truth is that the scope of things I am explaining is so large that regardless of how much I try, I cannot finish the explanations in one sitting. No matter how hard I try to convince you, your distrust in me would simply not go. On one hand you say you have great regard for me and on the other you simply insult me all the time by questioning my integrity."

"Vaishali," I was a little unsettled by her angry outburst and made a weak defense, "I have never questioned your integrity … I am simply trying to make sense of what I have experienced so far in this village. So far as returning to my room in the early morning hours is concerned, it was pure fear that prevented me from doing so. I appreciate all your efforts at making me comfortable but I guess my fears have gotten the better of me so far."

"Need I remind you that you are a paranormal investigator, Mr. Banerjee and your purpose of coming here is to help me out of my paranormal predicaments? Does it suit a person of your stature to be so afraid? Didn't you know when you took up this profession that very often you would have to deal with your fear? It is strange indeed to see that instead of making any attempts to allay my fears, all you are trying is to come out of your own fears," She continued in the same vein.

"Vaishali, I know my duties as a paranormal investigator," I too spoke loudly while in full knowledge that what she just said was not completely bereft of substance, "but how can I help someone who does not even discuss her problems with me? You have never told me what your problems are, have you? Whenever I offer help you suggest that no one can help you out of your problems. If I haven't been able to make any effort to bring you out of your troubles, the major reason behind that has been your not sharing your troubles with me."

"Maybe I would have done that eventually when I would have thought the time was right to do so … am I not entitled to my space for thoughts and judgments?"

"Of course you are but you could at least have told me what you know about all that I have confronted so far at *Prithaka*. When you say that my life is under no threat as long as you are alive, you indirectly convey that you have good knowledge of the things I have faced. Couldn't you just tell me everything about these incidents, Vaishali?"

"But that's exactly what I am doing now, Mr. Banerjee. What do you think I have been discussing with you so far?"

"Well, you mainly deliberated upon consciousness."

"O come on Mr. Banerjee," she said in a tone of frustration, "I don't expect you at least to talk like a complete novice in the area of the occult. You have yourself written in so many articles about ghosts and spirits being nothing other than disembodied consciousnesses. It is strange that now when I talk about consciousness and its characteristics, you consider it irrelevant to our proposed discussion on the paranormal activities you have encountered at *Prithaka*."

"Look, I am not suggesting that talks on consciousness are irrelevant to what I want to know. All I am objected to is your leaving the discussion midway. If you didn't have enough time to discuss the entire issue, you could have spoken on its essentials. By leaving it midway you have done little to help me cope with the happenings around me," I softened my tone down.

"Mr. Banerjee, patience is what you need. I am far from having finished my explanations. Please understand, there are no essentials of the issue we are discussing. I believe there are just two ways to go – either you know them in full or you do not know them at all. Surface knowledge of these things could only add to your bag of confusions. Although you have little trust in me, yet I shall request you to rest assured that you are safe and will be safe till the very end of your quest at *Prithaka*. I also promise that you will be safely back in New Delhi after your stint over here."

"But Vaishali…"

"Please Mr. Banerjee, speak no more. It is far beyond noon … it is time we go back and eat something. After lunch you could have a good rest in the room that you were so afraid of in the morning with complete trust that no problem will touch you. I would want you to have a good sleep as you have had a pretty difficult night. I will wake you up sometime in the evening. Then after having dinner we could go to *Mayur Paththar* again to resume our discussion," she looked up at me expectantly for a response.

"What do you say, Mr. Banerjee," she said again when I didn't speak.

I found her proposal an acceptable one though there was little else I could do other than accepting it. So I nodded.

"Good," a shade of a smile went alongside her words, "please trust me and you will not regret. I want to be a friend to you, Mr. Banerjee, a trustworthy friend. Please allow me the space I need to be your friend."

The benign sparkle of her eyes left me with little reasons to distrust her. I nodded again.

"Thank you so much … today in the evening we will start from where we left. I will try and finish my explanation of things, all right," her smile turned more earnest.

I couldn't help nurture a smile myself.

13 A GLIMPSE OF THE TRUTH

I went off to sleep after lunch in the same room. Except for some inexplicable sounds as though someone was breathing in the room which broke my sleep once, nothing extraordinary happened. The breath-like sounds induced some fear, no doubt, but the weight of my fatigue had the better of this fear and I fell asleep again. By the time Vaishali woke me up, I was very well rested.

We exchanged very few words at the dinner table and during our walk to *Mayur Pathhar*. As before, Vaishali easily climbed the rock and I climbed it clumsily with her support.

And then the discussion started again. This time, thankfully, the exchanges took a less obscure turn. They were more in line with what I wanted to know.

"I guess it is firmly established that a spirit is nothing but a disembodied or unembodied consciousness."

"Yes, that part is firmly established indeed," I responded.

"Okay, now tell me what do you understand by evil spirits?

"Spirits that wish to harm the living, I believe."

"There is, of course, no doubt about that," she laughed, "but that is rather too simple an explanation."

"Well ..." I fumbled with words and realized that actually I knew very little about the subject. In fact, what I knew was not too far ahead of what an ordinary person quite uninitiated into the study of the paranormal would know. It felt pretty shameful.

"You must have studied about evil spirits, Mr. Banerjee, haven't you? You also must have dealt with quite a few of them as a paranormal investigator."

"To speak the truth," I preferred being unpretentious, "I don't know much about evil spirits. My ideas are rather bland. I believe just like humans, spirits could be broadly classified as good and evil. Spirits, which are of course nothing more than free consciousnesses, that harbor benevolent feelings for other consciousnesses, embodied, disembodied, or unembodied, are good, while those that are sadistic and derive pleasure from the pains of others are evil. The evil ones attempt to cause pain to other consciousnesses to satisfy their sadistic selves. I am afraid, I know no more."

"Never mind, Mr. Banerjee, I really admire your truthfulness."

"It is demeaning to have such poor possession of knowledge about evil spirits despite being a paranormal investigator but that's how it is."

"It is not demeaning at all, Mr. Banerjee," she reassured me, "you call yourself a paranormal investigator, don't you? The expression *investigator* says it all. You are investigating the possibilities, you are not claiming the knowledge of the truth. And in any case, a paranormal investigator cannot know all about the paranormal. Your area of focus as a paranormal investigator could be far different from the subject of evil spirits."

"Your words are very comforting, Vaishali," I felt better, "please tell me about evil spirits."

"Fine," she said thoughtfully, "let's first talk from the perspective of religion. Many religions talk about God and Anti-God. Of course, God is believed to be more powerful than Anti-God but the latter does have enough powers to cause nuisances in the lives of those who love God and want to follow His ways. God does intervene every now and then to save His followers but it is not infrequent to see devotees falling victims to the Anti-God.

"But why does God allow that? Why would He want His followers to fall prey to His adversary?" I asked.

"Mr. Banerjee, that's a question thinkers have pondered over for centuries together. There is, however, still no definitive answer. I will explain the answer that appeals to me most. Look, God actually has no adversary. Nothing is beyond God and everything that is there is an emanation from His being. So Anti-God or Satan, as he is called in many religions, is also nothing more than a part and parcel of God."

"Evil is also a part of God, you mean?"

"It has to be. God is believed to be the supreme. No one can surpass God as there is nothing beyond or different from God. Every aspect of existence, tangible or intangible, is actually a manifestation of God. So evil cannot exist if God doesn't want it to exist. Also evil does have to have its ultimate causal agency somewhere. That causal agency lies within the being of God ... it has to be there somewhere within God as there is nothing that is beyond or different from God."

"In that case is God worthy of respect?"

"You are a writer, aren't you?"

"How does that relate to my question?"

"First answer me," she spoke with greater force, "are you a writer?"

"Yes, I am, I believe," I said nodding.

"And you also write fiction?"

"Yes."

"Are all your characters and circumstances you write about are good?"

"No, it can never be that way. Such a story will make little sense."

"So there are bad characters and difficult situations in your stories?"

"Of course."

"That's exactly why God's ways are both good and bad. He is like a writer. He derives pleasure from his creations, and creations, you would appreciate, are often bland if there is no mix of things. An all good creation would not appeal to anyone."

"I am not quite convinced, Vaishali," I moved my head.

"I am not asking you to agree with me. This is just a viewpoint. I am myself not sure as to what is the truth. I just tried to answer your question as to why should God command respect given the fact that evil forces also come from Him? He may be respected because He is the creator and derives pleasure from his creations, just the way a writer derives pleasure from his or her stories. Anyway, coming back to what we were discussing … God and Anti-God both exist. Likewise, there are angels and fallen angels. Now, who are angels? Those ethereal beings who are on God's side. And fallen angels? Those who are on Anti-God's side.

Needless to say, the forces of God which may be called *good forces* and the forces of Anti-God, also called Satan in many traditions, which may be called *evil forces* are in a state of perennial battle. Sometimes the good forces win and sometimes the bad forces overwhelm the good."

"So it is not always the good that wins?"

"Leading writers on sorcery, many of whom were great sorcerers and sorceresses themselves, believe that evil also has a chance against the good. Many religions contest that idea. According to these faiths, it is always the good that triumphs. Traditions of sorcery in this part of the country however do not agree with that idea."

"I think," I said, "many religions will also contest the idea that evil also emanates from God."

"You are absolutely right, Mr. Banerjee but that's not what all traditions of sorcery accept."

"Hmm hmm."

"Now, let's understand what is God or Anti-God for that purpose? A good spiritualist will tell you that God is nothing but consciousness and everything that emanates from Him is also one or the other form of consciousness. Matter, energy, time and what not … everything, real or abstract is a form of consciousness. So why should God be held special? That's because God is the primal consciousness – the root of all other consciousnesses."

"Indeed, so Satan, angels and fallen angels are all consciousnesses according to this view."

"Yes, Mr. Banerjee. Likewise good spirits and evil spirits are also consciousnesses. With that understood, let us now focus on evil spirits. Evil spirits are of two types – one that had manifested in a human body and then got disembodied at the time of death, and the other that had never manifested itself. Quite clearly, I mean disembodied evil spirits and unembodied evil spirits."

"What about disembodied spirits from animal bodies or inanimate substances?"

"Those are pretty harmless. Until a consciousness grows sufficiently high to become entitled to a human body, it is not considered worthy enough for being classed as good or evil."

"Okay Vaishali, carry on."

"Now, disembodied evil spirits can harm in many ways, the worst being the killing of the victim. Most of the poltergeist activities, cases of possession and harmful paranormal phenomena such as tragedies at haunted houses are because of disembodied evil spirits. But the unembodied spirits are much more dangerous. Do you know what is a demon?"

"An unembodied spirit, I believe," I replied.

"Not exactly," she cleared her throat, "it is true that by its very nature, a demon is always an unembodied spirit but all unembodied spirits are not demons. A demon can be reckoned as a direct agent of Satan and is far more powerful and evil than an evil disembodied spirit. A demon is very intelligent, far more intelligent than a spirit disembodied from a human body, but it casts its intelligence on achieving evil ends."

"What can it do?"

"Possibly everything bad that you can think of," a pall of gloom and fear came over her face.

"What's wrong Vaishali?"

She didn't reply. The fear that had caught her seemed to firm up its grip.

"Anything wrong?"

"What is right, Mr. Banerjee? Everything seems to be going wrong," She spoke with difficulty.

"If you are not feeling well, we can stop the discussion now."

"No, I am almost done."

"Okay, then let's wrap up quickly," I suggested.

"Mr. Banerjee," she continued, "the maximum damage an evil spirit or a demon can cause is death. But the demon often makes the death very horrific and painful. Sometimes the death caused by a demon is so painful, that the pain also lingers beyond the death. What we are dealing with at *Prithaka* is …"

"What? Demoniac phenomena?"

She nodded as a cloud of fear descended over her eyes again. I found myself cold as this truth surfaced. I can't say how long thereafter did we continue to sit there but it must have been quite long. When she spoke again she seemed to have won back her composure.

"You don't have any reasons to be afraid, Mr. Banerjee, rest assured."

"What about you?"

"Maybe we can talk about that some other time," she coughed, "I guess this is where we should close the discussion on consciousness. I have spoken enough to form a ground for you to understand the paranormal phenomena that you say have gripped you. However, you shall realize that you are under no threat when I tell you more about the paranormal activities at *Prithaka*. What you know at the moment is just a glimpse of the truth. Let's go now."

We got up and walked.

14 THE ROBED FIGURE AGAIN!

I was back in the same bedroom but there were no fears in my mind. Vaishali's assurances that the room was safe somehow felt very believable now. I stretched out on the bed with my mind crowded with the ideas on consciousness that Vaishali and I had discussed. As a part of my research on ghosts and spirits and other paranormal activities, I had done a good deal of study on consciousness and related subjects. I also had some grasp on many of the ideas she talked about. Yet after the discussions, I felt hugely enriched in the subject. It was as if someone had given me very fresh insights into it and reinforced what I knew about the subject to a degree I had never imagined possible. More importantly, she also provided the connecting links between what I knew and the fresh knowledge that I gathered. I now admired Vaishali all the more for her knowledge and rational interpretation of things. But I still had little idea as to what she was up to. I could sense from the discussions that she was also into magic like her mother but she had given me little hints as to what was really on.

I had rested enough during the day and therefore sleep eluded me. For a while I watched the curtains swell up and down in tune with the winds. My mind went to my dear friend Saikat. What was he doing now? How would he have reacted to the sequence of events at *Prithaka*, I wondered. I was missing him terribly. If I wasn't in a position to form an opinion about Vaishali so far, it was only because my dear friend was not by my side to help me with things. This was just one of the few cases in which I was having to work alone. And as fate would have it, this would turn out to be one of the most challenging cases of all. A deafening sound brought me out of my thoughts. It was a short but a terrible sound! It was as if someone had made a sharp strike on a piece of metal. After a few moments, when I had come to terms with it, I rushed to the window and looked outside. I was sure that the sound had come from outside. As expected, nothing was visible. I looked around to see if there was a visible change in the surroundings. There was none. But as I turned around a corner of my eye met a light somewhere. This arrested my motion and I looked out again to find out what it was. I did spot it in a while. It was again a flickering light to my right moving along the slope of the highest hillock visible from my window. I had my heart in my mouth at the thought of what happened last night when I spotted the flickering light. I wondered if an eerie figure would be standing behind me when I turned around, just as it had happened last night. I turned around to have my worst fears come true! There it was. The same figure in the dark robe! And it looked more threatening than last night. It appeared as though it would suddenly lunge forward and consume my existence in the most devilish way possible.

"Wh … who?" I reacted with my voice hardly even audible to myself.

The figure stayed put for a while and then seemed to have advanced by a small yet a perceptible distance. As I began to choke, it struck me again that in situations such as these one's fear could be one's biggest enemy. That's because one's fear could act as food for the ethereal being one is confronting. It was difficult to be in charge of myself again but luckily a part of my mind was still strong enough to put up a brave face. The robed figure floated further towards me and was now almost in touching distance. However, I had by now gained enough strength to at least put up some amount of resistance should it attacked. The robed figure retracted as before in a flash. I could again sense that it was not walking. Though I could not see where its feet were or if it had feet at all, I somehow was convinced that only its robe and no part of its body was in touch with the floor. It was moving like a wave. It stood for a while near the door and then moved backward with even greater alacrity till I could see it no more. A disturbing thought came to my mind. The second appearance of the figure somehow felt like an indication of my impending death. The thought was further fuelled when the visual representations of death as given in various books on occult and other ethereal disciplines flowed into my psyche. Indeed, the robed figure looked like one such representation.

"Vaishali, Vaishali," I shouted in indignation but got no response.

"Vaishali, where are you?" I shouted again.

Yet again no response followed. What followed were the sounds of someone breathing heavily from outside the window. I tried to move towards the window but realized that I had lost control over my limbs. With a lot of difficulty I did finally manage to go over to the window and as luck would have it, I got entangled in one of the curtains. Releasing myself from the curtain turned out to be quite an ordeal. I never imagined that the grasp of a soft curtain could be that formidable. The more I tried to release myself, the greater was the entanglement! Then a chill ran down my spine at the thought that the entanglement could be the deliberate act of the being that was breathing heavily. The thought soon turned into a conviction when the pressure of the curtain multiplied from all sides. Now I felt I was in somebody's arms. The pressure increased further. Thankfully, the idea that one should not give in to one's fears in situations such as this was still in my mind and I began to resist. As I applied more strength, the arms appeared to loosen their hold around me. And then suddenly all the pressure was gone! I released myself from the curtain and struggled for breath. The idea that the second appearance of the robed figure somehow signified my impending death was fortified by what just happened. Fear gripped my mind. I had never been that afraid before. As I slowly began to regain command over my mind and body, I heard the heavy breathing again. I rushed downstairs calling out the name of my hostess as loudly as I could but there was no response. I wasn't carrying a lantern and it was pretty dark but my pupils were adjusted to the dim conditions. Therefore, I didn't have much difficulty in locating the door of her room.

"Vaishali, Vaishali," I knocked vigorously at the door.

No one responded. Then I pushed the door and it opened with a creaky sound. It was almost pitch dark inside. This was the first time I was inside her room. I could see nothing. Either there was no window or the window was completely covered with perfectly opaque materials. What was this girl up to? I found myself completely out of wits. Why did she give me such a long discourse on consciousness? Yes, it is understandable that knowledge of consciousness and its myriad ways is crucial to understanding spirit phenomena and other paranormal happenings but it now felt pretty improbable that she had discussed consciousness at such consummate length with me with a view to explain the paranormal phenomena at *Prithaka*. In all probability she had had such a long discussion with me on consciousness simply to avoid a direct talk on the spate of paranormal activities that could kill me anytime. So could all her niceties have been mere playacting, I wondered. I now had little reasons not to believe that she had acted like a vamp.

"Vaishali," I spoke again but this time in a softer tone.

A dead silence was the only response.

"Vaishali, are you here?"

No, there was no response even this time. It felt that she was not in her room. I advanced further into the room with no idea as to where I was headed. A thin line of dim light coming through the linear space between the door and its frame was my only guide. I moved my hands around to check if I had any further space to move. But why was I walking so deep into her room, I myself didn't know. I reasoned, with whatever little reason my stressed and confounded psyche was still left with, that staying there for long was not a good idea. However, I took the decision of leaving the room a bit too late for its door closed with a bang. I rushed at it and moved my hands around on its wood frantically in a bid to locate a possible handle for opening it. There was none! I moved my hand up to see if there was a bolt at upper corner of the door towards its loose end. Yes, there was a bolt indeed. However, it offered me too small a grip to open the door. Was I trapped? Well, that seemed pretty probable. So was it a terrible vamp I had been dealing with so far? What would happen next – my death? Was someone there in the room to deliver the final killing blow? What led me to move so far into the room? Was I under some ethereal influence already? Alongside negotiating with a torrent of questions, I tried all I could to open the door. But there seemed little hope. The door had almost got jammed into its frame and could open only if someone pushed it from outside. I moved back into what could be the middle of the room resigning to my fate. I groped in the dark for a bed or something on which I could at least sit down for I felt too drained to keep standing. I would have sat down on the floor if my movements had not been obstructed by what felt like a bed. I felt it with my hands, it was a bed indeed. I sat down waiting for whatever fate held for me. There was nothing I could do now. I wondered if this room would have some light with the coming of the day. It was possible that the window and other openings, if there were any window and other openings that is, had been covered in such a manner that the room remained pitch-dark all through the day unless its door to the dining space was opened. Then I heard a movement around! No, I was not alone in the room! I heard it again and yet again. It sounded like a bird fluttering its wings. The movement happened again and it felt closer. Then there was some movement on the bed also. Thereafter, the two movements happened together. I could feel my mind and body giving in to the horrors around me. I had no strength left for any further resistance. It was all over! I recalled my loved ones as I prepared myself for death. Death could now come from any side and at any moment. But then death didn't happen? What happened was what I had least expected in the given circumstances. The door flung open with as much suddenness as it had shut down! It was an incredible sight – the open door! As I consumed moments to believe that the door was really open, the thought that the door could shut down again fuelled my almost dead limbs into action. I stood up and flashed out of the room. The sight of the dining space was such a huge relief. I had encountered so dark a set of circumstances in Vaishali's room that the dim light conditions of where I was standing now appeared bright.

I moved forward in the direction of the living area. Would going back to my bedroom be the right thing to do, I wondered. No, it would certainly not be prudent to go back to that room. In fact, no part of Latika Griha appeared safe. So I decided to move out of the house and sit somewhere in the meadows waiting for the dawn. I got yet another surprise to find the main door open. Somehow the open door appeared vicious despite the strong impulse that I should be out of the house at the earliest. I realized that my intuition was right when I moved closer to the door. At a point roughly between the door and the metallic gate stood the same robed figure! For a moment I thought of going back to my room again but then decided against it as regardless of where I went, the robed figure could reach there in a flash. Instead, going out of *Latika Griha* appeared to be a better bet. That's because if I was destined to take on this robed figure, then it was better to take it on in the open rather than in the confines of a room. Being out of the house could still give me some amount of chance to run away from it although I understood that running away from an ethereal being is a near impossibility. After some thought I was convinced that moving out was indeed the best option. Even waiting in my position inside the house with a view to act according to what the robed figure did next didn't feel like a prudent idea for it could be in touching distance from me in the twinkling of an eye giving me absolutely no time to react. So I finally stepped out of the house. To my left and right were lawns with tall grasses with occasional appearances of bushy outgrowths. I wondered if I should try to escape by running through one of these lawns. Suddenly the robed figure drew close to me and now there was no scope to run away. The fear was crushing me and I found myself almost paralyzed. I tried to retract but couldn't. There was just no strength in my limbs. The robed figure trembled and then took its hands out. The hands looked human. In fact, they looked very familiar. Then it used its hands to uncover its face. It was Vaishali behind the robes!

15 THE FLIGHT

As I continued to gaze at her face in utter disbelief, the beatific smile adorned her lips again. Her smile had a therapeutic effect on me. I felt much lighter and the fear disappeared altogether. I could feel my limbs moving again.

I was about to speak when Vaishali placed a finger on her lips.

"Shhh…" Her smile widened.

She turned around and moved towards the gate. As I tried to make sense of things, she slightly turned her face and gestured me to follow. The distrust I had developed for her in the face of the trauma I had just been through disappeared in a jiffy. Rather I felt really comfortable and safe in her company. Without a thought I started following her. The gate seemed to open on its own as she moved through it. I had been a witness to such mind-boggling unusual events at *Prithaka*, that the gate opening by itself felt too small an occurrence to merit attention. I continued to follow Vaishali as she hastened her motion. And soon she moved even faster. However, I didn't have any difficulty in keeping pace with her. In a while I realized that we were moving at breathtaking speed. I wondered how we were walking that fast. Or were we running? The meadows, trees and hillocks simply flashed past us. I felt lighter, much lighter as though some huge weight had been dissociated from my being. I mused on the possibility if I just died – maybe the spirit just got released from the bondage of the body. Even if it was so, I cared little for I simply relished the lighter state of being I found myself in. We sped up even more and soon everything around looked like a blurry continuum. The cold winds ran amok. They felt incisive as if I was braving an endless streak of randomly moving blades. Now another thought crossed my mind – I couldn't possibly be dead for if it had been so I couldn't have felt the winds. Can the spirit feel the winds just as a physical body does, I wondered. I didn't know the answer. It is possible that a spirit could have some sensations of the body. But whatever the truth was, it hardly mattered. The only thing that mattered now was my incredible airy existence and I wanted to hold on to it. Our speed went up further. It was now I realized that I was neither walking nor running. I was floating with my feet a few inches over the ground like the robed figure who was none other than Vaishali! So I was dead after all, I mused on my state of existence again. How could otherwise I be floating? Could a living man float like this? Well, again I was not sure of the answer. Was I dreaming? No, surely not. Things were too real to be a dream. I was certainly floating but had no idea how. But where were we headed? Although nothing around me was distinctly visible, I had an intuition that we were on our way to the peak of *Mahachoti*, the highest hill in the region. And the speed went up still further. By now I had almost got into what I can best describe as a musical harmony with the lightning speed of my flight despite the sword-like strips of wind touching me from all sides and I cared least as to what lay ahead of me. I wouldn't mind even if the most disastrous state of being awaited me for the lighter state was worth living even if it led to something acrimonious. I closed my eyes and was soon in utter ecstasy. For a long time thereafter, or so it appeared, I continued to be in that bliss.

I felt the flight ending abruptly and my feet landing on the ground. I couldn't, however, open my eyes for the meditative state was too strong. Shortly, I began to feel heavier. It was as if something had got stuck to me. What was it? Did I just come back from death? The feeling of being in a body grew stronger although I wasn't sure if I was ever out of it.

"Mr. Banerjee," Vaishali's voice flowed into my ears.

I opened my eyes and found nothing … virtually nothing! Where was I? I was about to move forward but someone stopped me from behind.

"No Mr. Banerjee," Vaishali's words flowed into my ears again, "there is no scope for moving forward, at least not with your physical body."

"Where am I?" I said.

"I am sure you can find that out yourself," Vaishali responded.

I could now make out that she was speaking from behind me.

"What are you doing behind me, Vaishali?"

"I am supporting you so that you don't trip over."

"Trip over …" I was completely puzzled.

"Look down, Mr. Banerjee," she said.

I looked down and figured soon that I was atop a steep hill. I was somehow sure that we stood at the highest point of *Mahachoti*. A little forward or a little backward could mean death but then the idea of dying did not frighten me at all.

"Where are we standing, Mr. Banerjee?" She sounded all the more lyrical and caring.

"We are at the tip of the *Mahachoti Hill*," I replied.

"Wow," she laughed, "how do you know?"

"I don't know how I know."

"Maybe you do," her breath touched the back of my neck.

"I don't know."

"Why? Didn't someone tell you where we were headed during our flight?"

In the face of all the strangeness that dictated my stay at *Prithaka*, the fact that she knew about my intuition about heading towards *Mahachoti* during the flight didn't feel too queer.

"You didn't answer me, Mr. Banerjee. Didn't someone tell you that we were on our way to *Mahachoti* while we were floating?" Vaishali pressed for an answer.

"Well, I had an intuition."

"O really, you had an intuition!" She laughed heartily.

Although her laughter virtually mocked my understanding of things, I didn't mind for there was now a friendly tenor in every action of hers.

"Why don't you tell me what actually happened?" I joined in the laughter.

"Of course I will, that's why I have brought you here. First, let's move to a safer position."

Vaishali helped me to a more secure place in the *Mahachoti*. Her hands felt ruggedly strong as she maneuvered my rather cumbersome body over the twisty edges of the peak. We were still close to the peak sitting under a massive Deodar tree.

"Are you fine?" She asked.

"Yes, I am."

"Any problems with breathing … these heights could be very nasty at times."

"No, I am doing great, Vaishali."

"So you had an intuition that we were moving towards the *Mahachoti*?" She returned to the point with some more laughter.

"That had been my belief till you laughed it away," I loved the joviality of the air between us.

"The truth is Mr. Banerjee," she said as she moved the locks spread over her face by the naughty winds, "I communicated the information to your mind."

"That we were going to *Mahachoti*?"

"Yes."

"You mean you established a telepathic connection?"

"Absolutely."

"My faculty of getting surprised had got somewhat dented in the face of the ceaseless chain of surprises that *Prithaka* has opened up upon me. However, I must say, your words seem to have mended that faculty for I find myself surprised again at what you just said."

"If you find my telepathic connection with you surprising, then the further revelations will simply overwhelm your faculties."

"O please overwhelm me immediately, I am dying to know what exactly is happening around me."

"Let me begin my next streak of explanations with some fundamental facts that you might have already guessed by now, okay?" She now took her robe off looking very happy as though relieved of some strenuous ethereal duties.

"Okay, Vaishali."

"First, the robed figure is none else but me … you know it already, don't you?"

"Yes."

"I believe the primary fear because of which you didn't want to go back to your room was that the so-called robed figure could hurt you. Now you know that you had no reasons to be afraid of the robed figure because it was me all along. That is why I have been telling you all the time that you were perfectly safe in your room."

"I understand that," I said as she took a pause for a breath.

"Now, you have also been extremely intrigued by the movement of the flickering light over the highest and the steepest hill visible from the window of your bedroom."

"O yes, that flickering light puzzled me inside out."

"First of all, let me tell you that the hill on which you saw the light is the one we are sitting on right now."

"You mean we are on the same hill that is visible from that window? And that hill is *Mahachoti*?"

"Absolutely."

"I had actually wondered once or twice if it was *Mahachoti*. I must say it has an intimidating look."

"Well, I would beg to disagree on that. I would rather say

Mahachoti is the most beautiful and the most spiritual hill around. Tourists take interest in *Mahachoti* because of its height and steepness. They are so foolish. They are completely unaware that this hill has a heart and a mind of its own. It can talk to you just the way a friend talks to you if your senses are subtle enough to establish a communion with it."

"That means my senses are also not subtle enough for it doesn't communicate with me."

"No, Mr. Banerjee, your senses are very subtle to receive the waves of the ethereal realms. Unfortunately, you have placed covers of material reason and logic over your senses. Sometimes when your spiritual faculties become active enough to realize their true potentials, these covers get removed and you begin to feel the ethereal. Some of the incidents you have described in your book *My Paranormal Files: The Bureau* wherein you found yourself enmeshed in the web of the ethereal are actually indicative of those moments when these covers get removed. The day you master your own being in a manner so as to remove these covers at will, you would be receptive to all that is happening around you. Communicating with this hill would then be just a small thing vis-à-vis what you would be able to do or achieve."

"That sounds nice, Vaishali, but I am not too sure if being in such a state at all times would be a good thing."

"Of course it is not good to be in such a state on a perennial basis. We are humans and we are not supposed to be carrying that state all the time. But those of us who can control their subtler senses can switch on or switch off that mode of existence at will," she said somewhat excitedly.

"Can you do that at will?"

"Yes, I can. I have developed these powers after years of practice."

"And you believe I too can have these powers?"

"I don't have the slightest doubt on that count."

I deliberated on her words and smiled.

"I will now come back to the flickering light," she continued, "well, Mr. Banerjee, that flickering light was nothing but a part of my consciousness moving over the hills. Sometimes an elevated form of disembodied consciousness could appear as a light to one who is receptive to ethereal phenomena. Ninety nine point nine nine percent of the population will see nothing if such a disembodied consciousness passes before their eyes but people like you who are receptive to ethereal phenomena can see it. I must add that even people like you cannot see such an ethereal presence at all times. It is only when their spiritual faculties are active, can the likes of you see it. I guess on both occasions when you saw the light, you were in some kind of a subtle state or the other. You might have woken up from sleep and still have been dwelling on the border of your conscious and subconscious minds or you might have got into a deep state of thoughts thereby moving into a meditative state. Whatever the reasons might have been, subtler facets of your senses were in play when you spotted the light."

"You are right, Vaishali, on both occasions I was in such a state."

"I know, I know," she smiled.

"This means you can throw the consciousness out of your body at will?"

"Yes, I can. However, what you saw on the hill was not my whole consciousness. It was just a part of it."

"That's really interesting Vaishali. So it is possible for you to be in and out of your body at the same time?"

"Yes, I can do it."

"It is like dividing one's consciousness into two and keeping one of the parts inside one's body and throwing the other part to move around in the open."

"You could say that Mr. Banerjee only if you treat consciousness as something divisible. If you choose to treat consciousness as indivisible, then you could imagine it as having expanded beyond the limits of the body. Again, none of these statements presents the full truth as the attributes of consciousness can never be explained in words."

"Indeed, Vaishali."

"Now I will come to the next question that might have driven you to the limits of confusion. And that question is who am I – an ordinary girl or a witch? After having seen me doing things that would rather be reckoned as paranormal not only by an average human but also by people who have some understanding of the occult, you might be inclined to think of me as a witch. But the truth, Mr. Banerjee, is that I am neither an ordinary girl nor a witch."

She looked up at the heavens and then closed her eyes. The winds continued to play with her hair.

16 HER MOTHER'S PREDICAMENT

For a long time she didn't speak as the night accentuated her bewitching looks. Being so close to her was nothing short of ecstasy. Sometimes her hair met my face and I still cherish the memories of those moments. She was about to reveal her true identity and I was eager to know the truth and yet I didn't have the slightest impulse to disturb the spell of silence that preceded the disclosure. Folds appeared on her forehead at times. Perhaps she was trying to assume command over some mental turmoil. Shortly, the folds came no more possibly indicative of her having conquered the turmoil. The sweetness of her being grew more and more idyllic with passage of time. The dim light reflecting from her cheeks had a glow of its own. It was as if the light was being fuelled to brightness by her spotless skin. Then I spotted a drop of tear trickling down her nose. I still didn't say a word for the tear seemed like a natural and necessary consequence of her cogitations. Then a calm descended on her face. She had apparently fought her way through a disturbing thought. The line the tear had made ended on her upper lip. The gleam of her lips caught my attention. Nature must have used its choicest skills to carve her lips. Driven by the impulse to feel them I raised my hand but stopped short of running my fingers over those exquisite lips at the sudden realization of the mindlessness surrounding what I was about to do.

Her sweetness made me lose all my sense of time and I can't tell for sure how long the spell of silence continued. When she finally opened her eyes, I was still lost in the charm of her lips. In fact, I didn't even realize for a while that she had opened her eyes.

"What are you looking at, Mr. Banerjee?" Her words shook me up as we exchanged a smile.

"Well … nothing," I somehow put up a response.

"It is not good to lie, tell me what were you looking at?" Vaishali's beatific smile would have stolen my attention again if I had not forced myself to look down."

"I … I …" I wished I had enough courage to speak the truth.

"No problem," the caring tonality of her words was unmistakable, "you don't have to tell me anything now. I can sense that someday you would certainly tell me all that you have kept guarded in your heart."

As I pondered over the possible sense of her words, she continued, "Let me now finally tell you who am I. You might be a little disturbed to know the truth but I guess time has come for you to know the reality."

"Rest assured, I will not limit myself to the surface understanding of your words. I will go deep and try to gauge their true import."

"Okay, Mr. Banerjee, the truth is I am on my way to becoming a powerful sorceress," Vaishali looked up at me to check my reaction.

I was by no stretch of imagination unsettled by what she just said. I had rather expected her to say something like this. However, I wasn't sure if I understood her words. That's because as far as I knew there was no difference between a sorceress and a witch. The expressions *sorceress* and *witch* are almost always used as synonyms in English language.

"You seem to be confused if not disturbed," She managed a faint smile.

"I am not disturbed but surely confused."

"I know what has confused you. You see no difference between a witch and a sorceress. So my argument that I am not a witch but a sorceress doesn't quite make sense. Isn't it?"

I nodded yet again wondering as to how she knew what was hovering in my head.

"In common parlance, *witch* and *sorceress* may mean the same but those who have good understanding of occult never mix up the two. In very simple language the difference is this – a witch practices magic with a view to gain ethereal powers for self-gratification; on the contrary, a sorceress practices magic to unfold the mysteries of the physical, mental and spiritual universes. In fact, a sorceress does not treat the physical, mental and spiritual worlds as separate realms. Rather, a sorceress deems the physical world as contained in the mental world and the mental world as contained in the spiritual world. Are you following me, Mr. Banerjee?"

"Yes Vaishali," I nodded, "but could you elaborate upon this perception of a sorceress, I mean – physical world being a part of the mental world, and the mental world being a part of the spiritual world."

"Sure Mr. Banerjee," the affection in her tone had grown, "the physical world scarcely has an existential value unless there's an observer who could interpret it with his or her mind. Therefore, the physical world is hardly anything more than a mental perception of the observer. Your perception of the physical world could be completely different from my perception of it and yet both our perceptions may be deemed as correct. Therefore, there could be nothing such as an absolute perception of the physical world. A human's eyes are sensitive only to the electromagnetic waves of what is referred to as the visible range in the spectrum. Imagine what would happen if a human's eyes suddenly become sensitive to the x-rays instead of the waves of the visible range. His or her perception of the physical world will change all together. He or she will see bones all around instead of skin. Likewise, one's perception of the physical world will be like that of a bat if one gets sensitive to the ultraviolet waves and like that of a snake if one gets sensitive to the infrared radiations. So you see, it is all in the mind of the observer when it comes to perceiving the physical world. No two living beings, even if they belong to the same species, could have the same interpretation and consequently the same perception of the physical world. Therefore, a true sorceress or sorcerer always thinks of the physical world as a part of the mental world."

"Yes indeed," I was already deeply drawn into her explanations.

"Now, one's mental world is one's realm of thoughts and interpretations. Such a world, you would appreciate, is much subtler than the physical world. Every human has his or her own mental world. You could intuitively sense that one's mental world is actually an emanation of one's consciousness. You would also appreciate that consciousness is the primal element of the spiritual world. That's why a sorceress would rather think of mental world as an intrinsic part of the spiritual world. The spiritual world is the ultimate world. There is nothing that is not a part of the spiritual world. Everything, whether material or abstract, belongs to the spiritual world. Have you understood, Mr. Banerjee?"

"Yes, I have, Vaishali," I said.

"Okay, now I will tell you more about my mother. My mother, I have already explained, happened to be one of the finest sorceresses of her times. She mastered the art of magic. The ultimate goal of true magic lies in understanding the truth underlying consciousness and becoming proficient in dealing with all kinds of consciousnesses. There is no other goal of true magic because if one could have conscious control over one's own consciousness as well as over consciousnesses of those that surround one, there is simply nothing that one couldn't do. Whether it be the consciousness of the apparently living or the apparently non-living, a sorceress can communicate with it. By communicating with consciousness of an entity, my mother could manipulate the way it behaved. Now, my mother could virtually talk to everything – plants, animals, roads, hills, rivers and everything else you can think of. If you allow me to use the expression *spirit* for *consciousness*, then I would say she was at ease with the spirits of all entities around her. She had at her beck and call the spirits of the five elements of the universe. All she had to do was to make a wish and these spirits would ensure that her wish was fulfilled."

"That's really amazing, Vaishali."

"Let me now tell you a little more about the spirits of the five elements of the universe. It goes without saying that for reasons of limitation of language, all I can do is to present a very simplistic picture of these elements. Each one of these elements comprises countless spirits. For example, earth has countless spirits, each with the essential attributes of *earthiness*. Likewise, fire also has countless spirits each carrying the essential traits of what you may call *fireness*. The same applies to air, water and sky. It is strange but true that an expert magician or sorceress could deal with any of these spirits as though she is dealing with a human spirit. My mother knew plenty of earth spirits, fire spirits, air spirits, water spirits and sky spirits. She would simply use them to gather more knowledge about the elements of the universe. In order to gain knowledge, she would sometimes have to use these spirits to manipulate the world around her. As a part of her experimentations to know the unknown, she would often make the earth spirits cause minor tremors, fire spirits cause fires, air spirits cause storms, water spirits cause inundation of lands and sky spirits cause rains and hailstorms. All this might sound like a fairytale to a commoner but now that you have already had a demonstration of what spirits of earth, air and sky can do, you should have no difficulty in placing your trust in what I am saying."

"You mean this flight we have had was actually made possible by the spirits of earth, air and sky?"

"That's right, Mr. Banerjee. I am still not an expert like my mother in dealing with the spirits of the physical universe but I have some knowledge."

"And that knowledge is enough to cause such an extraordinary flight from *Latika Griha* to the peak of *Mahachoti*," I laughed.

"You call it extraordinary! If you find this extraordinary how will you be reacting to the greater feats of sorcery? What I did was very simple. I just directed some of the spirits of earth, air and sky to work together to make the flight happen and they carried out my orders."

"But that is an incredible feat in my view."

"That's because you are not a sorcerer, Mr. Banerjee. In the light of what a true sorceress or sorcerer can achieve, this flight of ours should not even be deemed as an act worthy enough to be called a magical feat."

"I wonder what more things a sorceress can achieve."

"There's hardly anything that a sorceress of the level of my mother cannot achieve. However, a true sorceress like my mother does not use her magical powers for material gains. She would use her powers only to gain knowledge and elevate herself spiritually. Not even once did my mother use her powers for self-gratification. In fact, if a magician begins to use her powers for self-gratification, then such powers begin to wane away."

"But she did cause storms and tremors, didn't she?"

"Yes she did," she replied, "but not with the purpose of giving herself pleasure. Her incredible feats of magic were always the effects or what you may technically call *necessary corollaries* to her experiments. She never performed these feats for public exhibition or for gaining name and popularity. She was extremely secretive about her activities and would act as an ordinary woman in the midst of commoners. However, with time as she turned into a truly great magician performing magic of the highest level, she could no longer keep things concealed from the public. Many had seen her flying and walking over water and fire and perform other incredible acts of magic. Unfortunately ..."

"Perhaps the people around her didn't take her magic very kindly."

"You have guessed that correctly, Mr. Banerjee. Instead of appreciating her quest for knowledge and recognizing the science behind her experimentations, people branded her a witch. People can be really foolish, you see. My mother had to live up with endless humiliation and insult. In an assembly of villagers it was decided to socially ostracize her. Some villagers went to the extent of demanding that her house, that is, *Latika Griha* be demolished and she be forced to leave the village. My father, despite being a good man, didn't quite give her the kind of support she needed at that time. He did love my mother a lot but never appreciated her passion for the occult. My father did not mind as long as my mother limited her pursuit of the occult to studying books and travelling to various parts of the country and abroad for gaining knowledge about the occult and the paranormal. However, he was strictly against my mother's conducting experiments of magic. My mother never wanted to hurt him but her quest for knowledge was too strong for self-control. She continued with her experiments and the gulf between them soon became irredeemable. Out of desperation, my father took to drinking. Meanwhile, in response to the demands of some villagers that *Latika Griha* be destroyed and my mother be shunted out of the village, another village assembly was called by the elders. By that time the differences between my parents had become common knowledge and one elder suggested that my father hated my mother because she was indulging in sexual activities with the agents of the devil, and that if she was allowed to continue her illicit activities, then the entire village would soon be controlled by the devil eventually resulting in the destruction of the village and the death of every villager. Despite hundreds of explanations by my mother, the villagers didn't listen. It was decided to demolish *Latika Griha* and banish her. My mother took recourse to law and was immediately given interim relief. Shortly thereafter, her petition was allowed and the pronouncements of the village assembly were held as illegal and overstepping of the powers conferred upon the assembly under the concerned statute for local self-government. The village elders were also warned against such arbitrary action that was completely in contravention with the laws governing village assemblies or *panchayats*, as they are called in the vernacular languages. The villagers, especially the village elders, took this setback as an insult to them and retaliated one day by attacking *Latika Griha*. Hundreds of men, young and old, ruthlessly damaged the house from all sides. They called my mother names and demanded that she left the village immediately. Some of the aggressive rioters broke open the front door and barged into the house. My father was in a drunken state at that time and did little to resist the attack. In any case, even if he had been in his senses, he could have done little to prevent the mob from damaging our property. My mother and I took refuge in a small cabin in the terrace. Luckily, this cabin was built in such a manner that it looked more like a part of the wall roughly along the edge towards the west of the terrace rather than like a cabin. That was why the mob couldn't discover us. Later, in the middle of the night, long after the mob had left, we came out and went downstairs. It was very dark. Apparently, all the lanterns had been destroyed. With a lot of difficulty we found our way to the kitchen. She fidgeted with her things in a drawer and managed to locate a candle. My mother lit it up and in its meager light we got a rough glimpse of the horrors around us. It was clear that the rioters had destroyed everything that came their way – furniture, wall lanterns, decorative pieces, glass items, utensils, doors, windows, walls, shelves, and even my toys. When I started whimpering, my mother put a finger on my lips and asked me to be quiet lest the sound should attract some rioter to barge into the house again. We looked around for my father. My mother whispered his name but he didn't respond. We went upstairs again and checked every room. It was really difficult to see in the flickering light of a single candle that my mother was holding. No, my father wasn't upstairs. We wondered if he had left the house for good. No, he hadn't as we would soon come to know. We walked down the stairs again and looked for him everywhere in the ground floor. When we had given up hope of seeing him in the house, I tripped over at a point close to the bottom of the staircase. I think you have guessed why I tripped over. Indeed, I stumbled over my father's lifeless body. I can still remember the horror in the eyes of his corpse. As my mother moved the candle over the body, we saw the brutal wounds that had been inflicted by the heartless intruders. Think of our plight! We couldn't even cry at this shocking tragedy fearing another possible attack. For a minute or so she sat close to my father's body like a statue with virtually expressionless eyes. Then she looked at me and said, 'I have to act and act fast. What I am going to do now would be the toughest challenge of my life. The two of us can survive only if I am successful in meeting this challenge.'

Tears flowed uncontrollably as she held me tightly in her arms.

'I am so sorry, my darling. I am so sorry,' she said kissing all over my cheeks.

'What are you going to do, mother?' I asked.

'I will do only what is left to be done, my child. Otherwise, these ruthless people will lynch us both to death the moment they see us. If we had the slightest chance of running away from here, I wouldn't have considered doing this. But my child, there is absolutely no chance of an escape. So I must do it. I feel so bad about you. At your age you will have to witness this horrific procedure of sorcery.'

My mother tried hard to cry silently but the pain in her heart often undid her efforts. Every time a sound or two emanated from her throat, she put a hand on her mouth lest her cries should fall into the ears of those who were after our lives.

'I wish I could keep you away from all that I am going to do now but that could cause you great harm … so you must be by my side when I do this,' she continued crying.

'But mother, what are you going to do?' I asked and cried too with her," Vaishali's voice cracked as her emotions got the better of her.

17 THE LEGEND OF SARVANANDA

Vaishali took some time to get hold of her emotions and resumed her account, "I asked my mother repeatedly as to what she was talking about doing. For a long time she didn't give a clear reply. She was afraid that I would not be able to digest her ideas. However, as she felt she had no other option but to keep me by her side while she carried out her ideas, she did finally tell me what she wanted to do.

'I am going to perform a ritual, my child,' she said.

I didn't see what was so special about it. Ever since I could make sense of the world around me, I had been privy to the countless rituals she had been performing as part of her experimentations. So how would this ritual be any different? I said, 'So what, mother. I have seen so many of your rituals.'

'But this is very different, Vaishali. At your age it might be too much to absorb.'

I had never seen my mother so nervous. She had beads of sweat all over her face into some of which the lines of tears had diffused to cause ugly stretches of moisture."

"How old were you at that time, Vaishali?"

"Around seven."

"O how cruel fate could be," I remarked, "it is pathetic that you had to brave all that at such a tender age."

"There was more to follow, Mr. Banerjee. Can you guess what my mother told me?"

After a brief thought I moved my head, "I can't form an idea, Vaishali. What did she tell you?"

"She said, 'I have to do *shavasadhana*.' This was the first time I had heard that expression. 'What will you do, mother?' I was curious. '*Shavasadhana*, I will have to do *shavasadhana*,' she said and began to cry again. 'But what is *shavasadhana*, mother?' I asked. When she explained the ritual, I almost vomited my entrails out. It was the most sickening idea I had heard till then. Do you know what it is, Mr. Banerjee?"

"I can take a guess. *Shava* means a corpse and *sadhana* means spiritual practice. So *shavasadhana* should mean spiritual practice with a corpse ... I mean some kind of a spiritual practice in the vicinity of a corpse. Is that what it means?"

"You are close to the correct meaning. No doubt, *shava* means a corpse. *Sadhana*, strictly speaking, means spiritual endeavors to accomplish an intended goal. Therefore, *shavasadhana* means spiritual endeavors through a corpse to achieve the goal of one's choice. It is a tantric practice which is also very popular with the practitioners of sorcery and witchcraft in this part of the country."

"It sounds somewhat disgusting."

"Well, that's understandable," a faint smile came over her lips, "for most who are uninitiated into tantra or sorcery or other forms of magic, the very idea of being close to a corpse would feel disgusting."

Shortly thereafter she had a hearty laugh.

"What happened, Vaishali? Why are you laughing?" I was completely clueless.

"I have hardly told you anything about *shavasadhana* and you already find it disgusting. I wonder how you will react if I take you deeper into the subject."

"Why don't you try me?" I smiled.

"Well, I have little choice but to try you. That's because unless I tell you more about this ritual, I will not be able to explain what my mother did for our survival."

"I am ready to learn more about it, Vaishali. In fact, I am dying to learn more about it."

"Right then, Mr. Banerjee ... let me satisfy your curiosity. I am not an authority on this ritual but I will try to explain what I know," she elucidated, "*shavasadhana* happens to be one of the most difficult tantric rituals. The purpose of *shavasadhana* depends upon the practitioner. It could be done for one or more objectives such as gain of knowledge, propitiation of Goddess Kali, accomplishment of material goals, and achievement of magical powers. Can you guess on what does the practitioner have to sit while performing *shavasadhana*?"

"Don't tell me she has to sit on a corpse."

"But Mr. Banerjee," she laughed again, "the practitioner does indeed have to sit on a corpse."

"That sounds ..."

"That sounds what? Disgusting?"

"Yes."

"Why? A corpse is simply a lifeless material manifestation just like the soil we are sitting on now."

"What you are saying is the peak of rational analysis. Such degree of rationality often necessitates that humans give up their humanness and turn into machinelike entities. The disgust for a corpse springs from humanness. It is not easy for an average human to be treating a corpse and other lifeless entities such as soil and rocks on the same footing."

"I beg to disagree, one doesn't need to lose one's humanness to be a rationalist of the highest order. What you are referring to as humanness is actually a set of mindless weaknesses. I would rather believe perfect humanness to be a state bereft of such mindless weaknesses. It is only when one transcends such weaknesses, does one become a perfect human."

"Well," I said nodding, "you are right but not many people have the mettle of transcending these mindless weaknesses. I guess that's true of many spiritual aspirants as well."

"You are right. Spiritual aspiration is of different kinds and degrees. Not all spiritual practitioners are spiritual aspirants of the highest order. Some of these men and women are after material objectives. These people should never be reckoned as true spiritualists. The witches and shamans usually fall in this category. Many known to be sorcerers and sorceresses also seek self-gratification. The truth is very few of these people have the courage and maturity to perform *shavasadhana*. Unfortunately, some of those who do have the nerves to perform *shavasadhana* do so for material reasons rather than for spiritual growth."

She took a pause for reorganizing her thoughts and continued, "A legend goes that there was a spiritual aspirant by the name of Vasudeva who once worshiped Goddess Kali through tantric means at Kamakhya temple in Assam. After he finished, a divine voice informed him that in his next birth he would be his own grandson and that by performing *shavasadhana* in that birth he would accomplish salvation. Vasudeva confided the secret of *shavasadhana* in his trusted servant called Purnananda. As foretold, Vasudeva did reincarnate as his own grandson. His name in the new avatara was Sarvananda. Sarvananda didn't show any spark of brilliance in his early days. In fact, he grew up as a rather mediocre person. His father was one of the royal astrologers in the court of the King of Tripura. One day Sarvananda accompanied his father to the court. The men at the king's court thought that he would also be a brilliant astrologer like his father and thus requested him to demonstrate his command over astrology. Sarvananda messed up the whole thing. He proclaimed that day, which happened to be a new moon day, to be a full moon day. People laughed at his ignorance and his father, quite obviously, was embarrassed to the limits. Sarvananda left the court humiliated. The servant Purnananda, who was by now an old man, observed the somber mood of the young boy on his return and asked him as to what had gone wrong. Sarvananda cried uncontrollably and narrated everything that had happened in the court. Purnananda, who had received training of Tantra from Vasudeva, realized that it was time for Sarvananda, the reincarnation of none other than Vasudeva, to perform *shavasadhana*. He took him to the forest and explained what he would have to do. When Purnananda was confident that Sarvananda would be able to perform *shavasadhana*, he offered his own body for the ritual. He told Sarvananda that he would remove his essential consciousness, what we normally call *sukshmamedha* in Sanskrit, from his body and thus the body would turn into a virtual corpse. Sarvandanda would have to sit on that corpse and recite the mantras that he had taught him. Purnananda explained that when Goddess Kali appeared before him after the successful completion of the ritual and asked him to make a wish, Sarvananda must ask her to first resurrect Purnananda and then do as he desired. Thereafter, things happened just as planned by Purnananda. He removed his essential consciousness from the body and Sarvananda sat over it and chanted the mantras with all devotion. After *shavasadhana* was successfully completed, Goddess Kali appeared and said, 'I am very pleased with your devotion, Sarvananda. I am eager to fulfill your wish.'

Sarvananda said, 'O Mother, please resurrect Purnananda and do as he desires.'

Goddess Kali smiled and brought Purnananda back to life.

Purnananda said, 'Mother, Sarvananda performed this *shavasadhana* just as he had been asked to do when he worshipped you at the Kamakhya temple while he was in the body of Vasudeva. Therefore, he must get salvation by the time his essential consciousness disembodies itself as foretold by the divine voice at Kamakhya. However, at the moment I desire that you save Sarvananda's honor. In the court of the King of Tripura, he proclaimed that this night would be a full moon night. This brought him untold flak as everyone knows that this happens to be a new moon night. O Mother, please make this a full moon night so that Sarvananda does not lose his honor.'

Goddess Kali granted the wish and a brightly shining moon appeared in the sky. All over the region of Tripura, people witnessed this unusual spectacle that defied all logic and astrological calculations. The people who humiliated Sarvananda were stunned to find the moon in the sky in all its splendor. They now hailed Sarvananda as the greatest ever astrologer and the king immediately desired that Sarvananda be given one of the highest seats in his court. But Sarvananda by now had become an enlightened soul. All he wanted now was to spend his time in extreme devotion to Goddess Kali. That is where the legend ends. How do you find the legend, Mr. Banerjee?"

"It is an absorbing story."

"This legend more or less tells us as to what is *shavasadhana* and what kind of results can be obtained from it."

"Hmm, hmm," I reacted.

"I guess now I can resume the story of my mother. You are now in a better position to understand what she did."

"I too think so, go ahead, Vaishali."

18 HE IS THERE ONE LAST TIME!

"My mother said, 'I will use your father's corpse for my *shavasadhana.*'

'No mother, don't do it,' I shouted. This idea was simply not acceptable. Every part of my body rebelled against what my mother wanted to do.

'Look my child,' my mother explained, 'this is our only chance. If I do not use your father's corpse for *shavasadhana,* we will die before the sunrise. And if I perform the ritual, then there is a good chance of our survival.'

'Can't you use some other corpse?' I said rather innocently knowing fully well that it was impossible to arrange another human body.

She smiled and said, 'You know the answer, my child. So, do I have your permission?'

I didn't reply.

After sometime when she knew I would never happily say *yes*, she said, 'Look my child, if I perform the ritual with your father's corpse, I may be able to talk to him for one last time. I am sure you would also like to talk to him once before he is cremated, wouldn't you like to tell him how much you love him before we cremate his body?'

I was stunned to know that my father would be able to talk one last time if my mother performed *shavasadhana*.

'I can really talk to him again?' I asked.

'Yes, but just one last time.'

Indeed, I wanted to tell my father how much I loved him. So I nodded my consent."

"She would have done it anyway even if you hadn't consented, wouldn't she?"

"No, she couldn't have."

"You mean your consent was important?"

"Yes, it was. Now I know it was. Before I got into sorcery myself, I also used to think that her bid to obtain my consent was simply an exercise to make me comfortable. But it wasn't just that. Many books by experts on *shavasadhana* suggest that every participant in a *shavasadhana* must agree to the arrangements of the ritual even if he or she has no direct role to play in it. That's because if a participant is unhappy or does not agree with the arrangements, he or she could be badly harmed by the dark creatures that might get released from their respective worlds during the ritual. I am sure you understand that for the purposes of *shavasadhana*, even a mere spectator is deemed as a participant." She took another pause for thoughts.

I looked at the sky for a hint of sun but there was none. It was still a very dark night and I had no idea what time it was.

"My mother first cleaned the wounds on my father's corpse," Vaishali continued, "then she turned it over and asked me to get the paste of sandalwood from her room. I took the candle and slowly walked towards her room. I still remember how hard it was for me to find my way alone in the house. As I walked up the stairs I heard my mother whisper, 'Don't be afraid. Nothing will happen.' Her room was in the first floor, two rooms away from your current bedroom. When I reached the door of her room, I felt a cool breeze on the back of my neck. I turned around but there was nothing. I pushed the door open and went over to the rack where the sandalwood paste was kept. I picked it up and hurried back. When I was about to cross the threshold, I saw something whitish dazzle past my field of vision. I was completely shaken but could not shout. My voice was badly choked. For a long time thereafter I stood at the door trying to regain my balance. My mother's voice helped me sum up courage. I heard her say in a very low pitch, 'What happened Vaishali? Don't be afraid. Please hurry.' I moved out of the room and hurried towards the staircase. It was then that I had to brave this figure again. Now, I had a better glimpse of it. It was a white figure. It resembled a human. It suddenly emerged close to the staircase and moved towards me. First, it was a slow walk but then it was a brisk movement. As it moved past me, I felt that cool breeze all over my body. The candle fell down from my hands as my head whirled. I would have fainted if it had not been for my mother's timely arrival at the spot. 'Vaishali, Vaishali,' she whispered into my ears, 'don't be afraid. Everything is just fine. Come with me.' She picked up the candle and pulled me forward. I struggled to keep balance and staggered the next few steps. My mother patted my back. 'It's okay, it's okay, come on,' she said. She held me tight till we were back at the place where my father's corpse was lying. The corpse had been completely undressed. My father's shirt was barely lying on the body. The rest of the garments lay scattered at a distance. 'I had to do this,' my mother explained when she found me somewhat perplexed at the corpse having been unclothed, 'for *shavasadhana*, the body must be made completely naked. You might be feeling very awkward but I had no choice, my dear. I hope you understand, don't you?' Awkward it was, no doubt, and for a child of my age, the strangeness of things happening around could be disturbing enough to cause nervous breakdown. But I somehow stayed put. 'Do you understand why I have taken the clothes off your father's body?' she asked again. I nodded. 'Now, listen my child, you must not fall asleep. You might see some terrible creatures and hear some horrible noises. Just don't be afraid. When *shavasadhana* is performed, many evil beings try to cause disturbance. No matter what you see or hear, don't be afraid. Have confidence in my words. Nothing will happen to you. However, if you stray too far away from the ritual, then these evil creatures from the dark worlds would be able to harm you. That is why I am forced to keep you close to me while performing the ritual. Another thing, while I am on your father's corpse, you shouldn't try to talk to me. Remember, if you try to talk to me, all my effort will go waste and then there would be no chance for our survival. I have to finish the ritual as soon as I can. Too much of delay could be fatal. I am sure those men are waiting for the dawn. Unless I do something quick to save ourselves, nothing would be able to prevent those men from killing us. So please cooperate. Are you following what I am saying, my child?' I was too nervous to respond. My mother took me in her arms and showered all the love and warmth she could. 'Take it easy, my dear. We have to live, both you and I. Tell me, my darling, won't you help me tide over this terrible problem?' I finally nodded. She put me down and repeated her instructions. Then she put her focus completely on the ritual. She applied sandalwood paste all over my father's body. Then she pulled a knife out from an inner pocket of her robe and slit the top of her left wrist. I shrieked in disgust. My mother looked at me and placed a finger on her lips and moved her head. I understood that she would not be able to talk till the ritual was over and that I had to keep calm regardless of what happened. My mother then drew a sign on my father's back with her own blood. I had known that sign right from the time I could sense things. Even I use it sometimes these days. It is one of the most powerful signs used by sorceresses in our part of the world. Then she blew onto the sign to dry it up. In a while when the sign had somewhat dried up, she pulled out a small packet containing whitish powder and spread it all over the sign. From my experience in sorcery, now I know what that powder was. That was powder made out of dried livers of a number of reptiles. Reptiles, you would appreciate, have some strange powers. Their sensitivity to the world around is somewhat akin to the sensitivity sorceresses develop after years of practice. The powder absorbed all the moisture of the sign. Thereafter, my mother mounted my father's back and looked at me. I tried my best to oblige her. After passing a faint smile, she closed her eyes and started chanting some strange mantras. I had been privy to a number of her rituals that entailed chanting of weird mantras. I had already begun to recognize the patterns of many of these mantras. What she spoke now, however, was completely different from what I had heard her chant while performing other rituals. The mantras she repeated now consisted of heavy sounding words. Some of them felt threatening. Very soon she was through with the first cycle of mantras. Then she started the second cycle and it sounded even heavier and more threatening. Soon enough the second cycle was over making way for the third. In this way the cycles of mantras continued, each cycle being heavier and apparently more threatening than the preceding one. My eyes were soon heavy with sleep but the fear that my falling asleep could spoil the ritual kept me awake. My mother was now deep into the ritual and looked completely oblivious of my presence. Mantras flowed spontaneously out of her mouth. She spoke some of the mantras in a voice that didn't sound hers at all. Then I heard two voices instead of one chanting the mantras. Fear gripped my spine and I almost fell prey to an impulse to shake my mother out of her trance. However, better sense prevailed and I let things continue. It was not easy to keep courage for long as strange sounds filled the atmosphere. My mother was now speaking as if thousands of people were speaking from inside her. Then there was a knock at the door. I had my heart in my mouth. Who could it be? The intruders again? It seemed I had little choice but to bring my mother out of *shavasadhana*. Before I could do so, the door flung open. There was no one outside. I realized that neither I nor my mother had spared a thought for the door that had remained unbolted after the intruders left! I could sense the chill in my spine even more strongly at the thought that ever since we had come downstairs, we had been living dangerously with not even a bolted door to protect us. I rushed to shut the door and bolt it. There were two latches on the door – one roughly in the middle that I could reach with my hand and the other at the top that was beyond the height I could reach even with the best of my jumps. I pushed the one that was within reach to fasten it and wondered what I could do to fasten the other one as well. The best thing possible was to stand on a stool and fasten it. I rushed to get one. When I returned with it I found the door open again. How could that happen, I was completely out of my wits. I remembered very well having fastened the latch in the middle of the door. A strong breeze blew again almost pushing me backwards. My nerves froze the next moment when a devilish creature suddenly emerged at the door. It was ugly to say the least. It had no skin to hide its flesh which was full of dirty looking liquids dripping in gory torrents from a number of points. The eyes were almost non-existent and the nose not more than a stub. The orifice that probably served as its mouth had a nauseating whitish jelly like substance all around it. It moved forward cumbersomely dropping blobs on the floor. I could not shout for I was left with no voice. Suddenly, it sped up its steps and in a matter of seconds it was in touching distance from me. I stood there simply waiting to die. What happened next was the greatest miracle I had witnessed till then. 'Stop Zieste, don't you dare touch my daughter,' it was my father's voice. I turned around with my life force flowing again. He was standing next to my mother, handsome, neatly dressed and full of promise. He actually looked much younger, at least ten years younger than how he looked when I last saw him alive. 'You will be completely finished if you cause her the slightest of harms.' I ran towards my parents and was soon in my father's arms. My mother smiled and fondled my hair, 'See, didn't I tell you that you would get to meet your father again.' 'Don't you worry, Vaishali, I will set everything right,' my father said as he kissed me all over my cheeks. Meanwhile Zieste, the beast, had moved quite forward. He looked fearless and ready to attack. 'Let me handle this sickening creature first,' said my father as he put me down. Then he rushed at Zieste and thereafter all I could see was a flash. Moments later I found the two of them jostling on the pathway outside the entrance that leads to the gate. It didn't take much time for my father to vanquish the ugly creature. There was another flash and thereafter it was only my father standing outside the door. Zieste had disappeared without a trace," Vaishali looked at me perhaps to check my reaction.

"I am listening to every word of yours and willing to believe everything," I smiled.

"Great," she smiled back, "should I continue?"

"By all means, Vaishali, go on."

19 REVENGE

"My father got back into the house and said, 'I don't have much time and there is quite a lot of work to do.'

'Time to teach those people a lesson,' my mother said.

'You mean those who intruded into our place?' my father responded.

'Yes,' she said as her voice cracked, 'they didn't just intrude but also killed you ... they must be taught a lesson.'

'They must be taught a lesson, that's fine,' he replied, 'but for intruding, not for killing me.'

'Why? You will forgive your murderers?' My mother said.

'It seems you think those people killed me, they didn't,' he said.

'Then who killed you,' she asked.

'Your greatest ethereal enemy,' he responded.

My mother looked dazed at the revelation.

'You mean Islakais?' She wanted a confirmation.

He nodded," Vaishali cleaned her throat.

"Who is Islakais?" I asked.

"Islakais happens to be one of the most terrible demoniac entities. He is known for all kinds of evils. Islakais is believed to be an enemy to anyone who wants to unfold the mysteries of the universe," Vaishali replied.

"Why? How does it affect him if the mysteries of the universe are unfolded?"

"He is one of the creatures from the darkest realms of the Devil. He represents ignorance and does not want anyone, whether it be a human or an ethereal being, to be enlightened."

"So he was against your mother because she was on her way to unearth some of the mysteries of the universe?"

"Exactly, he often acted as a disturbing force when my mother would meditate. Islakais was responsible for the failure of so many of my mother's experimentations. Although he orchestrated his evil designs from a world different from the physical world my mother belonged to, yet the disturbances caused by him were too nasty to be ignored. He used to threaten my mother every now and then of dire consequences if she continued with her experimentations and rituals. However, my mother continued her quest for knowledge much to the chagrin of Islakais and other demoniac beings like him. He kept on disturbing her which sometimes amounted to hurting her physically. But she continued on her path and soon had enough powers to battle him. Progressively she grew in spiritual strength and a time came when both of them roughly had equal powers. My mother's unceasing experimentations and *sadhana* were about to make her more powerful than Islakais when that terrible event happened."

"By *terrible event* you mean the attack by the villagers and murder of your father?"

"Yes, that's right."

"Is Islakais openly visible?"

"No, he is an ethereal creature."

"Then how did your father know that it was Islakais who murdered him?"

"Don't forget my father had returned from death. He had been dead for quite a while and during that time he had enough exposure to the ethereal realms to know as to how he died and who caused the death. In any case, the *shavasadhana* performed by my mother accentuated his learning experience in the ethereal world. I guess, before he died he didn't know anything about Islakais or that he was my mother's greatest ethereal enemy."

"What an unexpected turn of the events, you and your mother thought that the intruders killed him, instead he told you that the killer was Islakais!"

"Absolutely! My mother was shocked to learn this. That's because Islakais or some other entity from the dark realms can get entry into the world of ours or what you may call the world of living only during the time a sorceress or a magician or a *sadhika* performs a ritual. If during a ritual, Islakais or some other demoniac entity enters our world, a good sorceress would immediately know that. That's why before finishing the ritual, the sorceress uses her powers to send such entity back into the world of darkness. However, if a sorceress fails to detect the entry of such a creature into the world of living or after having detected its entry fails to send it back into its own world, then the creature could play havoc with the life of the sorceress and her loved ones."

"In case a sorceress who is not very good at her craft fails to detect such entry, or upon detection fails to send such an entity back to its own domain, then can such entity affect the lives of other people, I mean people other than the sorceress and her loved ones?"

"No, such an entity that stays back can only affect the lives of the sorceress who made the mistake and her loved ones. It does not have the powers to harm others," Vaishali replied.

"That means Islakais was out in the open because your mother had made a mistake in one of her rituals?"

"Absolutely, you have guessed it right. 'When did I ever make a mistake in my rituals?' My mother exclaimed in a state of shock.

'Mistakes happen, Latika, even the greatest of experts make mistakes,' my father responded.

Tears rolled down my mother's cheeks as she said, 'Then it is me who is responsible for your death ... I will never be able to forgive myself.'

'Don't ever say that, Latika,' my father smiled and walked up to my mother and took her in an embrace, 'it is none of your faults. Anyone can make mistakes. Perhaps the mental turmoil you had to negotiate all these days caused some slip in your concentration while you were performing a ritual. It is all right. In any case, the kind of life I was living was not worthy enough to be continued. To speak the truth, I am very happy to be dead. Though it is no new knowledge for you but I can tell you that the world of the dead is much sweeter than this world of the living. And I am so thankful to you for having performed *shavasadhana* on me. By doing so you have given me an opportunity to tell you and Vaishali how much I love you both. I know I have neither been a good husband nor a good father but trust me - I have always loved you both, loved you much more than anything else in the world.'

My father broke down too and they got into an even tighter embrace. This was the first time I had witnessed my parents in such a loving stance. I had longed to see the two of them sharing an amiable equation. Look at the stroke of fate! It had to happen after my mother resurrected him by *shavasadhana*. Finally, after the three of us had spent some time in such hitherto unseen warmth in the family, my father said, 'I have very little time left. Let me first go and fix the problem with the villagers.'

'What will you do,' my mother said, 'I don't want you to kill them.'

'Don't worry, I will not kill them physically. But death they must have ... the death of their calm lives. I will ensure that every villager leaves this village for good at the earliest. These villagers must pay for their sins.'

My father left the house. I and my mother sat on the staircase huddled together. After about half an hour, we heard many anxious noises taking rounds. I can still remember people yelling things like 'O he has come back, run for your lives', 'Don't kill us, please don't kill us, we promise to leave at dawn', 'Let our children live at least, they didn't harm you or your family, did they', and 'Apologies, please forgive us, please forgive, we will do as you say, we will leave and never ever come back to this village again'. After about a couple of hours, minutes before dawn my father was back.

'I have done all that I could, Latika,' he said, 'I went to every part of the village and asked the villagers to leave lest I should kill them. Driven by the fear of death, each villager agreed to leave with spouse and children. I believe in just about a week's time, you and Vaishali would be the only inhabitants of *Prithaka*.' Then my father laughed and continued, 'Do you know, I floated inches above the ground and asked them to leave. Some of the stubborn ones did try to resist initially. But I used the powers that you have given to my consciousness by *shavasadhana*. I caused burns to their bodies by merely glancing at them. Some of them I just tossed around. And some of them who were too adamant left me with little choice – I placed their children at precarious high points of the nearby hills and brought them back only after they buckled like slaves.'

'Are you sure all of them will leave? You will be gone very soon and if they decide to stay back, I shall not have much to do if they choose to attack again,' My mother said.

'I now have the powers to sense the future, Latika. Trust me, they will all leave. They are scared to death and will not risk their lives or the lives of their near and dear ones by continuing to stay in the village. And they will never again dare cause any harm to you and our child,' My father gave his assurances.

'Thank you so much,' my mother said.

'No, my dear, thanks to you,' he smiled, 'because of you I did make myself somewhat useful. Maybe this stint of extended life will improve my karmic connections.'

He picked me up in his arms again and showered endless kisses before putting me down. Then he looked at my mother and said, 'There is one thing I couldn't do. I wish I could do that as well to make the two of you completely safe and secured.'

'What are you trying to say? Do you mean the villagers could still be problematic for us?' My mother asked.

'No,' he moved his head, 'I have already told you that the villagers would not cause any harm to you or Vaishali. But ... but that scoundrel ...'

'Are you suggesting Islakais could harm us?' She asked with

anguish in her eyes.

'Yes indeed,' he nodded, 'Islakais could certainly harm you. Unfortunately I can't deal with him as his powers far exceed mine. Latika, you must take special care of the child. That scoundrel has already shown up twice before her. Islakais is the only anxiety I would now be carrying with me to the next world,' he said while fondling my hair.

'You mean Vaishali has already confronted Islakais?' She asked with extreme panic in her eyes.

'Yes, Latika, she has already confronted Islakais twice. Although I doubt if he had any intent of harming her during these encounters, but this entity certainly made his presence felt to Vaishali when you sent her upstairs to fetch the sandalwood paste,' my father explained.

'That's right, she was taking too much time and that's why I went upstairs myself,' she responded.

'Indeed, you found her almost crumbling down over there, didn't you?' my father said.

'Yes, I had to support her all the way back to where your body was lying. Was she crumbling down because she had confronted that demon?' My mother asked.

When my father nodded, she looked at me and said, 'Did you see a frightening whitish figure, Vaishali?'

'Yes, I saw it twice,' I responded.

'O no,' my mother began to sob, 'this sickening entity is after our daughter as well … it is all because of me.'

'Don't blame yourself, Latika,' my father moved over and put his arms around her, 'mistakes do happen in life. Instead of being angry with yourself about having committed the error that allowed the demon to haunt us, you must now think as to how you can send him back to his world. I am sure you can do it, can't you?'

'I think I can but I will have to work very hard,' she replied.

'I am sure you will succeed, my dear,' he smiled.

Then he embraced my mother again before moving away.

'Love you Latika … love you Vaishali, God bless you both,' he lovingly waved at us.

'Love you too,' my mother responded with tears in her eyes.

'I love you too, daddy,' I too spoke with eyes full of tears.

Thereafter, his body fell lifelessly on the floor. We cremated him the next day. While he was being cremated, some of the villagers were leaving the village. We saw the movements around us. My father had indeed assessed correctly. Within a week's time I and my mother were the only ones left in the village."

20 THE DEMON'S THREATS

"Did they come back later to *Prithaka*?" I asked.

"Who?"

"The villagers who left," I said.

"No, they never came back. None of the villagers had the courage to return to *Prithaka*."

"Then how does the village have a population now?"

"They are all new inhabitants. None of them are the old timers or their descendants. All those who left the village sold their properties. It took quite some time for *Prithaka* to have a sizeable population again."

"I believe the new inhabitants have also not been kind to you or your mother."

"That's right," she replied, "they have also been quite unfriendly. However, they have not been as hostile as the previous lot. These new inhabitants never tried to harm us physically. In fact, they never had enough courage even to protest against my mother's practice. My mother made great efforts to be friendly with them but her reputation as a witch never left her. When *Prithaka* had a good number of people, it was decided to socially ostracize me and my mother. Though no public proclamation was made to ostracize us but the message nonetheless reached every household in the village that nobody should have any connection with us. However, I must say, the social ostracization this time was far less severe as compared to the magnitude of isolation we were subjected to by the earlier lot."

I looked up at the sky when she took a pause. There was still no hint of sun there.

"It is still very dark," I remarked.

"I know. Aren't you enjoying the darkness?"

"Yes, I am but isn't this night appearing extraordinarily long?"

"You want it to dawn?"

"Not really, I was wondering why this night is so long."

"Well, if my sense of time is working right, it should take another couple of hours to dawn. It must be close to four now."

"Only four!"

"Why? You thought it should be much beyond four?"

"I felt so, yes. I was under the impression that we started much after midnight from *Latika Griha*. And I guess, we have spent around four hours over here."

"We have spent much more than four hours over here."

"In that case why is there no hint of sun in the sky?"

"That's because no hint of sun is supposed to be there in the sky now. You feel dawn should be round the corner because you have erred on your judgment of the time we started from *Latika Griha*."

"How can it be?" I said.

"It is, Mr. Banerjee," Vaishali had a little laugh, "you have indeed erred on judging the time we started from there."

"But Vaishali," I argued, "we were at *Mayur Paththar* just hours back. After you finished explaining what evil spirits are, we returned to *Latika Griha* and rested there for a while. I believe we spent a little more than an hour at *Latika Griha*, during which time I had yet another paranormal experience, before we started that incredible flight of ours to reach this point. Now, tell me – if it was already past midnight when we finished discussing the gamut of consciousness at the *Mayur Paththar*, and then spent close to a couple of hours in going back to *Latika Griha* and resting there, what would have been the time when we started the flight for *Mahachoti*? By my estimate, it couldn't have been less than two-thirty. Even if I am to ignore the time we spent on the flight, the time now should at least be six-thirty and the sun should clearly be out in the sky."

"You are making me anxious, Mr. Banerjee," she spoke in a clear tone of concern.

"Anxious, why anxious?"

"It seems you have lost sense of time all together."

"Why? You think my estimate is completely wrong?

"You are talking about your estimate being completely wrong, you don't seem to have any estimate at all. Well, I guess I know the reason."

"What are you talking about, Vaishali?"

"Mr. Banerjee, we were not at *Mayur Paththar* just hours back as you just said. Around twenty eight hours have passed since we were there. As for the flight from *Mayur Paththar to Mahachoti*, we started it around quarter to twelve. Maybe we reached *Mahachoti* by eleven-fifty and since then we are here."

"Come on Vaishali, how can it be? You mean more than a day has passed since we finished our discussions on consciousness at *Mayur Paththar*?"

"Exactly, Mr. Banerjee."

"You are trying to suggest that we have been resting for close to twenty four hours before starting for *Mahachoti*?"

"We have not been resting all the time, Mr. Banerjee. We woke up in the morning, had breakfast, spent some time on the same rocks by the side of *Tarangini*, came back and had lunch, then I went for some work while you took rest in your room, thereafter we had dinner when I returned, then you went back to your room, and finally maybe after another couple of hours when the time was quarter to twelve, did we meet outside *Latika Griha* to start our flight."

"Look Vaishali, if this is a joke, it's a very bad one."

"Do you think I would be making such a cheap joke sitting over here at *Mahachoti* at this hour?" The anxiety in her voice grew.

"But I don't remember a thing you said."

"That's because you have been made to forget things. I am still happy that you at least remember things till the point our discussions ended on *Mayur Paththar*."

"But who has made me forget things?"

"Islakais, who else?"

"I don't quite understand this."

"You will very soon. First tell me everything that you remember since we returned to *Latika Griha* from *Mayur Paththar* after finishing our discussions on consciousness."

I told her everything that happened in as much details as I could right from the time I stretched out on my bed absorbed in my thoughts to my discovery that the robed figure standing outside *Latika Griha* was Vaishali herself.

"You mentioned a deafening sound, didn't you," she reacted, "you heard a deafening sound that brought you out of your thoughts?"

"That's right. It was a terrible metallic sound. It took me quite a while to come to terms with it."

"After you came to terms with it, you rushed to the window and shortly thereafter you discovered the flickering light on the hillock. Then you were worried that you might find the eerie robed figure standing behind you when you turned and that's exactly what happened."

"Yes Vaishali."

"Now I know what trick Islakais played on you, Mr. Banerjee."

"What did he do?"

"The deafening sound he caused robbed you of the memory of the day. We had a normal day as I have already explained. In fact, when we were having dinner I also made an effort to prepare you for the flight. I told you that we would shortly be going on a mystical journey to a beautiful place, and that we would discuss the paranormal activities that you have confronted at *Prithaka* in

162

that beautiful place. You were happy to learn about the prospective mystical journey and the interesting talks that were to follow. Then you went to your bedroom to have some rest before what could be a night full of revelations. It seems since you had already had a good sleep in the evening, you didn't feel sleepy and spent time on ruminations. Thereafter, the nasty demon made that sound making you lose track of everything that happened during the day. The deafening sound made you feel that you had just returned from *Mayur Pathhar* whereas you had actually spent one full day before you heard that sound. The sound was, quite needless to say, an ethereal tool at the hands of the demon."

"But why did Islakais do something like that? Is he trying to warn me?" I could sense she was speaking the truth and had no reasons to doubt her.

"He tried to warn me, Mr. Banerjee," she said, "it is a warning that if I don't stop, he could play such mischief every now and then."

"You don't stop what?"

"My practice of sorcery."

"He wants you to stop being a sorceress?"

"That's right. He doesn't want me to be even remotely as strong as he is, and he knows that if my practice continues it will not be long before I match him power by power."

"But why is he trying to harm me?"

"No, Mr. Banerjee, he is not trying to harm you. To cause harm to you is beyond his powers as you are not related to the sorceress, my mother that is, whose mistake allowed him to continue in this world. The maximum he can do is to play such mischief. But don't worry, I don't think it is within his powers to play such mischief often. Besides, these actions are pretty innocuous ... they cannot harm you. He can harm me and not you, Mr. Banerjee."

"So you mean these warnings have little weight?"

"Very much so, Mr. Banerjee," she gave a reassuring smile, "even he knows I will not be intimidated by such threats. Now tell me, should I continue my account, do you still have the stamina to listen?

"I have infinite stamina on that count, Vaishali. Please go on."

21 SORCERY IS HER DESTINY

"Well, for a long time after my father was dead, my mother seemed to harbor a fear that she just wouldn't share with me," Vaishali continued, "Even as a child I could sense the constant fear she was living under. She got me admitted to the Government Girls School in Shyamalpur. It was quite evident that she was hugely worried about me. Most children from *Prithaka* would go to their respective schools in Shyamalpur by specially designed horse carts for the purpose. But my mother did not let me go with other children by horse carts. Initially I thought that I was not allowed to mix with other children as there was an unwritten understanding amongst all that the two of us would be kept separate from every social activity. I later discovered that that was not the reason. Most horse cart drivers were from *Shyamalpur* and they had nothing to do with the social ostracization. If my mother had decided to send me with other children, their parents would certainly not have liked it but at the same time wouldn't have dared to object to such an arrangement. It was my mother who didn't let me commute to school with other children. It was not that she didn't want me to be in the company of others. Rather she didn't want me to be without her at any point of time. She had hired a horse cart permanently for the purpose of my daily to and fro travel. She would accompany me to the school and then wait there till my classes were over, and of course then she would join me on the horse cart back home. This arrangement continued till I finished middle school. You can understand, my classmates would often tease me for my mother's constantly hanging around me. I had been nicknamed as *the protected one.* When I was in senior school I insisted that she stopped coming with me. She wouldn't listen at first but finally gave in to my demand. I was happy to have the newfound freedom in my movements but that happiness soon waned away when I found that the weirdness in her conduct had taken a different dimension. Her concern for my well-being reached the point of causing extreme irritation to me. Every day she would wait for my return from school anxiously, quite like a family member of a soldier who has gone to war, with bated breath, half expecting the worst, and praying for the best. The moment I entered the house, she would anxiously inspect my face, neck, hands and legs to be sure that all my limbs were intact. I also noticed that she was now trying to keep her practice of sorcery as far away from me as she could. I was no longer privy to her rituals and experimentations. At times her attempts to keep her practice hidden from me reached weird proportions. I asked her several times as to what was the predicament that made her behave so abnormally all the time but she always replied by saying she had no worries. Around that time I had developed a strong interest in her books. One day when she discovered that I was reading her books, she reproached me in quite an abominable manner. She said, 'You must not read all this. These books are not meant for you. You should rather read your text books.' I was stunned at this strange behavior and even more convinced that she was dealing with a terrible problem. My mother continued to be secretive about the problem till I had cleared my college. The day I finished my graduation in psychology from the Government College, Shyamalpur, she was so happy. She had prepared a delightful cake and we had a nice little celebration. Little did we know while we enjoyed about the terrible stroke of fate that awaited us. After we finished a sumptuous supper, I expressed my desire to pursue a career as a psychologist in one of the main cities. My mother broke down when she heard this. It was the first time I saw my mother crying like that since my father died. She said that she couldn't let me be a psychologist. When I asked why she said, 'Because I have failed.' I couldn't make sense of what she said and asked her as to what she had failed in and she replied that she had failed in her practice of sorcery. When I demanded an explanation, she asked if I remembered who killed my father. When I answered in the affirmative, she said that Islakais was still out in the open and despite her best efforts she hadn't till that point of time succeeded in sending him back to his realm. Then she said that she had been trying to push Islakais back into his dark world ever since my father died but the demon had successfully resisted her efforts.

'I am tired now and my strength to fight the demon may run out any time. I am aging, my dear, and my skills at sorcery are hardly improving,' she cried.

'What will happen if you do not manage to send him back to where he belongs?' I asked.

'The worst can happen, my dear, the worst. Till this time I have succeeded in preventing him from causing any harm to the two of us, especially you. All along I have been keeping a close eye on you so that I could protect you from any of his possible attacks. But what will happen if he gains more strength and overpowers me. Then he would be able to cause the most terrible harms to both of us,' she replied as she cried uncontrollably.

'You mean he could kill us if he manages to overpower you?' I said.

She nodded.

'So this has been your predicament all these years?'

She nodded again.

'Can something be done to prevent him from causing us harm?' I could sense the gravity of the problem.

'I have the least worry for myself, Vaishali. I am only concerned about you,' she continued to cry.

'You didn't answer my question, mother?' I demanded a concrete reply.

'There is just one way, my dear,' she said.

'And what is that one way, mother,' I could already sense what mother wanted to say.

'That you should become a sorceress too, Vaishali,' mother said, 'then we would be able to fight Islakais with our combined powers. If we fight together, his chances of succeeding would be grossly reduced.'

'I will have to learn sorcery?' I responded after a long thought.

'Yes, my dear,' she nodded, 'there is just no other way.'

'You think we can send him back to his realm with our combined powers?' I questioned.

'We can certainly try,' she said, 'I am really feeling very bad to be asking you to be a sorceress too. I completely acknowledge that it is all my doing that has brought things to such an impasse. I should have been more careful with my rituals. I would attribute the mistake that allowed Islakais to sneak into our world purely to my overconfidence. Those were the days when I had begun to have too much faith in my abilities as a sorceress. I ignored one of the basic tenets of real magic – a magician should never be overconfident when it comes to dealing with demons and spirits regardless of how powerful he or she has become or how experienced he or she is.'

Her words made me ponder over the strange games of destiny. What a weird turn of events it was – it was she who had once discouraged me from reading her books, and now it was she again who wanted me to suspend, if not completely annihilate, all my career plans so that I could follow her footsteps.

'I am feeling miserable, my dear, that you can't even pursue a career of your choice,' she seemed to read my mind, 'I never thought that the circumstances would be this bad. I firmly believed that my constant endeavors will someday send this demon back to where he belongs. That is why the possibility that someday you would also be required to be a sorceress never crossed my mind. I am sure you understand that I never quite wanted you to be a sorceress. A sorceress lives under constant threats from spirits, demons and other evil ethereal entities. I chose to be a sorceress because my desire to unfold the secrets of the universe has been far stronger than the fears of being harmed by such entities. But I never wanted you to choose such a life for yourself. That's why I always discouraged you from reading books on magic and sorcery. When you were a very little girl, I had no choice but to keep you by my side while performing my rituals. But after you were old enough to make better sense of things around you, I tried everything I could to keep my pursuit of the occult as separate from you as possible. It is indeed very painful for me today to be asking you to be a sorceress.'

Well, Mr. Banerjee, that's how destiny had set it up for me to turn towards sorcery. To speak the truth, I wasn't too disappointed about the prospect of becoming a sorceress. I had a strong interest in the occult and I knew I could be a good sorceress. I wanted to start my training immediately."

"Your mother taught you?"

"No, Mr. Banerjee. She wanted to teach me but fate wouldn't allow it. I had to be my own teacher."

"You mean she ... she died before she could start teaching you?"

"Well," the smile on her lips now echoed a deep seated pain in her heart, "she was killed before she could start teaching me. It was the evening of the same day I had finished my graduation, I mean the day she asked me to take to sorcery. It was close to midnight and I was in my room reading one of the most elementary guides to sorcery. I still remember I was reading about Lezuina, an ancient sorceress from the Caribbean region and how she mastered the art of levitation by learning to generate zero gravity circumstances when I heard my mother's soul tearing shriek."

22 SHE MUST FIGHT

"I rushed to her room," Vaishali continued, "and found her lying on the floor with eyes still with dread.

'He,' she said very faintly.

'What happened mother?' I held her hand tightly.

'He, he … he was here,' she was in a state of extreme shock.

I tried to make her sit but couldn't. She scarcely had any strength to make an effort to get up.

I rushed to the ground floor and picked up a bottle of cold water and then hurried back to her room. By now her condition looked all the more precarious. I quickly sprinkled cold water on her forehead, cheeks and neck. This seemed to help her as a shade of normalcy returned to her movements.

'Try to get up mother,' I tried to help her sit again.

She shook her head to suggest that she didn't have enough force left to get up.

'What happened mother?' I began to sob.

'Water,' she spoke with immense difficulty.

I was badly unsettled and in no position to think coherently. I didn't even realize that she was asking for some water to drink. Instead I thought she wanted more water to be sprinkled on her body. So I sprinkled some more on her forehead.

'Water,' she shook her head and spoke with greater force.

Only then did it strike me that she wanted to drink some water. With a lot of difficulty she gulped down the small quantities of water I poured into her mouth. I stopped when she shook her head again. It took her quite a long time thereafter to be able to speak with greater clarity.

'I don't have much time, Vaishali, listen carefully,' she said.

'What has happened to you, mother?' I cried and could sense that her end was near.

'Don't cry, my child, please don't cry,' she put up a brave face, 'this is no time to cry. You must listen to every word of mine carefully. Otherwise he will do to you what he has done to me.'

'Islakais you mean?' I took her hands in mine.

'Yes, now listen and don't interrupt me. I wish to finish before the pain Islakais has induced in my body consumes me fully. Look my dear, I have been maintaining notes of my works regularly for the past three decades. You will find thousands of pages I have written on my practice and inferences. You will find these notes arranged in a logical sequence in the old chest under my bed. These notes could be very instructive for you. You should read these notes very carefully at the earliest and practice the methods of sorcery I have suggested. Do not start reading the books of my repertoire till you finish reading my notes and practice to your satisfaction all the methods mentioned in them. You will make better sense of the books if you have a firm grasp of what I have written. I can guarantee, if you read and practice what I have written in these notes, in just about a couple of years you would be a good enough sorceress. You will also find in these notes the possible methodologies that might be employed to counter Islakais. I am hopeful that you would be able to use what I have written to your best advantage. The problem is you don't have much time in your hands. A comprehensive reading of these notes and concurrent practice of the methods given therein would take a minimum of two years, as I have already mentioned. Islakais is all ready to attack you and therefore you wouldn't even have two days in your hands once I am dead, let alone two years.' She took a pause and drank some more water.

'If I have no chance for survival, why are you telling me all this, mother? Let us both die peacefully,' I remarked.

'No my dear, you have to fight. You do have a chance. Please understand that demons do not have the same amount of powers in all physical terrains. The ancient books have exhaustively dealt with this issue. According to these writings the magnitude of ethereal powers of a demon in a given geographical area would depend upon the time the demon has spent in that area. This means if a demon has spent a considerable amount of time in a physical terrain, then it would be very powerful over there. On the other hand, if a demon is new in an area, it would have very few or no powers at its disposal. Islakais has spent quite a lot of time in *Prithaka*. So he is very powerful over here. When I say you don't have even two days in your hands after I am gone, I mean you don't have two days in *Prithaka* and the surrounding areas. From my practice I know that Islakais's powers do not extend roughly beyond a radius of five hundred miles from *Prithaka*. If you go to a city that is far beyond this radius, you could be safe. In which city did you have plans of pursuing a career as a psychologist, my dear?' She said.

'I thought of going to either New Delhi or Calcutta.' I replied.

'Both these cities would be safe for you. Unfortunately, you wouldn't be safe in any place forever. Islakais would surely follow you to whichever physical terrain you choose for yourself. He would then wait there till he is strong enough to attack you,' her pain was beginning to show up in her voice.

'What if I keep shifting places?' I asked.

'That is not practically possible. You have to settle down somewhere in life. One can't be on the move all the time, Vaishali. And in any case, this idea might not work. If he realizes that you are constantly moving, he may station himself in any one place for a substantial period of time and become powerful there with the intention to wait there till you land up in that place. It is possible that you might never go to that place but then it is also possible that you actually land up there someday. So you will never know as to which place is safe for you and would always have to live in uncertainty and fear. It is also not advisable to keep shifting because certain places, including cities, might emanate vibes that are in coherence with his powers and in those places he might get powerful very soon. You can't be taking chances with him all the time. I would rather suggest that you settle down in a place and study and practice sorcery over there so that you become powerful enough yourself to repulse the possible attacks of Islakais. After you become a very powerful sorceress, you could choose to stay in any place. But you should never stop practicing. You must keep working on your magic so as to grow in powers all the time. Once you are in the groove of sorcery, I believe you will begin to enjoy it. I hope you are following me, my dear.' Her breathing was becoming more and more inconsistent.

'Yes, I am following you, mother,' I nodded.

'It is not easy to practice sorcery in a big city like New Delhi or Calcutta. You cannot possibly levitate yourself or material objects out in the open or overtly perform any ritual the result of which could defy common sense. If you do so you will attract a lot of attention and that could mean a death blow to your endeavors. Crowds that are driven by common sense find it hard to accept things that are uncommon. If something uncommon comes their way, they try to change it to what they reckon as logical and socially acceptable. It is, therefore, of extreme importance that a sorceress keeps her practice as secretive as possible. This maxim does not just apply to sorceresses living in cities but also to sorceresses living in small and relatively unknown places such as *Prithaka*. Ideally, any magician or sorceress should settle down in a remote place like *Prithaka*. The reason is clear. A remote and secluded place such as this one allows a lot more scope for secrecy as compared to a more happening place. Unfortunately, your practice of sorcery would not have the cushion of remoteness and seclusion since you would be stationed in a city. But in a way it is good that you would be in a city. Many magicians believe, and I am one of them, that it is not easy for demons to cause nuisance in a place that is crowded and replete with jazzy and glitzy facets of life. My experience in dealing with demons suggests that the rate at which a demon grows in powers in a flashy city is far less than the rate at which it gains powers in an isolated and dull place like *Prithaka*. So I do back your decision to be in a big city but be warned ... you must take special care to keep your practice a secret. A time will come in your pursuit of sorcery when the intensity of the results of your activities will be too high to hide from the public eye even if you choose to practice at the death of night. That is the time when you should decide to relocate yourself in a small township or village. You could even come back to *Prithaka* if you want because by that time you will be good enough to resist every effort of Islakais and he would have no advantage whatsoever for being in *Prithaka*. But you will be that powerful only if you are regular with your practice and persevere through your failures. Neither be too disheartened about your failures nor be too elated about your successes. And of course never be overconfident no matter how powerful you become,' mother explained.

'But mother, will I have to keep fighting Islakais all my life? Isn't there a way I can send him back to where he belongs?' I asked what was hovering in my mind for a long time.

'I am glad you ask that question, my dear, I would have come to it anyway,' mother replied, 'yes, there is a way of sending him back to where he belongs. You will know what that way is by the time you finish reading my notes and practicing the methods I have described exhaustively. There is no point my discussing that method now as at the moment you know very little about sorcery. Don't worry, you will certainly know what you have to do to send him back when the time comes. All I can tell you now is that the method to send him back is not easy but as an experienced sorceress you would be able to do it. You might be wondering as to why I couldn't send him back. Well, I couldn't do it because the powers I amassed were never enough to match his strengths. You will appreciate that after your father died, I lived under a constant peril ... all the while I had to see that you were safe. My worries never allowed me to focus hard on my craft. As a result, my growth as a sorceress did not happen at a desirable rate. The demon, on the other hand, constantly grew in strength by virtue of spending time at *Prithaka*.'

'But why couldn't you send him back when he had just got out in the open? At that time your powers must have been greater than his?'

'I didn't even know that he was out in the open till your father, after being resurrected, told me about him. Yes, when he was new at *Prithaka*, he wasn't too powerful and I could have sent him back but he always stayed out of my sphere of control. Apart from being evil, he is also very intelligent. He knows exactly what to do and when. After having spent a good amount of time at *Prithaka*, when he realized that he was powerful enough to confront me, he dared into my sphere of control and since that time we have been in a constant state of battle. Unfortunately, today he got the better of me.'

'But mother' I vented a doubt, 'Islakais did kill daddy. He was new at *Prithaka* at that time. How could he then be so powerful so as to kill daddy?'

'My dear,' she explained, 'your father was a very weak man. He was very weak both physically and mentally due to constant drinking. Islakais, despite not being too powerful at that time, had enough strength to attack and murder that frail man. But he couldn't do anything to you or me. Don't you remember that he crossed your way twice the same day he killed your father?'

'I remember,' I responded.

'He crossed your way twice but couldn't do anything to you, could he?'

I moved my head.

'Why couldn't he harm you at that time? Please understand I had no idea when he crossed your way that he was out in the open. So you were not under my protection when you saw him. And yet he couldn't harm you. That's because he didn't have enough powers to do so. Once I knew that he was out in our world, I used my powers to create a shield around you and myself. With time I kept raising the strength of these shields so that they remained impregnable to Islakais. It is not easy for a sorceress to be maintaining two such ethereal shields to fight a demon of Islakais's strength. But with my accomplishments in sorcery I managed to fight Islakais for a very long time, much more than a decade now by maintaining and constantly strengthening the shields. I had been successful in doing so till this very day. But finally the demon had his way. Moments back he broke into my shield and played havoc with my physical, mental and psychical balances. I don't think I will last this night,' Tears now rolled down her cheeks.

'Please don't say that, mother,' I bent over her and cried uncontrollably.

'Have a hold of yourself, Vaishali,' she pushed with all the strength she could garner, 'you can't afford to break down, my child. You have to fight the demon till he is back in his domain.'

'Don't just leave me like this, mother, I can't live without you a single moment,' my flood of tears continued.

'No Vaishali, you can't do this,' she protested, 'you must not act with such immaturity. Don't forget, you are the daughter of a sorceress. You must know that there is nothing such as death. My consciousness can never die. This body will stay back but my consciousness will enter a different world, a world that is infinitely better than this one. I have written a lot about consciousness, especially disembodied consciousness, in my notes. If you read them thoroughly you will learn a lot about what is consciousness and why is it not possible to understand it with the arguments of the material world. Consciousness could be understood only through experience. So rest assured, my consciousness is not dying. To speak the truth, even my body will not die. You might have heard people say that only the body dies but the soul or consciousness does not die. Even those people do not understand what consciousness is. The truth is neither the soul nor the body dies. Even when my consciousness leaves this body, this body will not be devoid of all consciousness. It will have its own consciousness just as every other inanimate object has its own consciousness. The material objects around us that we often brand as *inanimate* are actually living. It is just that most humans do not have the intelligence to sense their life. When you become an accomplished sorceress, you would know that these material objects are nothing but manifestations of consciousness. You could call them *consciousness in material form*. So my dear child, do not shed any tears for my so-called death. Nothing will die – neither my soul nor my body. Of course you will have to cremate the body and it will disintegrate and no longer remain in this shape but the consciousnesses it is made up of will re-arrange themselves but not die. Consciousnesses are meant to stay, my dear.'

Her words helped me regain balance and I wiped my tears and brought smile on my lips.

'Good, my child,' my mother smiled too, 'that is how you should behave. No tears please. Now let me finish off by telling you the last few things. I have already told you that regardless of where you go, this nasty demon will follow you. You have also understood that he will need to spend time in that new place before he could cause you any harm. Now, the question is how you will know that the demon has become powerful enough to cause harm to you in the place you are located,' her excruciating pain showed up in her voice even more clearly.

I clasped her hands tighter and smiled as I knew that is what she wanted to see in her last moments."

23 THE SIGN

Her tears glistened even in the dark conditions as Vaishali continued her narrative, "It seemed mother was losing her voice but I knew she wouldn't give up just like that. And I was right. She summed up all the remaining vital forces of her body to finish the account, 'My dear, no demon can attack without giving a prior indication of its intent. That's how nature has arranged things for these ethereal creatures. Now, what sign Islakais would give you in the place you locate yourself before attacking you, I simply can't tell. You would always have to remain alert and be on a lookout for any such possible sign. If you practice sorcery in accordance with the principles and procedures I have laid out in my notes, you will have an intuition strong enough to detect any sign coming from Islakais. Now, the last words before I leave this shell behind ... the shield that I have created around you with my powers to resist the onslaughts of Islakais is strong enough to protect you for a little more than two days. That means even after cremating my body in the morning, you will have enough time to run away from *Prithaka*. All you need to take with you at the moment apart from your essential items is the chest carrying my notes. Go to any place of your choice but be sure it is far enough to be presently immune to the powers of Islakais. That chest also has all the bank documents. You will never have to worry about money, my dear. There is enough money in the State Bank of Shyamalpur to last you a lifetime. You may, if you think it appropriate, open a new bank account in the place of your relocation and have that money transferred from the State Bank of Shyamalpur to the new account. Since you don't have to worry about sustenance, you could put all your focus on the practice of sorcery. That's all I have to say my dear. I have been holding my soul from thrusting out of my body ... I can't do it any longer. I am so happy to see you smile, Vaishali, keep smiling all the time. I love you, my dear.'

I continued to smile as she breathed her last. A serene look came over her lifeless body. It was as though she was still smiling. I didn't want to shed tears. I found reason in her argument that a sorceress's daughter could not act like a commoner. A commoner grieves on the death of his or her loved ones for he or she believes that that is the end. But a sorceress's daughter has no reasons to follow the footsteps of commoners. After being privy to the strangest possible phenomena that transcended all barriers of matter, space and time, it would be asinine on my part to cry uncontrollably over my mother's corpse, I reasoned. Well, my reasons were fine but then you will appreciate, Mr. Banerjee, that a sorceress's daughter is also a human. Despite my attempts to dispel my grief, my humanness got the better of my reasons as tears escaped my eyes.

I waited for the daylight and then through one of my mother's confidants called Chinu sent a message to Dr. Gaurav Suri, a renowned doctor in *Shyamalpur* to visit *Latika Griha*. Dr. Suri happened to be one of my father's very good friends. Even after he passed away, Dr. Suri kept close contacts with us. In just about an hour he was before me. I still remember how I flung myself into his arms and cried ceaselessly with all my reasons for not crying taking a backseat. After he examined my mother's body and wrote the death certificate, I arranged for the cremation with the help of a village priest. Initially, the priest was a little reluctant in supporting me as he too wasn't different from the society that had ostracized us but his fears that if he didn't arrange for and perform the last rights of a sorceress, some great harm might befall him and his near and dear ones overwhelmed his reluctance.

I bathed after the last rites in keeping with the Hindu traditions and then prepared for my journey to New Delhi. I took only the very essential items with me and of course the all important chest. Then I asked one of the assistants of the same priest to arrange for a horse cart for me. The horse cart arrived towards evening. Although there was no train from *Shyamalpur* to New Delhi till the next morning and I would have to spend one whole night in the waiting room of Shyamalpur Railway Station, I preferred to move as spending a single night at *Latika Griha* without my mother didn't feel like a very safe prospect. I shut all the doors and windows of *Latika Griha* tightly and bolted them. Then I took a round of the house as a flood of memories rushed past my mind. Finally, when I was locking the entrance door, tears began to flow from my eyes. After all it is not easy to leave the place you belong to. It was like leaving behind the aura of my parents, the symbols of my being, and the umbilical cord that had till that day sustained me. As I walked towards the horse cart, I turned back once to have another glance of *Latika Griha*. That turning back, I reckon, was one of the greatest turning points of my life. I realized that my subtle senses were working already. I could sense the consciousness of the house. I could hear the *Latika Griha* whimpering. Its love for me was unmistakable. That was the first time I experienced the gospel truth that what look to be inanimate objects also have consciousness; in other words, nothing in the universe is actually inanimate. I wanted to comfort the house. I wanted to tell *Latika Griha* that I wasn't leaving it permanently and that I shall be back after I was a powerful sorceress like my mother. It wasn't easy to communicate with it at first. But I tried again and again. Finally, I did communicate with it. The house told me that it was upset but I was doing the right thing by following my mother's advice. I told *Latika Griha* that I would certainly return and it responded by saying that it would wait for me. I smiled and moved into the horse cart. And there I was – on my way to a new place, a new vocation, and a new life!

After arriving in New Delhi, I stayed in a small hotel close to the New Delhi Railway Station. I was on the hunt for a good accommodation, if possible in a secluded area. One of these days a newspaper advertisement caught my attention."

"I guess it was an advertisement from Neha."

"You have guessed it right. I was interested for two reasons – first, the job was of my taste, and second, it promised salary plus accommodation. I called up and fixed up a time for the interview. The interview, as you might be aware, went off very well. It was not long thereafter when we became great friends, just like two sisters. I can't thank God enough for bringing Neha Ma'am in my life. Not only did I learn a great deal about ethereal phenomena, I also got to stay in a room in the office itself."

"Didn't you find that place pretty stifling?"

"It was small, no doubt, but it perfectly met my needs."

"Okay," I responded, "so you had no problems practicing sorcery over there?"

"I was just coming to that Mr. Banerjee," she said with a faint smile, "You know Neha Ma'am doesn't work for more than three to four hours a day. And that is perfectly understandable. A séance drains out a lot of energy from the medium. The loss of energy could be very high if ectoplasm emanates from the body of the medium in the course of a séance. That is why genuine mediums like Neha Ma'am never want to do more than one séance a day unless of course there is some extreme urgency to conduct more than one. My work in her office was cut out – I had to maintain her appointments, receive the visitors, ensure that her rooms were clean, arrange for the séances in keeping with the ritualistic principles, and sit during the séances to meet her incidental needs. I was prompt with her work. It didn't take me much time to meet her requirements. She was very impressed with the way I was working. Shortly after our working together, she virtually left all the office affairs for me to handle. She would then come only for the séances. This allowed me a lot of time to study and practice sorcery. I strictly went by my mother's advice. I read her notes and practiced the methods she had mentioned in them. Indeed, nothing could have been more instructive. The notes were really beautifully arranged. They were almost like a *how to do book*. My mother's writing followed the most logical pattern – starting with the very basics, moving up step by step to more and more difficult practices leading the learner to the intermediate and then to the advanced levels. Within a year I was very much capable of practicing sorcery at the intermediate level. It was not easy to master the advanced techniques but I persevered through my failures and indeed in another year's time I was an advanced learner. Now, I was in a position to successfully perform some of the most advanced tasks in the field of magic. I could now levitate my body and material objects, hold communions with the consciousnesses of inanimate things, sense the presence of spirits and interact with them, and have some amount of command over the five elements of the material universe. But I never got overconfident just as my mother had said. I also never failed to act in accordance with her advice that I should always remain alert and be on a lookout for any possible sign that Islakais might produce before launching an attack. Things seemed to be moving beautifully. I hardly failed in my practice of sorcery. Neha Ma'am showered so much of sisterly love on me that I never missed my parents. And of course there was no sign of Islakais anywhere. Everything, just everything, seemed to be going my way. Though at times I felt very bad about having concealed the fact of my being a sorceress from Neha Ma'am, but I hardly had a choice. Ideas such as I was cheating her by keeping my sorcery under closed covers often burnt my mind and soul and yet I had to carry on with my secret endeavors lest I should find myself in a hapless situation wherein I would be able to do little other than become an easy prey for Islakais. Every now and then my heart reproved me for what was nothing less than keeping a sisterly soul who had showered untold love on me in the dark and pushed me into telling her the truth. However, on each such occasion my mind repulsed the efforts of the heart. Now when I look back at the skirmishes between my heart and my mind, I feel good that the mind vanquished the heart every single time. If I had fallen prey to the forces of my heart, I wouldn't perhaps have been able to accomplish what I have accomplished so far as a sorceress. Although Neha Ma'am is an angelic soul, she might not have empathized with me if I told her the truth as she might deem it as a breach of trust. The result could be my being thrown out of the job and of the accommodation, which would in turn seriously jeopardize the prospects of my emergence as a sorceress with enough powers to combat a demon like Islakais. The conditions around me were ideal conditions for the purpose I was in New Delhi, and to give them up for the sake of some of my emotional appeals would be completely asinine."

"So except for the moral dilemma everything was fine," I observed.

"Yes, Mr. Banerjee," Vaishali nodded, "but things changed one day. Someone slid into our office a strange looking envelope through the space between the entrance door and the floor. The moment I looked at the envelope I knew there was something wrong. Neha ma'am was also in the office at that time. She asked me to pick up the envelope and open it. Somehow, I didn't even feel like touching it. The more I saw it the more I was convinced that it was evil. However, I took care not to exude the slightest irregularity in my behavior as any such deed on my part could rouse suspicions in the mind of Neha Ma'am. So I picked it up. There was no address on the envelope. I opened it and pulled out the paper it contained. A chill went through my spine when I unfolded it. It was evil indeed. There was a symbol on the paper drawn with what looked like human blood. The strokes were pretty thick and in certain portions the blood didn't even seem to have dried up properly. This meant the symbol had not been drawn too far away in the past. Clearly, some strokes had been left wet deliberately to suggest that the symbol was freshly done. I had enough knowledge in sorcery by that time to know what that symbol meant. That symbol was used as a representation of death by some of the demons. So this was the sign of Islakais. I had never thought that Islakais would give such a clear sign to me. So the time had come for me to take him on. I wasn't sure still if I was ready for the combat but I didn't have a choice. I had to fight the demon now. There was no way for escape. Neha Ma'am sensed that something was wrong from the anxiety that clearly spread over my face. She asked me what was wrong. I had to tell a lie. I told her that it was a letter from my village and that something urgent had come up there. Therefore, I would have to rush to my village. Neha Ma'am insisted upon knowing what was wrong at the village but I didn't answer ... what could I have said anyway? There was no way I could have told her the truth." Vaishali took a pause.

The shade of anxiety on her face indicated that she was reliving those terrible moments.

24 BAISHNOB GRAM, THE VILLAGE OF LOVE

"I wondered if I was physically, mentally and psychically ready for the fight," Vaishali continued, "I realized I was not. Despite all my successes in the practice of sorcery, I simply didn't have the prowess of fighting Islakais head on. I remembered my mother having said that a time would come in my pursuit of sorcery when the intensity of the results of my activities would be too high to hide from the public eye even if I chose to practice at the death of night, and that would be the time to relocate myself from a city to a relatively quieter place, and if I wished I could even return to *Prithaka* because by that time I would be good enough to match Islakais in every possible way and he would be left with no advantage whatsoever by virtue of being in *Prithaka*. It was easy to reason that my powers in magic could certainly not be held equal to the powers one might have after reaching the stage wherein it is simply impossible to hide the results of one's pursuit of sorcery from the public eye because till that point of time I had no difficulties in keeping my practice a complete secret from everyone. Unmistakably I wasn't prepared enough for the battle. So what was the next best thing to do if I was not to fight him? Clearly, the best alternative would be to run away to a new place to buy time. I packed up some of my luggage and at the pretext of going to *Prithaka*, I left for Calcutta."

"Calcutta was safe for you at that time, wasn't it?

"Well yes, it was but I was unhappy still for much more than two years had passed and I wasn't still ready for the demon."

"Indeed, that's understandable, things didn't look too good for you," I nodded.

"Thankfully, things changed pretty quickly after I reached Calcutta. I decided not to rent a house in the main city to avoid the public eye. The countryside areas around Calcutta are also very developed with large chunks of population. Renting a house in one of those places also didn't feel like a prudent thing to do. So I did some research and finally ended up locating myself in a very remote village called *Baishnob Gram* which means *the village of Vaishnavas*. It was just the kind of place I wanted. Most of the people living in the village are devotees of Lord Krishna. They live in mud hutments with thatched roofs and have the simplest of lifestyles. Most importantly they are extremely welcoming. One Vaishnava family offered me a large hutment at a very low monthly rent. I spent the first few days studying their lifestyle. Most of them would wake up as early as three o'clock and bathe in the nearby rivulet and then assemble in a beautiful temple roughly in the middle of the village for the early morning *aarti* or what you call lamp ceremony in English. Thereafter, most get busy with their agricultural activities. The rest of the population, mostly women, manage the household works. Children go to a nearby school being run on Vedic principles. These and every other activity that form the simple village life continue till early evening. At seven, the Vaishnavas gather at the temple again for the evening *aarti*. By eight thirty there's hardly a soul who stays awake. It was clear therefore that I would have to carry out all my outdoor experiments roughly between eight thirty and three. I did exactly that and my efforts were hugely successful. I succeeded in experimenting with some of the most difficult methods of sorcery. My daily timetable was fixed – I practiced outdoor magic for six and a half hours when the entire village slept, and the remaining time I spent on sleeping and studying the notes of my mother. Very soon my command over the elements of nature was much better."

"So *Baishnob Gram* almost simulated the conditions of *Prithaka?*"

"I would rather say *Baishnob Gram* provided me with much better conditions than those available at *Prithaka*. Would you believe – the ideal conditions at *Baishnob Gram* helped me treble my powers in just about a month's time. I was now as good as my mother. I could do everything that she could do. I loved the surge of confidence in my being. However, I still had doubts if I could take on Islakais. The doubts were soon cleared. One morning, a senior member of the family that had given me the hutment came over and said with a beautiful smile, 'Hare Krishna, Ma, can I have a word with you?' I loved to be addressed as *Ma* ... I truly felt like a mother although the one talking to me was at least thirty years older than I, I reckon. There was so much of warmth in the way he addressed me."

"Bengalis sometimes affectionately address young girls as *Ma*. That is one way of respecting womanhood."

"Indeed, Mr. Banerjee," her smile indicated that she was reliving the moment when she was addressed as *Ma*, "interestingly, many men and women who are devotees of Lord Krishna all over the world address every girl and every woman as *Ma*. I don't see a better way of respecting womanhood. In fact, after having stayed in *Baishnob Gram* for some time, I have also begun to believe that there is no better way to greet a person than saying *Hare Krishna*."

"I agree, Vaishali."

"I was overwhelmed by his saintly disposition. I could feel a very pure consciousness enveloping my being. 'Hare Krishna, Ma,' he said again with the same angelic smile.

'Hare Krishna, Sir,' I replied.

'Could I talk to you for a while, Ma?'

'Of course, Sir, please sit down.'

'First you take this,' he came forward and gave me a box full of sweets, 'this is the *prasadam* of the morning *aarti*, Ma.'

'Thank you so very much, Sir.'

Then we sat down on cane chairs. Incidentally, the two cane chairs we were sitting on, a table and a rather simple wooden cot were the only furniture in that hutment. At times I found it pretty odd that such a large hutment should have such few furniture items. While the space of the hutment had been hardly used, the walls hardly had any space left for they were full of pictures of Lord Krishna's pastimes. I guess most of the houses in the village followed the same scheme of internal arrangement – minimum possible material objects and maximum possible use of wall space to depict the various moods of the Lord. That's how life is at *Baishnob Gram* – simpler than the simplest.

'Ma, I don't have the slightest intention to know what you are doing, let alone interfering with your activities. All I want from you is an assurance that what you are doing does not run counter to our feelings for Lord Krishna. I am sure you understand that everyone in this village has accepted Lord Krishna as the Supreme Personality of Godhood. Some of the advanced devotees amongst us have not just accepted Him but also experienced Him as the Supreme Personality of Godhead. I too have my own share of divine experiences. You would therefore appreciate, Ma, that any activity that even remotely shows disrespect to the Lord could cause a lot of pain in the hearts of devotees,' his tone conveyed a serious concern.

'I don't quite understand, Sir,' I spoke as softly as I could, 'are you suggesting that I have done something that is disrespectful to the Lord?'

'No, Ma, not at all,' he moved his head apologetically, 'I am not suggesting that at all. You seem to be a very good girl, Ma, and I have a fatherly affection for you but what people have seen in the last few days have led to some wondering if what you are doing is in harmony with our feelings for Lord Krishna. That is why I have come here for a simple assurance from your side that your activities are in agreement with our love for the Supreme Personality of Godhood.'

I was stumped by his words. Had the inhabitants of *Baishnob Gram* been watching my experimentations? Was the stillness of the village between eight thirty in the evening to three in the early morning a mere delusion? Had it been completely foolhardy on my part to conclude that the village slept during that time? Had I badly offended the feelings of the Krishna devotees?

'Tell me, Ma,' his smiling face brought me out of my deliberations, 'just tell me once that your activities are in harmony with our love for Lord Krishna, and I shall never disturb you again.'

'Sir, I will certainly tell you what you want to know but would you mind telling me as to which activities you are referring to?' I asked.

'What we have seen happening, Ma,' he said.

'What have all of you seen me doing, Sir?' I pressed for a clear answer.

'We have not seen you doing anything, Ma. But we do know that you are up to something. The effects of what you are doing are very clearly visible,' he smiled again, 'strange lights often spread out from your windows after dusk. I call them strange because they seem to be full of geometrical figures, also made of light, which rapidly change shapes. It is like watching inconstant figures of bright light floating against the backdrop of light that is comparatively less bright. Some people have even seen bright figures resembling humans moving around your hutment in the evening. Some villagers have witnessed orbs of light over the roof of your hutment. The villagers staying close to your hutment have even reported hearing sounds of weird nature taking rounds in the dead of night. A group of children that was playing nearby claimed to have seen bright human figures dancing around this place one evening. Let me tell you, Ma, that no one in the village has a complaint against you. All that the villagers want is an assurance from your side, that's all. In fact the senior most priests of the village have made it clear that nobody should interfere with your work if it does not run contrary to Krishna consciousness."

I immediately knew that I had reached that stage of excellence in sorcery wherein the effects of one's magic can no longer be hidden from the public regardless of how hard one tries to keep them within closed doors. Happiness in the true sense of the word filled my being for I was now, without a trace of doubt, a sorceress with great powers. Indeed, I could now take on Islakais. And perhaps even send him back to where he belongs!

'Won't you give me that assurance, Ma?' His saintly patience was truly remarkable.

'I wish to assure you, Sir,' I smiled back, 'that to the best of my belief my activities are not against Krishna consciousness. To speak the truth, I am also very fond of the Lord. Although I am not too sure if I am pure enough to be reckoned as a devotee of the Lord, I am certainly sure that I could never do anything consciously that is even remotely disrespectful to the Lord. Trust me, Sir, I have untold admiration and love for the inhabitants of *Baishnob Gram*, and can't imagine myself doing something that could hurt their feelings. Rest assured, Sir, my deeds do not run counter to your beautiful feelings.'

'That's all I needed to hear, Ma,' he folded his hands, 'Your words have removed all my anxieties. Now you can carry on with whatever you are doing and I assure you that no one ever will ask you another question.'

'But Sir,' I smiled again, 'my work here is done. With your permission I would now like to leave. I can't thank you all enough for the love and care you have showered on me. Honestly, I couldn't have finished my work so quickly if I had not received such extraordinary cooperation from all of you.'

'But Ma, why do you want to leave,' he sounded perturbed, 'has my seeking an assurance offended you?'

'No, Sir,' I moved my head, 'noble souls like you can never hurt anyone. I wish to leave because I have really completed my work.'

'Are you sure, Ma? I am sorry if I have hurt you,' the saintly man folded his hands again.

I couldn't bear the sight of that wonderful soul folding his hands before me again and again. So I got up from my chair and went up to him.

'Don't fold your hands before me, Sir,' I said kneeling down and holding his hands, 'you said you have fatherly affection for me, didn't you, Sir?'

He nodded.

'A father shouldn't fold hands before his daughter. Please believe me, Sir, I am planning to leave only because my work is finished. I wouldn't have thought of leaving if the job remained incomplete even by a trace. And never think your words offended me. You said nothing that could hurt me. In fact, you have been very soft on me. An average man in your place would have rather been very ruthless with me in the light of what the villagers have reported. I have never seen a man like you, Sir … so sweet, so patient, so composed and so caring. Now, if you really think of me as your daughter, then trust your daughter's words – I am leaving because the purpose of my stay in this village has been fully served.'

We both had tears in our eyes. I embraced him after we stood up and he said, 'May Lord Krishna bless you, Ma. May He be with you in all your endeavors.'

'Thank you, Sir,' I said wiping my tears, 'Your words will always remain in my heart as a perennial source of strength.'

Would you believe Mr. Banerjee, the entire village assembled to say *goodbye* to me? I had hardly spent a month over there and yet people seemed to be in true love with me. Many men, women and children had tears in their eyes. I cried too for their feelings were overwhelming. 'Come back whenever you want, now this village is as much yours as it is ours,' that's what the saintly soul in whose hutment I stayed said to me as I finally stepped out of the village.

Then I took a bus to Calcutta and caught a train bound for New Delhi from the Howrah station. I had great reasons to be happy now – I was now good enough to take Islakais head on, and I had a heart full of love showered on me by the angelic Krishna devotees.

THE SORCERESS

I called up Neha Ma'am from the train itself.

'Ma'am,' I said vibrantly, 'I am coming back.'

'O I am so happy to hear that, Vaishali,' she responded warmly as usual, 'I have been longing to see you again. Where are you now?'

'I am in the train, Ma'am,' I replied.

'How's everything in your village, now?' She asked.

'Fine, Ma'am,' I spoke as though I was returning from my village. In one sense I wasn't lying for I was returning from *Baishnob Gram*, a village I now felt like my own.

25 THE SECOND SIGN

"It was not sweet homecoming for me, Mr. Banerjee," Vaishali continued, "the taxi I hired from the New Delhi Station stopped for a while at the famous crossroads with the White Lady. Have you seen the White Lady, Mr. Banerjee?"

"Of course I have, it is a remarkable sculpture."

"No doubt it is very beautiful," Vaishali nodded, "but what happened next was not beautiful. As I watched its perfectly carved face, tears of blood appeared on its eyes. I believe I was the first person to see it shedding blood tears."

"It became a major event. It caught the attention of the entire world. All the news channels and newspapers covered the phenomenon in consummate details."

"For the world it was simply a mysterious phenomenon but I knew what was actually happening."

"You knew the cause for the blood tears?"

"Yes, Mr. Banerjee, I knew the reasons right from the time it started happening. Those tears of blood were not meant for anyone but me. From my study of mother's notes, I knew that sometimes a demon may give a second indication before a possible combat with the sorceress. A second indication from the demon could also mean that he has an edge over the sorceress. My mother had quoted from some ancient books on magic that explained that no demon would have the ethereal power to give a second indication or sign unless it is truly more powerful than the sorceress it is preparing to take on. I found my confidence shaken by the possibility that Islakais might still be stronger than I."

"But how could you be sure that Islakais was behind the blood tears or that it was a second indication?"

"A good sorceress has a strong intuition. Sometimes that intuition could be as strong as a mathematically calculated reality. The blood tears left me in no doubt about their cause. I was hundred percent sure that it was Islakais. There was another thing about the second indication of Islakais that shook me to the core."

"What was it?"

"It was the way the second indication came. Had the second indication come in a manner so as to be visible only to me, it would still be worrisome but not as worrisome as it was now. It had come in a way so as to be visible to the entire world. Such second indications could mean confirmed defeat for the sorceress. By quoting a couple of very reliable ancient texts on sorcery, my mother had very clearly written that if a sorceress confronts a second sign of this nature, then all she should try to do is to prepare herself mentally for her inglorious end at the hands of the demon."

"Such a horrific sign could dent anybody's confidence, Vaishali," I reacted, "I can broadly sense what you might have gone through at that moment."

"It was horrific indeed. I could almost see Islakais ruthlessly killing me. As the news of the White Lady gained popularity on television and in newspapers, my fears grew all the more difficult to live with. These news reports were constant reminders of what possibly lay ahead of me. Neha Ma'am could easily make out that there was something seriously wrong with me. She asked me a number of times but there was simply no scope for telling the truth. In a matter of days, the fear gripped my nerves so fiercely that I was hardly in a position to be of any assistance to Neha Ma'am. I lost my composure all together. I was not dealing well with her clients and I messed up a number of séances. Neha Ma'am, being a sweet soul, never rebuked me for anything. The frequency of my errors went up exponentially and yet she did not lose her equanimity even once. She was earning a bad name because of my mistakes but nothing could touch the serenity of her being. I knew that despite all the problems she was facing because of me, she would never ask me to leave. But I had a moral responsibility towards her. I had the least intention to see that sisterly woman suffer due to my presence. And in any case it was time now to take on Islakais. He could attack me any moment and I did not want Neha Ma'am to be a privy to this combat. What a shame it would be for me if she came to know my secret! What would she think? That I reciprocated her sisterly love with lies? It would perhaps be the greatest shock of her life. She wouldn't perhaps be inclined to trust anyone else after she saw through the veil of falsehood I had been wearing all the time before her. No, I couldn't afford to stay there anymore. But then where should I go, I wondered. *Baishnob Gram* came to my mind. Although the inhabitants of *Baishnob Gram* might find it pretty awkward to find me so quickly back in their village, that seemed to be the sanest choice. I would be safe there till I saw another sign from Islakais."

"So you decided to go back to *Baishnob Gram*?"

"No Mr. Banerjee," a smile of frustration came over her lips, "moments after I had begun to consider the possibility of going back to *Baishnob Gram*, I remembered having read in my mother's notes that the sighting of the second sign of the demon means that the demon has got psychic access to the soul of the sorceress. In other words, the demon has attached itself to the sorceress. So the demon would be in psychic connection with the sorceress no matter where she goes. Even if she goes to a new place, the demon would be able to launch his attack on her at any point of time and would no longer have to wait to gain powers to attack her, as would be the case if he had no psychic connection with the sorceress. Since I was alone in the office at that time, I quickly skimmed through my mother's notes to see if I had recalled correctly what she had written about the sighting of the second sign. My worst fears came true! I was spot on in assessing my condition. The very fact that I had seen the second sign meant Islakais had access to my soul. So it was same whether I stayed in New Delhi or in *Baishnob Gram*. It was the same everywhere! He could attack me at anytime in any place. So why not go back to my native place, I questioned myself. At least by being back in *Prithaka*, I would be able to have the satisfaction of dying where I belong. 'Let me also die where my parents died,' I said to myself."

"So you came back to *Prithaka*?"

"Yes Mr. Banerjee. Just as a loving elder sister would do, Neha Ma'am tried all she could to keep me with her. I am sure you understand how difficult it must have been for me to repulse her loving efforts. But I had no choice. No matter how heartless I appeared to her in turning down her repeated requests, I had to come back to *Prithaka* for if she ever came to know my secret she would be emotionally shattered. And if my inglorious death happened before her, there was high probability that sooner or later she would know the entire truth. So I packed up all my things thereby ensuring that not even the weakest clue was left behind which could lead to the disclosure of the reality, and left for *Prithaka.*"

She wiped the tear drops that had formed at the corners of her eyes.

"How long has it been since you returned to *Prithaka*?" I asked.

"Well, close to two months," she replied.

"And what about the combat with Islakais, Vaishali?"

"The combat is already on, Mr. Banerjee."

A brief spell of silence followed before she said, "So far I have been able to match him but I can sense the edge he has over me."

"So you have been fighting him for the last two months?"

"Yes, I am fighting him all the time. I can't even sleep properly, Mr. Banerjee. All the time I am on the lookout for a possible attack by this horrendous demon."

"How are you doing without sleep?"

"I do sleep in brief spells, Mr. Banerjee, but even during those brief spells of sleep I am conscious of what is happening around me. I have to keep my vital and psychic senses alert at all times."

"That is too much work, Vaishali … it must be draining your body."

"It is draining my body, mind and soul. I don't know as to how long I can go on living like this. It is possible that I die due to all my physical, mental and psychic energies seeping out of my being even before the combat with Islakais reaches a logical end."

"Don't say that Vaishali, nothing will happen to you."

"Come on Mr. Banerjee," she laughed, "I am not a child who could be comforted with such assurances."

I felt somewhat embarrassed at her reaction. Perhaps I should have been more careful with my words. Indeed, a girl who is dodging death all the time cannot find comfort in assurances that are based more on emotions and less on logic.

"I am preparing myself for the inevitable, Mr. Banerjee," she said, "no one can help me but I appreciate your coming here. I knew that you would come here to help me. I told you before that I knew you would come, didn't I?"

"Yes, you did but you didn't tell me as to how you knew about it."

"Please understand Mr. Banerjee, a sorceress of my level has a very strong intuition. The moment I left New Delhi, I knew that Neha Ma'am would approach you and ask you to help me. And given your zeal for unearthing paranormal mysteries, it was not difficult to intuit that you would do exactly as Neha Ma'am said."

I nodded in response.

"There are just a few more things you need to know before I wrap up this discussion. Those things must still be hovering in your mind."

"Yes, indeed ... there are some questions that have still remained unanswered."

"Don't worry, you will get the answers to those questions right away."

She got up and stretched her body and said, "Come, let's fly back to *Latika Griha* before there is sunlight.

"But you said I will get the answers to my unanswered questions right away," I said.

"Of course you will get the answers right away. Trust me."

She walked a few steps forward as I got up.

"Ready for the return journey," She said.

"Yes," I responded.

"Good," she said and began her walk.

26 QUESTIONS ANSWERED

I followed her effortlessly as her walk turned into a run and then the run turned into a flight. Moments before I was freely flying, I felt something detaching from my being. But as before, I cared least for what I had lost for this lighter state again felt far more soothing to be in. Then she spoke to me again through telepathy. Now, the communication was much clearer than the one we had during our flight to *Mahachoti*. It was almost like the two of us talking to each other under normal circumstances.

"Can you hear me clearly, Mr. Banerjee?" Vaishali asked.

"Very clearly, Vaishali."

"Great, so you do see the power of telepathy, don't you?"

"Absolutely, I must say you have great powers."

I heard her telepathic laughter in response.

"Are you ready to know the answers to your hitherto unanswered questions, Mr. Banerjee?"

"I am."

"Great, then go ahead – ask your questions one by one."

"Okay, my first question is who were the men I met in the train on my way to *Shyamalpur?*"

"Those were demoniac companions of Islakais. You are quite receptive to spirit phenomena, Mr. Banerjee. That is why you could see them. Islakais didn't want any help to come my way. He planted his companions in the hope that you would reconsider your decision of visiting *Prithaka.*"

"So he has been after me," I did press the panic button immediately.

"No, Mr. Banerjee," she explained, "I guess I have explained before that he cannot be after you even if he wants to. The rules of the ether world prevent him from harming anyone other than me. I have told you before that if a demon stays back in our world due to some mistake committed by a sorceress in her rituals, then it could have access only to the lives of the sorceress and her loved ones. It cannot have access to the lives of others. By *loved ones* I mean the kith and kin of the sorceress concerned. You are not related to my mother in any way. That's why he cannot harm you. At the most he can frighten you but I repeat – there's just no way he can harm you. So simply relax, you are completely safe."

Her words, no doubt, were very comforting but I also felt being somewhat selfish. It was as though all I was concerned with was my own safety and it didn't really matter how perilous a condition my beautiful hostess found herself in.

"Don't worry, you are not being selfish," her telepathic laughter took rounds in my head, "it is very natural to think about one's own safety. I would have done the same if I had been in your place."

"Who is the whitish humanoid I saw running through my window? Was it Islakais?" I asked after her words therapeutically cleansed my mind of the feeling of being selfish.

"Yes, it was Islakais. Again, you could see him because you are appreciably sensitive to spirit phenomena."

"What were those sounds I heard from my room while you were away, the ones you said were made by a cat? Who was there?"

"There was no one, Mr. Banerjee," she explicated, "it was all Islakais's doings. He generated those sounds to frighten you. The reasons are clear – he did not want you to continue staying with me. After all he doesn't want me to have even a semblance of a protection. And I am sorry, I lied to you at that point of time … there was of course no cat."

"After I arrived at *Latika Griha*, I found you constantly alternating between good and bad moods. Why?"

"I am sure you understand it is not easy to keep one's composure intact at all times when one is ceaselessly confronting the possibility of dying. Being a sorceress I know that there is nothing such as death and yet I am frightened by the thought of death engulfing my being. That's because despite being a sorceress I haven't ceased being a human. And I guess that's true of every sorceress and magician regardless of how far up the ladder of success she has climbed. Even if a sorceress is on the brink of unfolding the Absolute Truth, beyond which there is no knowledge, she will have some elements of humanness still left in her. And as long as there are elements of humanness in an individual, she is not free from the fear of death. Of course the fear of death does die for a sorceress who does actually unfold the ultimate truth for anyone doing so virtually merges with the Divine and death ceases to lose its meaning for her. I am far from unfolding the Absolute Truth. Therefore, the fear of death is pretty strong in me. So the alternating good and bad moods you are referring to are nothing but external expressions of strings of hope and hopelessness that keep moving through my psyche. Sometimes, the false hope that I might survive gives me a good mood, and sometimes when I confront the reality of the hopeless situation I am in, I get a bad mood."

"Are you in a hopeless situation?"

"That's a new question, Mr. Banerjee," she laughed, "I am sure this question hasn't been taking rounds in your mind like the others."

"That's right but I still want an answer."

"I have been explicit about my situation a number of times. Now that you want to hear it again, I will tell you again – yes, I am in a completely hopeless situation.'

As I took time assimilating her frank assessment of the situation, she said, "Do not think about the hopelessness that surrounds me, Mr. Banerjee. Go ahead and ask the next question."

"When I asked you as to what should I do if someone visited *Latika Griha* in your absence in the first afternoon that followed my arrival, you were pretty sure that no one would come. How were you so confident about it?"

"That's too simple a question to haunt you. The answer is clear – I am still socially ostracized and nobody visits me or my house. There's another reason why people stay away from *Latika Griha*. They are afraid of being in the vicinity of the house of a sorceress lest some harm should come over them. When you asked as to how I was so confident that nobody would come, I didn't give you a clear reply as by that time I hadn't quite become candid about my issues with you. It is not that I didn't want to tell you about myself and my lot, but I wanted to tell my story by slowly building it up in a logical order. If I just said that I was in a state of social isolation in response to your question, then it would be like pulling a string somewhere from the middle of my story. Such a reply entailed the possibility of causing confusion to you and the absolute certainty of causing embarrassment to me."

"Okay," I asked the next question, "how did you know that I was trying to extract information from you by insisting on being told as to how you were sure that nobody would visit *Latika Griha* in the same afternoon?

"I have already told you that a sorceress of my level has great intuitive powers, and that sometimes the intuition could be as strong as a mathematically calculated reality. So the answer to your question is – I knew it from my intuition."

"Who touched the heel of my left foot at the staircase when I was heading to your room with the intent of waking you up so that I could ask you about the paranormal happenings that were constantly happening around me?"

"It could have been anyone, Mr. Banerjee," she said, "either Islakais or one of his accomplices. You could guess the intention – Islakais wanted you to leave *Prithaka*."

"And who held me from around the curtain?"

"Again it could be Islakais or his accomplices."

"If these entities can touch me, can't they harm me, Vaishali?" My fears spoke again.

"No Mr. Banerjee, they cannot harm you. This correlation is not a valid one – I can vouch you are safe."

"Okay, now tell me Vaishali, has that huge pendulum clock always been hanging from the wall close to your bedroom or did it emerge there all of a sudden?"

"So you haven't forgotten the clock, Mr. Banerjee," Vaishali laughed.

"How can I forget that clock, it kicked the life out of my being," I responded.

"Well, I must confess what I told you about the clock was another lie. Indeed, that wall clock was never there. It did emerge there at the instant you spotted it! However, I must say in my defense that I didn't lie to you with any evil motif. I lied because I didn't want you to be scared of the unusual things happening around you such as a huge clock materializing from nowhere."

"I have no doubts about your intentions, Vaishali. But how did the clock suddenly emerge there? Was it another attempt of Islakais to frighten me?"

"No, Islakais had nothing to do with it. I caused it to emerge there, Mr. Banerjee. What you saw was not a real pendulum clock. It was an illusion that I weaved for you."

"But why Vaishali?"

"Actually I misread the situation. When you scoffed at the fact that there was no clock around, I thought of putting one there. I made the wrong assumption that your tempers will cool down at the sight of a clock. However, it had an exactly opposite effect on you."

"How could the toppling of the bucket cause such a large sound … I am sure it wasn't the sound of the bucket toppling over."

"You are right. The sound was caused by a bunch of ethereal entities."

As I pondered over her replies, she said, "Any more questions?"

"Yes."

"Go ahead."

"Where do you go to during the afternoons?"

This question made her laugh heartily.

"Have I said something very funny?" I said.

"Mr. Banerjee," she responded still laughing, "I have to arrange for the provisions, don't I? And you do understand that there are no shops at *Prithaka*, I have to go to Shyamalpur to buy the things. Besides, I do enjoy spending some time all by myself on the meadows. Sorry about my laughing at your question but I found it to be too simple to fit in with the other questions. Go ahead, ask your next question."

"Tell me something about your bedroom and the experience I had over there. Why is it so dark? There doesn't seem to be a single opening for light. Who shut the door of the room? What was fluttering like a bird after I sat down on the bed? What were those movements in the bed itself? And who suddenly opened the door?"

"Dark conditions suit my needs for advanced occult practices. That is why I have kept the room dark. I have covered all the openings so that I could do my work well even during the daytime. Now, who shut the door so suddenly? I am sure it must have been Islakais himself or one of his companions. What was fluttering close to you and what were those movements in the bed? Both the fluttering movements and the bed movements must have been caused by the one who shut the door just to make you feel more miserable. As regards who opened the door, well, it was me. I flew through the entire house but found you nowhere. Clearly, you were in my bedroom. When I found the bedroom door tightly shut, I knew immediately that Islakais or his companions have locked you up in my bedroom. So I rushed out of the house and tried to open that door with my powers. It wasn't easy to open that door as it had been jammed very tightly into its frame with evil forces constantly pressing on it. After a lot of effort I finally managed to vanquish the demoniac forces and the door flung open."

"So you saved me?"

"You were already safe in the sense that the demon or his accomplices couldn't have harmed you but if you had remained confined in that room for some more time, then your own fear could have caused you some terrible harm like …"

"Like nervous breakdown?" I asked.

"Yes. What else, Mr. Banerjee?"

"This question is about this magical flight."

"I will be more than happy to answer. What is the question?"

"Tell me more about this flight. I have noted that soon after the process of the flight begins, the body feels lighter as though something has got detached from one's being, and within moments of the flight ending, the body seems to gain its lost weight as though what got detached from one's being gets re-attached to it. Explain these phenomena."

"Well, Mr. Banerjee, I have already explained to you earlier that as I made advancements in my craft, my command over the elements of the nature got more and more pronounced. At the moment, I have very good control over some of the spirits of every element of nature. I also explained sometime back that this flight is nothing but the result of the combined efforts of some of the earth, air, and sky spirits. The earth spirits help nullify the effect of gravity. The air spirits help lift our bodies in air, and the sky spirits help maintain the trajectory of the flight. Why do they help us? Well, I command them to help us, that's why. Many of the earth spirits, water spirits, fire spirits, air spirits, and sky spirits that were once subservient to my mother are now subservient to me. These spirits can go to any extent to carry out my orders. This flight is just a small example of what they can do for me. As for what gets detached from the being just after the flight begins and gets reattached to it soon after the flight ends ... well, we sorceresses call it the *mahajadatattva*, which broadly means gross inert aspect ... the gross inert aspect of one's being is often the principal reason behind one's being earth-bound. By shedding the *mahajadatattva*, one's flight becomes possible. But do not make the mistake of thinking that *mahajadatattva* is a bad aspect of the being. Material life of a being would be impossible without *mahajadatattva*. It could act as an impediment only when one partakes in ethereal phenomena."

"You just said you now have very good control over the spirits of the elements of nature."

"That's right," she nodded.

"Can't you direct them to keep Islakais in check," I said.

"These spirits can achieve only what lies within their powers. They cannot do things that are beyond their abilities. Fighting Islakais or his companions are far beyond their powers," Vaishali explained.

"Now these ethereal companions of Islakais you are often talking about – who are they? Did they also leak into our world due to the mistake made by your mother?"

"No, they are petty demoniac entities who accidentally leak out from the dark realm of ether into our world. There are many such entities hanging around in the world of the living all the time. It is not only humans who can go wrong, Mr. Banerjee. Even nature can go wrong as you can see ... the accidents that help such entities enter this world are nothing but mistakes made by nature. These entities, however, are not very strong in terms of ethereal powers. I can take on thousands of them easily. In fact, even a sorceress of intermediate level can vanquish these beings with ease. More often than not, these entities tie up with strong demons like Islakais to cause nuisance to people like you who are not practitioners of magic. However, for a man or a woman with strong heart and mind, these petty beings hardly mean anything."

"Understood," I responded, "thank you Vaishali, I have got answers to all my questions."

"Are you sure? If you have any further questions, please ask ... I will answer."

"No Vaishali, that's all."

As before, the flight ended abruptly as I found my feet touching the ground. Yet again I was in a meditative state and Vaishali helped me come out of it. She removed her robe. What a sight it was to see the beatific smile playing on her lips again! Behind her stood the unmistakable edifice of *Latika Griha*. She helped me walk and soon we were inside it.

"What time is it now, Vaishali?" After quite a while I spoke with my mouth again.

"It should be close to six. Why don't you go over to your bedroom and sleep?"

I looked at her.

"Don't worry," she said reading my mind, "that room is perfectly safe for you. It will do you a world of good if you could get some good sleep.

"What about you?" I asked.

"Don't worry about me, I will take rest in my own way."

I looked back once while walking up the staircase.

"This telepathic talk we had," I said, "it was…"

"We can talk about that later," she spoke before I could complete, "don't strain yourself too much. I guess you need rest. Please get some sleep, Mr. Banerjee."

I continued to look at her for a while before walking back to my bedroom.

27 A MOOD SWING YET AGAIN!

The sun's rays stealing in through the curtains were quite strong by the time I woke up. I had rested well. I looked around and found everything very well arranged. I remember having thrown my shirt carelessly on the chair close to the window. Now I found it neatly folded on the table. Clearly, Vaishali's day had begun much before mine. I wondered as to when she takes rest.

When I went downstairs I found her arranging the breakfast on the dining table.

"Good morning," she said beaming.

"Good morning," I responded.

"Did you have a good sleep?"

"Yes, I had. I am feeling very fresh."

"That's good to hear, Mr. Banerjee."

"Did you have a good sleep too?"

She just looked up at me in response with the vestiges of the smile still on her lips. I realized that I shouldn't have asked the question for the kind of state she was in, good sleep was out of question.

"I hope you like the breakfast. I made it in a hurry."

"I am sure it must be good," I said as I put a small cake into my mouth.

"How is it?"

"Delicious, if you can prepare food of this nature in a hurry, I wonder how your food will taste when you cook in leisure," I replied settling down on a chair.

"Thanks Mr. Banerjee, I take that as a compliment," she said and sat down to eat.

Meanwhile, I had noted that the big wall clock was no longer there. There were no reasons now for her to continue with her illusion.

"It is good that the illusion is gone, Vaishali."

She understood what I was talking about and nodded.

"Your illusions are as good as real objects," I remarked.

"Of what use are illusions if they don't look like real objects?" She laughed.

"Indeed, indeed," I nodded as I finished my share of cakes.

"You could have some of my share," she pushed her plate.

"No Vaishali, thank you, I have already eaten quite a number."

I picked up my cup of tea as my mind went back to the incredible last night experiences.

"What are you thinking, Mr. Banerjee?" Vaishali asked.

"I am still wondering," I said sipping tea, "if the experiences I had last night were real or some fantastic dreams."

"It seems *Prithaka* has made life really difficult for you," she said with a faint smile with crumbs of cake in her mouth, "perhaps you have lost track of the line that separates reality from dreams."

"You are right, Vaishali. *Prithaka* has completely changed my outlook on life. I can sense the power of the dictum that fact is stranger than fiction."

"What did you find so strange last night?"

"Everything about last night was strange. I would rather say that to call those experiences strange would be a gross understatement. They should rather be reckoned as fairytales coming true."

"I am happy, Mr. Banerjee, that I have been of some use to you."

"You call it *some use*? By making me a part of these experiences you have enlightened me with such experiential knowledge which would have taken a lifetime of spiritual practice to acquire."

"It is nice to know that you attach that kind of importance to the magical flights."

"Not just the flights, Vaishali," I rejoined, "I reckon the telepathic conversations were equally important."

"O that's interesting."

"I didn't have the slightest idea that telepathic conversations could be as good as real conversations."

"I must correct you there, Mr. Banerjee, telepathic conversations are also real conversations. If you are suggesting that telepathic conversations could be as good as talks at the material level, I must correct you again there for the truth is telepathic talks are more powerful than the common tête-à-têtes."

"I agree with you, Vaishali."

"I have something for you, Mr. Banerjee," she took out an envelope from her gown and held it out to me.

"What is this?"

"See it for yourself."

After wiping my hands clean with a tissue paper, I took the envelope from her hand, opened it and took out its content. It took me a while to realize that the card like thing that I was now holding was a train ticket from *Shyamalpur* to New Delhi.

"What is this, Vaishali?"

"Can't you see it, Mr. Banerjee," her tone suddenly felt like losing its warmth, "you are catching a train back to New Delhi tomorrow. I had this ticket booked through one of my confidants. He delivered it today in the morning."

"What … Vaishali … what are you talking about," the suddenness of what she said made my speech incoherent.

"A horse cart will be here early in the morning tomorrow to take you to *Shyamalpur* Railway Station," she spoke in the same vein.

"I don't quite understand this, Vaishali?"

"What do you not understand now? I have told you everything that you wanted to know. Your job at *Prithaka* is done."

"It was not merely to gain knowledge that I came to *Prithaka*. I came here to clean the mess that you find yourself in, Vaishali, and that job is far from being done."

"Excuse me for saying this but your words are giving me the impression that your mind is presently afflicted with extreme naiveté."

"Don't you think you should have asked me once before booking the ticket?"

"I don't think that would have helped," this was yet another instance of her mood changing abruptly. She was now speaking with distinct shades of surliness.

"What do you mean, Vaishali?"

"I mean exactly what I said. If I had asked you before booking the ticket, you wouldn't have agreed to leave *Prithaka*. That's why I didn't ask you."

"So you don't want me to stay here any longer?"

"Why do you keep asking questions, Mr. Banerjee?"

"That's because you always choose to do something strange, you are indeed a master at springing surprises," my irritation made itself felt in my tone.

"Doesn't matter what you think about me, I have made my stand clear."

"On one hand you call me an honored guest, and on the other you suddenly and quite insultingly ask me to leave. Tell me Vaishali, what do I make of these diametrically opposite stands?"

"I don't wish to talk about this anymore. I have some work now, I suggest that you go back to your bedroom and give yourself some more rest."

I got up with the ticket still in my hands and went back to the bedroom. My mind had turned into a pool of morbid thoughts.

Vaishali's mood swings were nothing new, but I still found difficult to digest what had just happened. Somehow her words made me feel unwanted ... someone no better than a liability. I reclined on the bed and closed my eyes. Her words *'Doesn't matter what you think about me, I have made my stand clear'* kept hovering in my mind making the sores of my heart all the more painful. And then I felt the corners of my eyes moistening up. The faculties of reason and logic in my mind denounced me for losing my balance but I could do little to regain my composure. The way she spoke to me was too caustic to be ignored. But why was I attaching so much importance to her words? Who was she after all? Nothing more than a potential beneficiary of my skills, I reasoned. The very next moment I saw the faultiness of that reason. Did she really need my help? No, there was no reason to believe that she needed my help. In what way could I help her? She was by herself such an accomplished sorceress and her understanding of ethereal phenomena was far greater than mine. Perhaps, only I stood to benefit from our exchanges. And I had benefitted immensely. I had gained invaluable knowledge from her association. What I learnt about consciousness and other ethereal phenomena connected to magic and sorcery from her couldn't have been learnt by reading even a thousand books. And a large part of this learning was of experiential nature. That's what made this knowledge very special. So the truth lay bare before my eyes. Perhaps it always lay there but I avoided seeing it. And the truth was she was in no need of my help and with my limited abilities I couldn't help her even if I wanted to. So she was right. I really had no more business at *Prithaka*. The best thing for me to do was to pack my bags and leave the next day just as she had said. It was no doubt very upsetting to think that I wouldn't be of any help to her but the sooner the truth was accepted the better.

The chain of my thoughts continued for a long time. It was late afternoon by the time I got up from the bed with my composure in place. I wondered if I should go down and see what Vaishali was doing. After some consideration I decided not to go downstairs and rather focus my energies on one of my professional requirements that I had not got the chance of meeting for quite some time now. I was in desperate need of updating my notes. That had been in my mind all the time but one set of circumstances or the other prevented any such effort. It was a good opportunity now to write down everything that I had experienced since the time I wrote down my notes last. I was not sure if my memory retained all the essentials of the experiences I had had at *Prithaka* since the time I wrote last. More delay could mean complete disappearance of some important learning points from my mind. So I took out the diary again and began to write. It was not easy to arrange the random experiences in a logical order. I avoided writing down the learning points in the form of a narrative, though that was the first impulse, as there was too much to write about and began to write in the form of short and succinct points.

"Please come for lunch," Vaishali's voice broke my concentration.

I looked up and found her standing at some distance.

"The lunch is ready," she spoke again and went out of the room.

I closed my diary and went downstairs. The food, as usual, had been neatly arranged on the table. She pulled a chair for me and I sat down. She put some rice on my dish and tenderly pushed two bowls, one carrying dal and the other potato curry, close to my dish before moving over to the other side of the table. Then she pulled a chair for herself and sat down. We didn't exchange a single word almost till I had finished my food.

"Should I give you some more rice?" Vaishali broke the silence.

"No," I moved my head.

"Dal or curry?"

"No, thanks."

"There's something more I have prepared. It's rice pudding, please have a little." She said as she took the last crumb from her dish and put it into her mouth.

Although her tone was not soft, yet there was an earnest appeal in what she just said. So I couldn't turn down the offer.

"All right," I responded.

She got up and went to the kitchen. In a couple of minutes she was back with a bowl full of rice pudding. Vaishali kept it close to me and began to arrange the used dishes and bowls for a wash.

"Won't you have rice pudding too?" I asked.

"I have already had a bowl," she replied and went to the kitchen with the dishes and bowls.

The rice pudding, called *payesh* in Bengali, had really been prepared beautifully. The reason I just mentioned the Bengali equivalent of rice pudding over here is because its taste was just like the traditional *Payesh* prepared by seasoned Bengali cooks. I loved the aromas of the *Basmati* rice of the choicest quality and the cardamoms.

"How is it?" She said after she was back in the dining space. Her tone had surely softened down by now.

"It is really good. It tastes like the typical Bengali *Payesh*."

"O really," a faint smile adorned her lips, "that means my effort has been successful. Actually I made a conscious effort to emulate the Bengali style. Neha Ma'am taught me this delicacy. O I miss her so much."

"Why don't you go and meet her once?"

She gave me a strange look for a while before moving towards the entrance.

"I will be out as usual for some time. Help yourself if you need anything," Vaishali said before she stepped out of the door.

I finished the rice pudding and went upstairs to my room and began to write. Thankfully, most of my experiences were still fresh in my mind. I went on and on with my writing till I realized that the light outside had dimmed. I was happy to see that most of what I wanted to be recorded had indeed been recorded. I put the diary back into my bag and wondered what I would tell Neha and Saikat once I was back in New Delhi. Clearly, my job at *Prithaka* would remain unfinished. The truth about *Prithaka* once again came before my eyes and I once again told myself that I actually had no job to do at *Prithaka*. There appeared to be no way to help Vaishali and even if there was a way, it was beyond my abilities to effectuate it. That was the truth I would have to acquaint Neha and Saikat with.

I lay down on the bed again with images of last night's experiences in my mind. The indistinct continuum of things that went past us during our flights, the exchanges at the top of the indomitable *Mahachoti* Hill, and the telepathic talks – what experiences I had had! As my psyche took me to finer details of the experiences, I had a sudden feeling that Vaishali was talking to me. The feeling flung me out of my reminiscences. Did I really hear Vaishali say something? I looked around. No, Vaishali was not in the sight. Yet again some blurry words of Vaishali seemed to fill my mind. What could be happening, I asked myself. Was it possible that I had heard her indistinct words through a telepathic cord? Or was I imagining things? Any of the possibilities could be true. I closed my eyes and tried to move deep into my consciousness to find the answers. Very soon I knew that something unusual was happening in my psyche. But I was not sure if it was a telepathic connection with Vaishali that gave the sense of unusualness. I didn't have to struggle long to be fully sure that a telepathic communion with Vaishali had indeed taken shape again. The indistinct words soon made way for clearly audible words. What followed thereafter was a patent communication. There was no scope for any ambiguity in what we said to each other. Every expression exchanged was charged with spiritual energy. I could now see the truth in Vaishali's argument that telepathic conversations are much more powerful than common tête-à-têtes.

"Can you hear me clearly now?" Vaishali's words flowed in.

"Yes, I can, are we again in a telepathic conversation?" I pressed for a confirmation despite not harboring the slightest doubt about it being a telepathic conversation.

"What do you think?" She asked.

"It feels like one."

"Well, it is a telepathic conversation."

"But it didn't begin smoothly like last night," I remarked.

"Ethereal phenomena do not happen in any set pattern. Tell me – would you like to have a talk with me now?"

"Yes, Vaishali.

28 I SAW THAT BEFORE

"You must be feeling very bad about the way I spoke to you in the morning," Her words flew into my being as the telepathic conversation continued.

"I don't want to talk about that, Vaishali."

"I am sorry, Mr. Banerjee, I didn't have the slightest intention of hurting you."

"I don't need any explanations, Vaishali."

"Please let me share my thoughts with you, Mr. Banerjee ... we may not get another opportunity for communication. After all you are leaving tomorrow."

"Why? Telepathic connections transcend the boundaries of space, don't they, Vaishali?"

"Yes, but I may not ..." The pain in her words registered in my psyche.

"Finish what you were saying," I said.

"This could be our last telepathic conversation, Mr. Banerjee ... if fate supports me, I would perhaps manage just one more telepathic conversation after this one, but as I just said that would happen only if fate is on my side.

"Why? What has fate got to do with our telepathic conversations? Are you suggesting that you would snap all connections with me after I leave *Prithaka*?"

"That's not what I meant."

"Then why do you think this could be our penultimate or last telepathic conversation?"

"Because ..."

"Because what," I found my composure stretched again.

"Because I might not live beyond tomorrow, I think my time has come," Her words were now laden with tears and helplessness; it was clear she had given up all hopes.

By now the telepathic cord had become so strong that I could almost peep into her psyche. Plops of gloom ceaselessly emerged from the core of her being and spread out in all directions.

"Don't say that, Vaishali," I found myself running short of words.

"My not saying so will not change the truth ... I am preparing myself for the end."

"Maybe that is not the truth ... maybe you are mistaken."

"I wish it were so, Mr. Banerjee. Sadly, what I am saying is the only truth. I can sense the final combat that will happen at the top of *Mahachoti* tomorrow after the fall of night. I can already see the fierce battle between me and Islakais robbing *Mahachoti* of all its peace. At first, I will match him power by power, and blow by blow. Very soon I will find my powers not good enough to battle him for long. Yet I will fight the hopeless battle. He will constantly attack the weaknesses of my being and my resistance will progressively go down. I will also be looking for weaknesses in his being all the time but I will find none. Then he will unleash the one last deadly blow ripping my being apart. Thereafter I will not be able to fight anymore for I will be left with little life force to carry on."

Vaishali did not speak for sometime thereafter. I could feel her organizing her thoughts. So I too didn't speak lest I should disturb her mental drill although I had a strong urge to let out the voice of my inner self that strongly rebelled against the idea that she would be vanquished by the demon in so inglorious a fashion. Before long she spoke again.

"Maybe I can faintly see what is going to happen thereafter. With a great effort I will gather the remaining chunks of energy and walk towards the peak of *Mahachoti*. I will stand at the peak and look ahead of me, perhaps thinking about you for you have been my last human connection. I will deem myself lucky if the final drops of life energy left in me turn out to be enough to establish yet another communion and surely the last communion between us. You perhaps will be sleeping at that time for it will be close to midnight. Doesn't matter how deep a slumber you are in, you will be wakened up by the weight of the communion. You might have heard that just before death one might see ethereal beings moving around freely in the space separating life and death. I am certain I will get to see these beings, beings that look like elves and fairies, all around me. And since you will be connected to my mind, you might also see these beings. Your eyes will then fall on the summit of *Mahachoti*. The summit will appear different as though something or someone is standing over it. The elves and fairies will often cross your field of vision making it very difficult for you to have a clear look at the summit. You will constantly adjust and readjust your position to have a better view. However, these beings will continue to block your line of vision every now and then. Disturbed by their flights, your mind will direct them to stay out of your field of vision. Being ethereal beings they will be able to hear the voice of your mind. They will now clear off. Therefore, you will have a better look at the summit now. Being in telepathic mode, you will be able to zoom in on the summit. Now, you will see me standing there with a look a resignation. You will say, 'Vaishali, what are you doing there.' I will reply, 'This is my destiny, Biswajit.' Yes, I will call you *Biswajit* and not *Mr. Banerjee*. I have always wanted to call you by your first name but somehow never quite managed to sum up enough courage to do so lest you should think of me as being discourteous and uncouth. But at that very instant I shall not care for the rules of civility. Incidentally, that will be the first and the only time I will address you by your first name. My reply will confuse you and you will ask, 'What is your destiny, Vaishali?' You won't get a reply this time. Instead, you will find a disagreeable smile on my lips. This smile will make you very sad … so sad that you will shed tears. And then it will strike you that I am not smiling at all, and that it is death smiling through my lips. You will feel utterly helpless when in the next moment you will see me bending down and allowing myself to fall freely into the arms of death."

"I have seen all this before, I have seen all this before," I was stunned by what she just said.

"You have seen all this before? When Mr. Banerjee?" Her words were laden with strong elements of surprise.

"Do you remember I had a very bad dream when you took me to *Tarangini* for the first time?"

"Yes, I remember. The dream was so bad that you actually shrieked in terror."

"That's right, Vaishali. I dreamt what you just described as the possible last moments of your life. I saw you standing at the summit of *Mahachoti* after a crowd of elves and fairies moved out of my field of vision on my demand. Your expressions were gloomy. Then we had exactly the same conversation that you just narrated. And then I realized that it was Death smiling through your lips, again just as you had narrated. Thereafter … thereafter, you know what happened. I simply watched the horror helplessly."

"Mr. Banerjee, is that what you dreamt?"

"Yes, Vaishali."

"Are you absolutely sure you dreamt exactly what I narrated?"

"I have no doubts."

"And you are also sure that you dreamt that sitting close to *Tarangini* when I took you there for the first time?"

"Yes, I am sure of that as well."

"Did this dream come again?"

"No, Vaishali."

"Now this means …"

"What Vaishali?"

"This means we didn't have our first telepathic connection yesterday … our first telepathic connection happened when you dreamt me falling from the summit of *Mahachoti*. The thought that we could get spontaneously connected never crossed by mind. Perhaps I should have known that with your kind of sensitivity to ethereal phenomena, our telepathic connection would not always need a single handed effort from my side to get established."

"I am not sure I have understood you, Vaishali."

"Mr. Banerjee, while you were sleeping on that day, I was imagining the possible circumstances of my death. I also wondered as to how you would see my death happening by standing on the rock I was sitting on, in case you do chance upon watching my death with our telepathic connection established from that point. I tried to see things from your perspective but did not make any effort to establish a telepathic communion between us. However, the telepathic communion did get established. That's because your sensitivity to ethereal phenomena pushed your psyche into getting connected with my psyche. I believe this happened because my thoughts about you were very strong, strong enough to find their way into your telepathic receptors. As a result you could see my thoughts in your dream."

"How strange things can be at *Prithaka*?"

"This has got nothing to do with *Prithaka*. This is about you and me," her words, I sensed, conveyed a hope.

"What about you and me?"

"This shows our consciousnesses are conducive to each other and could sometimes overlap on their own without any of us making any conscious effort to make them overlap. If I understand my mother's notes correctly, a person whose consciousness is conducive to mine could ..."

"Come on Vaishali, why do you leave things unsaid ... tell me clearly ... what a person whose consciousness is conducive to yours can do for you?"

"Perhaps my death ... no, Mr. Banerjee, I can't do this ... I can't do this."

In the very next moment the telepathic connection got snapped. I banged a fist on the bed in frustration. She broke off the telepathic cord at the most vital point of the conversation. However, from whatever she spoke I could intuitively figure out that there was some hope of untangling the state of affairs. It was also not difficult to make out that I was the one who held the hope for her. But then why wasn't she willing to tell me what I could do for her? Perhaps because any effort from my side could endanger my own life, I reasoned. Would I be willing to help her if she asked even if it meant placing my own life in jeopardy? – I asked myself. Perhaps I wouldn't if she had asked even a few moments ago but now things had completely changed. My inner self, and clearly a better self, now implored my conscious mind to go to any extent to help the sorceress even if it meant dying for her sake. After all I was at *Prithaka* to help her and to shirk away from my duties simply because there was a threat to my life would not be in keeping with the spirit of my profession, which by its very nature is full of threats from known and unknown realms. Not helping her in the existing circumstances would be like a firefighter not making attempts to extinguish a terrible fire because of risk to his life, or a soldier running away from a terrorist attack on innocents because of the fear of being struck by a bullet. No, I couldn't run away from the situation. My sense of duty would simply not allow that. If there was a way I could help her, I would help her regardless of the size of risks involved.

I knew what I was supposed to do next and I did exactly that. I rushed out of *Latika Griha* towards the meadows I intuited I would find her in. And my intuition wasn't wrong. She lay on her back on one of the raised lands with her eyes fixed on the dark skies. Vaishali, normally a very watchful girl, was so absorbed in her thoughts that she didn't get the slightest inkling of my approach.

29 HOPE

"Vaishali," I said moving close to her.

"Huh," she reacted as she came out of her thoughts.

"Vaishali," I sat close to her.

"Mr. Banerjee ... you ... here," she got up with a look of surprise.

"Why did you snap the telepathic conversation, Vaishali?"

"I don't want to talk about this."

"You will have to talk about this," I pressed her hand.

"Leave me alone, Mr. Banerjee," Vaishali released her hand with a jerk.

"I will not leave you alone, Vaishali," I now gripped her hand more firmly, "you got to tell me how I can bring you out of this mess."

"Leave my hand, Mr. Banerjee," she shouted, "you are causing me pain."

I freed her hand and looked down, somewhat embarrassed,

somewhat helpless.

"Now, why did you have to come here?" her tone was quite raised still.

I looked up without responding.

"Speak up, Mr. Banerjee … what prompted you to come to the meadows?"

"I have come here to know how I can help you."

"Help me in what?" She spoke in the same vein.

"Help you in fighting Islakais."

"What? Do you really think you can help me in fighting that demon?"

"Yes, I think so."

"Are you mad, Mr. Banerjee?"

"My inner self says I can salvage your life."

"O stop speaking like a lunatic, Mr. Banerjee," Vaishali shouted at the top of her voice.

"You stop behaving like a lunatic, Vaishali," I responded with an equal shout.

A strange overlapping of the echoes of our words followed. As a result, the eeriness of *Prithaka* appeared all the more heightened.

"Mr. Banerjee, I don't understand this," softness returned to her speech, "I appreciate your concern but there is nothing you can do. Haven't I made it very clear that nobody can help me out of my problems?"

"You have but I don't subscribe to that view."

"Please believe me, Mr. Banerjee ... you cannot do anything to help me."

"Maybe I can."

"From where has this madness crept into you?"

"You have said it yourself, Vaishali."

"What have I said?"

"You said that our consciousnesses are conducive to each other and can overlap even if none of us makes an effort in that direction."

"Yes, I did convey that telepathically, so what?"

"You also said that if you understand your mother's notes correctly, a person whose consciousness is conducive to yours does have some chance, howsoever small it may be, to help you out of the mess you find yourself in."

"No, I never said that," she raised her voice again.

"You didn't say it so explicitly but I could gather the import of your words."

"That's enough, Mr. Banerjee, I can't take this anymore."

"You know very well what I am saying is right."

"No, it is not."

"It is Vaishali. Do I need to explain to you that when the telepathic cord becomes very strong, the communicators can almost peep into the minds of one another? I could read your thoughts even though you didn't communicate very clearly that I could be of help."

"Mr. Banerjee, please …"

"Look Vaishali, I know why you are not comfortable with the idea of my helping you. You think that any efforts from my side to help you fight Islakais could place my life under serious threats and that's not acceptable to you. I respect your feelings but you must understand my position as well … I am a professional paranormal investigator and it is my job to protect you. By not letting me help you, you would be denying me the right to perform my duties. You would appreciate that that would not be the correct thing to do …"

"But Mr. Banerjee …"

"Allow me to complete, Vaishali. My duties constitute an essential part of my karma. You know how important a role karma plays in one's spiritual evolution. Thus it wouldn't be wrong to say that your attempts to keep me out of your problems would interfere with my spiritual evolution. To speak the truth, I have been working on your case right from the time Neha requested me to help you. Thus far I have put in untold physical and mental labor. Now, when the case is approaching its point of culmination, you simply cannot shut the door on my face. And if you do shut the door on my face, it will be nothing short of handing down to me the most terrible humiliation; that's because by doing so you would exude utter distrust in my abilities."

"Mr. Banerjee …"

"I haven't finished still. Do you understand how much anguish you would cause me by keeping me out of your problems? I will carry the burden of this humiliation all my life. And what do you think you are going to achieve by keeping me out of all this? That you will save my life? I am sorry to say that if your purpose is merely to save my life, then this is an indication that despite all your accomplishments as a sorceress, you haven't been able to understand the truth that every arrangement of material life is impermanent in nature. What is the use of pursuing the occult if you can't even appreciate the impermanence of things around you?"

"Mr. Banerjee, let me speak too," she shouted to stop my chain of arguments, "I guess I have already explained to you that even the best of sorceresses do not transcend the fear of death. I understand that things around me are impermanent, yet it is difficult to accept this impermanence. That is human nature. I am not above human nature – I have conceded that before and I concede that again. And indeed I am not letting you help because I fear you might die in the process. And don't tell me you are not afraid of death. You have been afraid of death all along. Maybe suddenly you have realized that the fear of death and your sense of duty do not go together. Tell me isn't that true?"

"Well … well…"

"Your reaction proves what I am saying is true. Who wants to die, Mr. Banerjee? No one, even I don't want to die. Sadly, I don't have a choice. But you have a choice. Why do you wish to place yourself in such danger? Please understand, thus far you are safe. At the moment Islakais poses no threat to you. However, if I let you help me, you would also be in the direct line of his attack. Do you understand that? The immunity you are enjoying from Islakais and his accomplices will no longer be available to you if I let you help me. This demon would then be able to harm you. And I would be able to do little to protect you. As regards my refusal to let you help me being the same as humiliating you, you do know that I can't even imagine humiliating you, let alone doing so in reality. Mr. Banerjee, I have never doubted your analytical powers but what can you do in the face of an ethereal attack? Is it wrong on my part to assume that you would not be able to tackle the horrendous powers of Islakais? Even my abilities are nowhere close to his, let alone the abilities of someone uninitiated into magic. Mr. Banerjee, your chances of succeeding against Islakais are as good as zero. I see no way how you could contest him. As regards your karma, well … if you remain alive, you have a chance to perform your karma in a manner so as to facilitate your spiritual evolution. But if you die, your karma for the present human incarnation comes to a full cessation. So what would be a better choice for you? To die and put a full stop on your karma, or to live and perform the right kind of karma so that you could merge with the Absolute Truth?"

"Thanks, Vaishali."

"Thanks for what?"

"Thanks for at least acknowledging that I do have some little chance to bail you out of the situation."

"When did I …"

"Again, you didn't say it directly, Vaishali, but your words spoke for the hidden corners of your mind."

"Why are you doing this, Mr. Banerjee? Why are you forcing me to place you in a hopeless situation?"

"Don't trouble yourself with these questions, Vaishali. Just let me help you."

"Why should I when I know that your decision to help me is driven by an impulse?"

"Don't say that, Vaishali. My intention has always been to help you. Otherwise, I wouldn't have been here at *Prithaka*. But I agree that I was afraid of death. You are right – nobody wants to die. Perhaps an accomplished yogi also wouldn't want to die except when he or she has completely transcended humanness. If a sorceress like you is afraid of dying, I cannot obviously be expected to be free of that fear. And I am not. I also agree that this fear was quite dominant over other sane thoughts in my mind even a little while ago. That's why if you had asked for help sometime back and told me that such help could cost me my life, I would perhaps refrain from helping you. But that situation has changed all together. I want to help you now regardless of the consequences. I don't want to think about death now, I rather want to think about how I can help you. Trust me, this decision of mine is not driven by an impulse. It is driven by the saner parts of my consciousness. Look Vaishali, you cannot beat the demon alone, and I cannot even face him for long, let alone beating him, but together we may be a formidable force. Together we may convert the bleak hope of defeating him into a reality."

"You might regret your decision later."

"No, I will not, Vaishali," I took the railway ticket out and tore it into two parts.

"I have never seen your kind of obstinacy, Mr. Banerjee," she said after some thought without being able to prevent a faint smile from coming over her lips.

I was thrilled to see the faint smile for it was indicative of her hope for survival getting fuelled, and her inclination to let me help her.

"So tell me what do I have to do?" I said.

"What makes you feel I am now ready to accept your help?" The faint smile now gave way to a more patent grin.

"Don't forget we could be telepathically connected anytime," I smiled too, "for the moment that smile of yours has played the role of the telepathic cord."

"You are very good with your words," she laughed heartily, "you can make me laugh like this even in such anxious moments."

"So tell me what can I do for you?"

"As for now, you could walk with me back to *Latika Griha*, have dinner with me, and then ..."

"And then ..." I smiled again.

"You win, Mr. Banerjee ... and then understand as to what could be the only way in which you could help me. Let me tell you again that the chances of your success are almost non-existent."

"The chances are almost non-existent but not non-existent," I said as we began to walk back to *Latika Griha*.

"You should think of writing a book on optimism," she laughed again.

Our exchanges became more and more vibrant and humorous as we walked over the meadows with fragrant breezes of *Prithaka* refreshing us all the time. By the time we reached *Latika Griha*, the hope that our combined strengths could turn the tide against Islakais had grown stronger.

30 WHAT A CHALLENGE!

Not that I ever had a doubt about Vaishali's culinary skills but the dinner she prepared that night was truly delicious. It was as if she had injected magic into the food. I ate with little regard to table manners as she watched with a glee. Before long I realized that I had overeaten and burped a couple of times. I looked up and found her smiling blissfully.

"Sorry, Vaishali, the food was too tempting to resist," I remarked.

"I take your burping as the best compliment for my cooking efforts."

"You are a great cook, Vaishali ... never have any doubts about that."

"Thanks again, Mr. Banerjee ..." Her smile seemed to wane away.

"What are you holding back again, Vaishali?"

"I was just wondering if you will ever again get the taste of my food," she now wore a look of resignation, "now that you have decided to help me, you would have to be on total fast tomorrow. You can't even take water ... you might be aware that such fasts are called *nirjala upavas* in the Hindu traditions."

"I don't mind being on *nirjala upavas* tomorrow, Vaishali," I smiled, "I have filled my stomach with enough food and water to last me a day with ease, but I wouldn't spare you on the days that would follow tomorrow – you would have to prepare your choicest of dishes for me on each one of the days I spend at *Prithika* thereafter. I have little doubts that I shall have many more opportunities to taste your food."

"I really appreciate your positive approach to life, Mr. Banerjee, but you will get to eat my preparations again only if we overpower that demon tomorrow, and let us face the reality – our chances against Islakais are very grim. There is little hope that our combined efforts will yield the desired results."

"Who is bothered about the results, Vaishali? I am only concerned with the efforts. One of the primal teachings of Lord Krishna has always acted as a guiding principle for me – one's focus should be on the efforts and not on the possible results. The glorious truths that the Lord passed down to Arjuna in the battlefield of *Kurukshetra* are meant for all ages. Let me recite the relevant *shloka* from *Shrimad Bhagvad Gita*, I know it by heart –

Karmanyevadhikaraste ma phaleshu kadachana
Ma karmaphalheturbhurma tey sangoastvakarmani

Do you understand what this means exactly?"

"Yes, Mr. Banerjee, I do … I have some idea of *Shrimad Bhagvad Gita* from my mother's notes. She held this scripture as the best prescription for the humankind. The *shloka* you just recited means – you have the right to your action but you don't have any right to the fruits attached to it; don't allow the fruits of your actions to become your motive, and also don't give in to inertia. Am I right,

Mr. Banerjee?"

"Indeed, you are right, Vaishali, but we must not be caught up in what could be described as the surface meaning of the *shloka*. We must look deeper into it."

"Why don't you help me look deeper into it?"

"Well, many self-proclaimed rationalists, some of which happen to be hardcore communists condemn this idea as impractical and pro-bourgeois. I still remember one of my communist friends saying, 'What a stupid verse this is, to suggest that one should only be concerned with one's efforts and not be bothered at all about the possible results is like saying that a worker should only focus on his work and not expect a salary. That is why this stupid idea is fit to be discarded for good.' My friend and others like him never realize how faulty their assessment of this verse is. The truth is the limitations of their intelligence prevent them from appreciating the essential aspects of this beautiful verse. It is they, and not the idea, that are worthy of condemnation. I have been lucky to study the commentaries of some great spiritual masters on this verse. These studies helped me understand what can be reckoned as the central and deeper truth behind this verse. I shall explain. Now, what is likely to happen when a person is completely focused on the effort? Obviously, the work at hand reaching its logical end is the most likely outcome. And if the work at hand reaches its logical end, then the chances of the desirable results become very bright. Instead, if one thinks about the possible results of the work at hand, then one's focus on the work gets diluted. If you wonder whether the work you are supposed to do would bring you success or failure, you would obviously be doing the work with limited attention. What do you think such efforts, which are devoid of appreciable attention, could lead one to? Clearly, more often than not, such efforts will result in failures. On the other hand, as I have already explained, efforts in which one puts one's heart and soul are likely to result in successes."

"I guess that is the way this verse should be interpreted. The import of what you are saying is this – the probability of success is high when one focuses on the effort and not on the results. The higher the focus on the effort, the greater the probability of the success."

"Exactly, so the truth is that this verse happens to be one of the most practical approaches to dealing with life. If you are truly serious about being successful, then this is the mantra for you."

"I completely agree, Mr. Banerjee."

"Great, now let us be clear with things – the work at hand is combating *Islakais*. Tell me what efforts are we required to put in."

"If I were to deal with *Islakais* all by myself, then I would be in a typical battle with him wherein both of us would be using our ethereal powers against each other. However, if we are to fight together against him, the mode of battle would be very different. Unfortunately, you would have to take the lead in our joint battle against him. In fact, you would practically have to do all the work, I will be in a hugely passive role. Does that frighten you?"

"Not at all, tell me what I have to do?"

"You shall act as Sarvananda while I shall be in the role of Purnananda."

I found myself frozen with fear! What after all was she trying to suggest? Did she mean I would have to perform *shavasadhana* on her corpse, just as Sarvananda had executed the ritual while seated on the back of Purnananda's lifeless body according to the famous legend she narrated to me at *Mahachoti*? Well, I hadn't erred with my interpretation of her words; she meant exactly what I thought.

"Mr. Banerjee, you would have to perform *shavasadhana*," she said softly, "There is no other way to fight *Islakais*. At this juncture, I guess, I must give you an opportunity to reconsider your decision to fight the demon with me. Tell me, do you still want to proceed with the joint operation?"

I tried to read my own mind with my face down. Was I willing to help her at any cost? Would I not even mind going to the extent of performing a *shavasadhana* for her sake? I couldn't find an answer as I groped through the murkiness in my mind.

"I am waiting for your reply, Mr. Banerjee. Now that you know what you have to do to help me, would you still be willing to help me?" She asked.

I couldn't give her a reply. Instead, I asked her another question, the answer to which I already knew from what she said earlier but wished hopelessly that the answer wasn't what I had in my mind.

"From where would you get a corpse?"

"I guess you know the answer. You will use my body to perform the ritual," she said the obvious.

"You will kill yourself?" I followed up with another question.

"No, don't you remember what *Purnananda* did in the legend? I will do exactly what he did. I will dissociate my essential consciousness from my body. You know I am capable of detaching my consciousness from my body, don't you?"

I nodded slowly.

31 I MAKE MY DECISION

"Once I disembody my consciousness, my body will turn lifeless for all practical purposes," Vaishali continued to explain, "it will be like a fresh corpse. For our purpose, we do need a fresh corpse. Thereafter, you will sit on the back of my body and perform the ritual."

"But how ..." I wasn't allowed to finish.

"Relax, Mr. Banerjee. I know you have a number of questions in your mind. Let me first explain the sequence of activities we will have to undertake if we really go ahead with this joint battle against *Islakais*. You would start with your *nirjala upavas* after a short mantra early in the morning. Then, I will teach you the cycle of mantras that you would have to chant while performing *shavasadhana*. You will practice the chanting all through the day so that you don't make any mistake during the ritual. If you make a mistake, that will be the end of everything – I will die for sure and you also are unlikely to live for long thereafter. *Islakais* might also succeed in trapping our souls so that he could use them for executing his demoniac plans. So you will practice and do nothing else till late evening. Then we will start our ethereal flight which will, quite obviously, end on the summit of *Mahachoti*. There I will give you my final instructions and then ... then ... well, it is quite embarrassing to be saying this but I have little choice ... then, I shall undress myself and sit in a yogic stance called *Padmasana*. In around ten minutes from that time I shall be out of my body. Please keep in mind that the disembodiment of consciousness that I shall execute tomorrow will not be the usual kind of disembodiment I practice. Normally, when I detach my consciousness from my body, it is connected to the naval of the body through an ethereal blue colored cord. This cord helps my consciousness to reenter the body whenever it wants. Tomorrow however I shall execute permanent dissociation of my consciousness from my body. That's because unless I do so, my body will not be fit for *shavasadhana*. My resurrection would therefore depend upon the successful completion of the ritual. If you fail to complete the ritual successfully, I shall be as good as dead. You could then perform my last rites and live on under the shadow of *Islakais* till he succeeds in killing you. Anyway, let's get back to the disembodiment of my consciousness. I have just explained that it shouldn't take more than ten minutes for the disembodiment of my consciousness to be complete. To be on the safer side, you will wait for fifteen minutes and then move over to my body which will still be in the same yogic posture. You will first have to make my body lie on its back and then turn it over. Thereafter, you will sit on the back of my body and close your eyes and chant the cycle of mantras repeatedly. *Islakais* and his accomplices will disturb you in every way they can to prevent you from successfully completing the ritual. I cannot myself imagine as to how they will try to disturb you – they might generate the ugliest and most frightful visions in your psyche, they might cause the most terrible storms around you, they might even physically hurt you ... the possibilities are endless. If you do manage to brave their mental and physical assaults by constant and correct chanting of the mantras till the point of culmination of the ritual, you will feel that a strong yet benign feminine power has approached you.

This power, as you would appreciate, would be that of Goddess Kali. This power will set up a telepathic communion with you and ask you to make a wish. Then you will make your wish, but be sure you do not open your eyes even at that stage. What wish will you make? Recall the legend – *Sarvananda* asked Goddess Kali to resurrect *Purnananda* and do as he said. Your wish will be in exact correspondence with that of *Sarvananda* – you will ask Her to resurrect me and do as I say. The benign power will resurrect me. You could open your eyes once you feel the movements of my body beneath you. After having come back to life in this manner, I shall ask Her to send *Islakais* back to his realm and punish him as she pleases. If everything works well, that's going to be the end of our joint venture. And if you make the slightest of mistakes, then you know what's going to happen. Have you followed what I have said?"

I took a while to come to terms with the horrific procedures of our possible joint venture and again nodded softly.

"So Mr. Banerjee," she smiled, "how are you feeling now?"

I looked up at her and smiled faintly, still incapable of a reply.

"Now that you have good knowledge of the ghastliness of our possible combined battle against *Islakais*, are you still willing to go ahead with the combined battle?"

I couldn't reply still.

"Mr. Banerjee, I am asking you for the last time … if you don't reply even this time, I will take your silence as a refusal to go ahead with the joint venture. Tell me, do you still wish to help me?"

No, still no word came out of my mouth. She smiled and got up.

"Don't worry, I will not blame you for not going ahead with it. I quite understand your dilemma. The possible joint venture is too ghastly to agree to," she said as she arranged the dishes, "to speak the truth I am happy that you have decided against it. I never wanted this joint venture to happen … I considered the joint venture only because you repeatedly insisted on it. Nothing would have come out of it anyway. *Islakais* is too formidable an adversary to deal with. I would have lost my life and you would have carried the burden of his presence around you till he killed you as well. Instead of two people dying because of the demon, it is better that only one dies. What do you say?"

She picked up the dishes and walked into the kitchen. I heard her placing them on the sink. Shortly she was before me again. The crisis hadn't been able to rob her of the beatific smile.

"Please don't feel sad, Mr. Banerjee. I am actually very happy that you have decided against the joint venture. It wouldn't help in any way. Don't think my respect and admiration for you have gone down because of your deciding against it. Rather, my admiration for you has grown all the more. I can't thank you enough for coming over to *Prithaka* with the sincerest desire to help me. It is a different matter that you cannot help me for the methods are too difficult and the chances of success too bleak. I advise that you go to the station early in the morning tomorrow and buy a ticket and then board the train to New Delhi. Don't worry about me, my destiny is unalterable. But I am happy that I have been able to spend my last days with a man like you. I suggest you go to your room now and have a short nap. I will wake you up early in the morning, good night."

"We are doing it, Vaishali," a wave of courage and confidence had built up inside me over the last few minutes. I could now think with clarity. I had to help her no matter what came. If I shirked away from the challenge, then I would never be able to face myself again. And in any case I had no business thinking about the possible results of the joint venture. The question of success or failure should not upset me, I reasoned. I should rather concentrate as much of my energies as I could on the job at hand.

"But …"

"There is no place for any *but*, Vaishali," I smiled, "we are going ahead with the joint venture."

She looked on with disbelief.

"Tomorrow we are fighting the demon together strictly according to the procedure you explained."

"Are you sure, Mr. Banerjee?"

"I couldn't have been surer."

"Think again."

"Thought and decided. I am going to get a quick nap. Do wake me up early in the morning so that I could chant the relevant mantra and start my *nirjala upavas*."

"Mr. Banerjee … it is going to be ghastly."

"I repeat – wake me up early in the morning so that I could chant the relevant mantra and start my *nirjala upavas*. It is advisable that you too take a quick nap, Good night."

I got up and lovingly pressed her shoulder before walking towards the staircase. And of course I didn't miss the faint glimmer of hope and joy in her eyes.

32 THE SHAKINESS OF MY BEING

Vaishali woke me up sometime between three and four in the morning.

"Take a bath quickly and join me in the living area downstairs," she said, "Please be careful, do not gulp any water, not even a drop."

I am in the habit of splashing water twenty one times on my eyes every morning in keeping with a yogic tradition. That day I was careful to cover my mouth with one hand while I splashed water on my eyes with the other. Thereafter, I bathed with utmost care not to allow any water to enter my mouth. When I came out of the washroom, I found a new set of kurta and pajama neatly placed on the bed. I knew Vaishali had kept it there for me to wear. Bathing and wearing new clothes are pre-requisites to almost all Hindu rituals. I quickly put the kurta and pajama on and went downstairs to the living area. She was waiting for me there. The shades of anxiety were unmistakable on her face but there was also an indistinct yet sure expression of hope.

"Sit down, Mr. Banerjee," she tenderly pushed a chair towards me.

I sat and so did she on a chair placed ahead of me.

"Repeat after me," she said and chanted a mantra.

It was a simple mantra and I easily repeated it after her.

"Say it again."

I chanted the mantra again.

She made me repeat the mantra eight times and said, "Now, your *nirjala upavas* has started as a build-up to the ritual you would be performing late in the evening. Not all types of *shavasadhana* need *nirjala upavas* but this one being one of the most extreme types requires that the performer observes *nirjala upavas*. The repetition of this mantra eight times marks the beginning of *nirjala upavas*."

"I understand, Vaishali."

"Now, I will teach you a cycle of nine mantras. They are not as simple as the one you just chanted. But I am sure you would be able to register them in your memory. Remember, this cycle of mantras must be recited endlessly till the feminine power approaches you. The mantras must follow the same sequence I am going to teach you now. Any mistake in the sequencing of the mantras could be fatal. Also try to avoid errors of pronunciation and diction. Although errors of pronunciation and diction do not matter much if the performer of *shavasadhana* keeps a good spiritual ardor, it is still better to minimize such errors if not eliminate them. So, are you ready to learn, Mr. Banerjee?"

"By all means."

Vaishali took out a paper from her gown and gave it to me. The nine mantras of the cycle were neatly written on it.

"I will now chant each one of the mantras in the correct order. While I recite a mantra, listen carefully and read it in your mind from the paper in your hand in synchrony with my recitation. Should we start?"

I nodded. She closed her eyes and recited the mantras with an air of devotion all around her.

"Did you listen and read carefully?"

"Yes."

"Let's do it again."

She recited the cycle again and I listened and read the mantras in my mind as attentively as I could. After we repeated the process a number of times, Vaishali said, "Have you understood how you would have to recite the cycle?"

"Yes, Vaishali."

"Now simply read the mantras in the correct order."

I read the mantras as best as I could.

She thought for a while and said, "Well, I must say that you are doing very well. But have you understood the meanings of the mantras?"

"Not really, Vaishali, my understanding of Sanskrit is very limited."

She explained the meanings of the mantras. Most of them were praises of Goddess Kali.

"According to my mother's notes, chanting of these mantras is the fastest way of propitiating the *adyashakti*, the primal feminine power of existence. I am sure you now know what you have to do next, don't you?"

"Yes," I replied confidently, "I shall have to commit the mantras to my memory now and practice reciting the cycle over and over again."

"You are right, Mr. Banerjee," she smiled, "please go to your room now and do the needful. I will come to you as a robed figure and give you further instructions through a telepathic communion. Any questions?"

I shook my head.

"Okay," her face shone with what I believed to be a newfound hope, "then I shall see you in the evening as a robed figure."

I went to my room and started the drill. Sometimes the powers of the mind get substantively enhanced when faced with a duress. I was lucky to find my mind exemplifying this process. It didn't take me long to ingrain the mantras in the correct order in my psyche. Thereafter, I started the cycle from my memory. I went on and on with it. A stage came when I could virtually see the mantras appearing on my mental screen with stupendous clarity. However, I was careful about not falling prey to a process that my dear friend Saikat often refers to as *laxity because of achievement*. In a nutshell, this expression describes a situation wherein one might tend to relax and feel overconfident as a result of some accomplishment, small or big. Such laxity could rob one of one's focus and zeal for greater accomplishments thereby resulting in a defeat or underachievement in the context of the work in hand. I made a conscious effort to eliminate all laxities and continued to recite the cycle of mantras. In what felt like an endless drill, another stage came when the mantras seemed to have become inseparable parts of my existence. I found them flowing in the material and abstract realms of my being. Still I made sure not to fall victim to *laxity because of achievement*. I kept reciting … reciting … reciting … reciting … and reciting. By the time the light conditions began dimming, I and the cycle of mantras had merged together into a single organic whole. However, my recitation continued. My throat had dried up and my vocal cords had strained but the very joy of successfully reciting the cycle kept me going. I was in full cognizance of the fact that I didn't have even the most miniscule scope for error. I guess this fear helped me in allaying all possible laxities. It didn't matter how well I was reciting the cycle at that time, all that mattered was how I dealt with it when faced with the real circumstances. The chills, tension and challenges of the real drill that just lay a few hours ahead of me could dampen my memory and blunt my confidence in no time at all – I realized this truth to the core. Apart from the weaknesses that my nerves might generate while I took on the demon, the disturbances, that he and his accomplices might subject me to, some of which could even come in the form of physical assaults, could play havoc with my recitation. As these thoughts crossed my mind, I could sense the smoothness of my recitation receding. This was the first time since I started the drill that I felt my anxiety gaining weight. No, I simply could not let that happen. I had to find the way to fight this anxiety. Then it struck me that creative visualization might eliminate the ripples from my psyche. I imagined the corpse of Vaishali lying at the summit of *Mahachoti* hill. I mounted on its back, closed my eyes and started reciting the cycle of mantras. I imagined fiery faces and weird looking shadows hovering all over my mind with the intent of distracting me in every possible manner. I, however, stayed put and continued with my recitation. Then the fiery faces struck what could be best described as the corporeal limits of my mind. Their touches were like terrible shocks of electric current. I was up to the task and didn't let the pain dilute my focus. Then the ugly shadows swept all across my mind in a bid to thrust my determination out of my being and yet I succeeded in thwarting their devious efforts. Then I felt a soft touch on my head. No, this was not a part of my creative visualization. I had indeed felt a touch, a real touch.

I opened my eyes and looked behind me with a start. There stood the robed figure at an arm's length! The light conditions had become too dim by now to see her clearly. The telepathic communion ensued immediately.

"Hello Mr. Banerjee, are you prepared for the challenge?"

"Yes Vaishali," I replied.

"Then follow me downstairs."

She flew over the floor and the staircase effortlessly and I followed her as closely as I could. It wasn't easy for me to tread behind her as the darkness was too heavy to discern the twists and turns of the path with ease. Thankfully, I didn't trip over. Causing myself a physical injury could seriously compromise the drill.

The entrance door of *Latika Griha* flung open as Vaishali approached it. She moved out of the house and so did I. The iron gate also opened by itself for us to move out of the compound. From the light conditions I could guess that the dusk was gradually making way for a very dark night. Vaishali's speed shot up immediately after we were out of the compound. Although I was keeping pace with her, my feet were still touching the ground. Her speed went up further and I also hastened up to keep pace.

"Don't worry Mr. Banerjee," she said telepathically, "you don't have to exert yourself. Just allow things to happen by themselves."

I ceased my conscious efforts to follow her and found myself following her pretty easily. In the twinkle of an eye I was flying too!

"Are you comfortable?" She asked.

"O yes, Vaishali," I responded.

I enjoyed the ethereal flight despite sensing the unpleasantness of what was to follow.

"Do you know the cycle of mantras by heart?" Vaishali asked.

"Yes, I do."

"You must not fumble with the mantras."

"I shall try my best."

I saw the moving continuum of things from the corners of my eyes as the ethereal flight continued. Crests and troughs and planes – we flew over all kinds of landforms. Even though the vision was blurred, my heightened senses could identify the broad shapes and sizes of things speeding past us. It wasn't long before I could make out that we were flying over the muddy path that led to the summit of *Mahachoti*. The ethereal flight was no longer enjoyable. The fears within me had begun to gain wait. To be honest, I did ask myself once more if I had done the right thing by deciding to help my poor hostess. No doubt I had a heart full of admiration and sympathies for her, but I was again unsure if that should have translated into the possible misadventure I had put myself in. I knew that I was still in a telepathic communion with Vaishali and she could easily read my doubts and yet I couldn't help being in doubt. As I felt the summit approaching, Vaishali expressed her displeasure with my thoughts.

"Mr. Banerjee," she said, "Your apprehensions are disheartening me. I had asked you a hundred times if you wanted to do this and even tried to dissuade you from taking this plunge. But you put up a brave face every time. Now when you are required to show that courage, you are cringing in a rather shameless manner. Apologies for using such harsh words but you surely understand that I am in a state of mind that is completely at variance from the kind of temperament I need to put up a resistance against *Islakais*. To speak the truth, your confidence had raised hopes in me and therefore I neither prepared myself physically or mentally to take on the demon. If I fight him now, I will be consumed by his diabolical powers in less than a second. You might not like to hear it but the truth is you have caused this misery to me. I would have in any case died at the hands of *Islakais* if you had decided not to stand by me. But then I would have the satisfaction of having spent my last few days in the company of a great and unpretentious friend. But by baring up the contradictory faces of your personality, you have denied me that pleasure."

33 DIVINE INTERVENTION

I sensed the anguish that I caused her and felt miserable. I closed my eyes in a bid to digest the embarrassment. What a shame it was! How on earth could my confidence evaporate in so shameless a manner? My heart cried, so did my mind and so did my soul. What followed next could be described as the greatest spiritual experience I had ever had till that point of my life! I saw myself passing through a huge ball of light. The feel of the light simply washed away all my shame. The deeper I went into the ball the more comfortable and blessed I felt. I was totally clueless as to what was happening. I was sure though that my eyes were closed. Thus what was happening was certainly not a material phenomenon. I went deeper into the ball and then I heard someone speak to me. The voice was *Divine* – it is simply beyond my literary abilities to describe the voice any better. Expressions such as *soothing*, *calming*, *therapeutic*, *pristine*, and *Godly* would badly fall short of describing the quality of the voice. I wish I could capture that voice in my being for all times to come and play it as often as I wanted so that I could give my loved ones a taste of Divinity! If I could do so, I would certainly make the reader of these lines get a feel of that Divinity as well. Since all that is not possible, I don't intend to describe that voice any further than calling it *Divine*. Maybe the expression *Divine* says it all.

"Biswajit, what has come upon you, my friend? From where has this frailty entered your heart?"

The warmth in the words was unmistakable. Every word appeared to be laden with love of the highest order.

"Who is that," I responded.

"It's me Biswajit, your dearest friend. I am the one you seek, albeit not with absolute devotion, and I am the only one who will never desert you regardless of the circumstances you find yourself in."

"You mean you are ..." I wondered if I was in communion with Lord Krishna, the Supreme Personality of Godhead, the one with whom I have been in an eternal relationship of love ever since my maternal grandfather narrated His feats, as recorded in the Mahabharata and hordes of other religious and spiritual texts, in my early childhood. I was so attracted to His indescribable beauty and powers that even till this day I can feel the strong aura of the Lord that my grandfather had created around me with his tales. 'Lord Krishna is most adorable. You can love Him in any way you like,' my grandfather had said, 'you could take him as a guardian, as a toddler, as a teacher, or simply as a friend. Through the Bhagawad Gita, the Lord has given the world the greatest of material, philosophical and spiritual truths, and as a part of that same discourse, He has made it clear that a devotee can aspire Him in any form and He shall come to the devotee in that very form. That is the Lord's commitment to His devotees.' The idea of having him in my life as a friend was most appealing, and ever since that day I have treated the Lord as my friend. Often I have complained to Him during my monologues or soliloquies about His keeping me distanced from the Absolute Truth, the truth which when known turns an ordinary being into a Divine Being. It is not my intention to talk about the relationship I share with Lord Krishna at this juncture for this relationship is too difficult to verbalize and even if I push myself hard to verbalize it, I might have to write book after book in that attempt only to find in the end that all my books on that subject put together describe just an iota of an iota of the bond I share with the Lord. Well, let me only say for now that the Lord is my friend and when I heard the Divine voice, I felt myself spiritually charged.

"Complete what you were saying, my friend," the voice responded.

"Are you Lord Krishna?" I said shedding tears of joys with my eyes still closed.

"You must help the sorceress, Biswajit," the friendly voice advised me without answering my question, "do not run away from the karma that you deem is right for you. You talk about the importance of keeping one's focus on the karma and not on the results and when it comes to practicing it, you choose to do the opposite. No, do not do that, Biswajit … do what you can do for your sorceress friend with all the focus you can gather without caring about the results … doesn't matter even if you die in the process of helping her. You will have to die one day in any case. Why not die in the cause of Dharma? If you die in the process of helping her, your disembodied consciousness will have the satisfaction of having done what it could do in the cause of Dharma before it disincarnated. If your attempt to save her fails resulting in the demon being a constant threat to you till it kills you, you will still have the satisfaction of having treaded on the path of Dharma. And if you succeed in sending the Demon to where he belongs, then you will have the satisfaction of having vanquished a dreadful spirit by following what your heart felt to be your Dharma. I am sure you understand that regardless of what results you achieve, if you follow the path of Dharma, you would always be the winner. So tell me now, Biswajit – will you listen to your friend? Will you follow the path that your heart deems as Dharma?"

"Yes my friend, yes," I said with tears flowing uncontrollably from my closed eyes, "thank you Lord for showing me the right path."

I could sense Him smiling. As I was about to open my eyes, He spoke again.

"No, Biswajit," the Lord said, "do not open your eyes. Your physical, mental, and psychic faculties are not strong enough to stand the luminescence present around you at the moment. I shall leave you now, and the moment I am gone, this sphere of luminescence will disappear, and you shall again find yourself in the telepathic communion with your sorceress friend. She shall not know about my intervention till the time is right. My conversation has been exclusively with you. Do not fuel any of your rational faculties that might suggest that this intervention of mine has been a result of the sorceress's powers to generate illusions so that she might be able to make you do what is advantageous to her. Goodbye for now, my friend."

I sensed the voice and its source mingling into nothingness. In less than an instant, the ball of light also disappeared. I opened my eyes that had become heavy with tears and found myself moving over the terrains of the *Mahachoti Hill* with the telepathic communion with the sorceress still intact.

"I don't understand this, Mr Banerjee," Vaishali said with a great deal of confusion, "one moment you are so full of negative energy, and in the very next moment you are brimming with positive energy. It is confounding indeed that a moment back you were hugely unsure if you had acted wisely by deciding to help me, and now you don't only feel that you made the correct decision but are completely confident of doing your best against the Demon. What caused this sudden shift?"

What I felt like a long dialogue with the Lord was nothing more than an instant for her. Things had happened just as the Lord had explained. She did not have the slightest idea about the appreciable spiritual heights I had accomplished with the grace of my Lord during what she felt to be an instant. Although the Lord had made it clear, I would have known it even if He hadn't that His appearance was not a magical trick of Vaishali. It was too Divine an experience to be a stroke of magic! Not even the demigods and demigoddesses could have generated an illusion of that magnitude, what to talk of human beings.

"I guess a stroke of Divinity," I replied.

"O really," her words were laden with awe, "that's wonderful, but I didn't sense any such spark of spirituality."

"Some experiences might be too divine to sense."

"I wonder how powerful a spiritual spark that was so as to banish your uncertainties and lack of confidence in a flash."

"It was surely very powerful."

I relished the raised spirits and the waves of joy taking rounds in her mind as we covered the last stretch of terrain of the *Mahachoti Hill*. We finally descended over the summit of *Mahachoti*. It was time now for action!

"Sit under a tree of your choice from where you can see the summit clearly. Don't go too far lest you should not be able to see me clearly," Vaishali said with our telepathic cord appearing even more intense.

I walked to a nearby tree that felt like sending out vibrations of hope and sat under its canopy which despite possessing a dominating look in the dark did not raise any fears in me. Actually nothing could raise fears in me now. Ever since the Lord made an appearance on the ethereal screen of my being, all I was left with was the intent to do my best, and although no part of my conscious mind was cast on the possible results, my heart was full of hopes that the sorceress would not die an inglorious death. She sat on the summit in a pose that is called *padmasana* in yogic traditions and closed her eyes.

"You can close your eyes and relax," the words flowed in from her mind to my mind, "for the next three hours or so we shall be in a state of *yogic nidra*, a special kind of sleep that is induced by spiritual methods. I will use my powers to induce *yogic nidra* in both of us. When we wake up, we will be as fresh as if we have had a good and deep sleep of thirty hours continuously. The *yogic nidra* will revitalize the physical, mental and spiritual faculties in us. Fresh faculties will help me dissociate my consciousness from my body in such a way that the luminous cord that usually stays in connection with the naval is also broken, and of course the rejuvenated spirits will help you perform the *shavasadhana* with tremendous intensity. So relax and let my mind have complete control over your being."

I cooperated with her and was soon asleep. We slept till it was close to midnight. When she woke me up, I felt thoroughly rested. I had never before slept a sleep of that kind.

"Are you feeling good, Mr. Banerjee?" The telepathic communion continued.

"Yes, Vaishali, I have never felt so fresh."

"The time for the battle has arrived."

"I understand, Vaishali."

"I am really happy to see your confidence."

"Indeed I am confident," I responded, "I am confident of doing my best."

"I am so happy, Mr. Banerjee," for the first time I could sense her beatific smile reaching out to me purely at a mental level, "You are a truly brave man."

An impulse that I should tell her that all my courage was because of my Lord crossed my mind in a flash. The next moment I realized that I shouldn't be doing so for if the Lord had wanted her to know of His intervention, He wouldn't have kept it covered from her in the first place. I also realized that all my thoughts except for those of the Lord were being conveyed to her. So the telepathic cord didn't reach out to those parts of my mind that were now full of Krishna consciousness. Even this was an indication that my interaction with the Lord was not meant to be revealed at that point of time. Vaishali, however, would learn all about it later at the approach of the right time.

She loosely caught hold of the edges of her robe and looked up at me.

34 THE RITUAL

"Mr. Banerjee, this is very embarrassing," she explained, "you understand that … I have to undress myself now."

"I know Vaishali," I could still sense the spiritual vibrations that the Lord had left behind and I tried filling my words up with these vibrations so that I could make her comfortable, "it doesn't matter. Using clothing for any purpose other than protection of the body is just one of the many falsehoods of existence humans have fallen prey to. Clothing shouldn't be a cause of pride, shame or embarrassment to spiritual aspirants like us. So relax."

"Your words are very comforting," the beatific smile again appeared on her lips, I hoped not for the last time, "I am so glad to have you as a friend. Perhaps I couldn't have done this before anyone else."

"I truly respect your confidence in me, Vaishali."

"But Mr. Banerjee, there's still something that I need to tell you as a part of my instructions and I truly hope you take these words in the right sense."

"Trust me, I will."

"I don't have the slightest doubts about the high level of rectitude in your personality but I must still make it clear that my undressed state must not kindle your carnal faculties even by the slightest degree. That's because the kind of *shavasadhana* you are going to perform requires that the performer must be free of all lascivious feelings … you understand that this is one of the most difficult forms of *shavasadhana*, don't you?"

"I do."

"Sorry to be asking you this but do you feel this requirement will be difficult for you to meet?"

"No, Vaishali, I am confident of keeping my senses under control."

To speak the truth, I am not sure if I could have kept Vaishali's condition with ease if the Lord had not intervened. But now there was no problem at all. For some time at least I was completely free of desires for impermanent pleasures. The spiritual vibrations that I felt in my nerves had made me immune to many mental frailties that could otherwise have been very difficult to handle. I had little idea as to what *Islakais* and his accomplices would do as I proceeded with the ritual but the thought that Lord Krishna had referred to what I was about to do as *Dharma* gave me untold confidence and courage for one who follows the path of *Dharma* never fails. Whether I died or lived, I would win and that assurance alone, I felt, was enough to take on *Islakais*.

She pulled the edges of the gown apart and in a while she was standing on the summit, completely undressed. I shall say no more than she looked divine for even the best of literary expressions will miserably fall short of describing how beautiful she looked. However, the basal tendencies of my being were under check. Perhaps that was because her naked appearance was too divine to kindle such tendencies. She looked at me. I smiled and nodded to reassure her that I was completely in command of myself and soon she smiled and nodded in response. Then she sat down in *Padmasana*.

"Now I shall give you my last instructions before I leave this body and detach the ethereal cord from its naval. I have discussed some of these points with you earlier. Are you ready for the final instructions?"

"Yes, Vaishali," I spoke with the same confidence.

"Listen, after I say *Om*, you must wait in your place for fifteen minutes. By that time I will have left my body. Then you will come over to my body which will still be in *padmasana*. The next step is to make it lie straight on its back. And then you will turn it over in a manner so that its breasts press firmly against the ground. Thereafter, you will mount on its back and sit as comfortably as you can. Then, you shall close your eyes and think of Goddess Kali. The next step of *shavasadhana* will be to start reciting the cycle of mantras. Please be careful, you cannot afford to make any mistakes with the order of the mantras. Recite them in the correct order in every cycle. One mistake and everything will be over. You must also be careful not to open your eyes while chanting the mantras. As you keep chanting, *Islakais* and his accomplices would do all sorts of dirty things. Some of their acts could be really nasty. With the grace of the Goddess you might be able to brave all their evil attempts to spoil the ritual. If you do manage to finish the ritual you will feel the *adyashakti*, the primal feminine power of existence approaching you. She will establish a telepathic communion with you and ask you to make a wish. With your eyes still closed ask her to resurrect me and do as I say. After she resurrects me, you will feel the movements of my body beneath you. It is at this stage that you could open your eyes and get down from my back. Be sure to stay close to me and not stray too far away. I will then get up and request the Goddess to send *Islakais* and his accomplices to the dark realm they are from and punish them as she pleases. Any questions about the ritual and what you are supposed to do?"

"When I open my eyes after feeling your movements beneath me, will I be able to see the Goddess?"

"No, as far as I understand the Goddess does not make a material appearance in the end of the kind of *shavasadhana* you are performing. However, you will easily know the Goddess's presence around you. Her vibrations are stronger than any visual perception."

"Okay."

"Any other questions, Mr. Banerjee?"

"No Vaishali. We can start."

"We will start but there are just a few more things you must know before we start."

"Okay, tell me then."

"The failure of our joint venture could entail some legal implications. You understand that I cannot return to my body if the *shavasadhana* fails. Under such circumstances, what you will be left with is my corpse. So that no legal imputations could be made against you by anyone, I have asked Chinu to come to the summit of *Mahachoti* if we do not return to *Latika Griha* by seven in the morning. He will come with all arrangements to carry my body down to *Prithaka*. Dr. Gaurav Suri will be waiting for you and Chinu at *Latika Griha*. I have told you about Chinu and Dr. Suri, haven't I?"

"Yes, you have," I nodded, "Chinu happened to be one of your mother's confidants who now serves you and Dr. Suri is a renowned doctor in Shyamalpur who was also your father's friend."

"You are right, Mr. Banerjee. So all you have to do in the event of the *shavasadhana* failing is to wait. You could expect to see Chinu long before the sun becomes too strong. I am sure he will bring a special cab with him that can move easily over the muddy roads of *Mahachoti*. After the two of you reach *Latika Griha*, Dr. Suri will examine my body and write the death certificate. Thereafter, Chinu will arrange for the cremation. You will have absolutely no problems in the legal context. But then there will be problems of course ... problems of ethereal nature caused by the dastardly demon. And then ... one day or the other ... I can speak no more," Tears appeared on her eyes.

"I will complete the sentence for you, Vaishali," I said smiling, "one day or the other the problems caused by the demon would be too nasty to survive."

"Don't say that, Mr. Banerjee," her voice cracked, "may Goddess Kali not allow such a thing to happen. May you succeed at *shavasadhana* by Her grace."

"Don't cry, Vaishali. I guess the last thing we must do at the moment is to dampen our spirits. Let's do our Karma to the best of our abilities and leave the results for Goddess Kali to decide."

"You are right," Vaishali wiped her tears, "it is time for me to start the process of disembodiment."

"Yes," I continued to smile, "but before you do so I have a request."

"A request?"

"Yes."

"What, Mr. Banerjee?"

"I want you to smile. Smile with all your heart once."

She looked on for a while and then the same beatific smile adorned her lips yet again. O how magical she looked! Like a pristine consciousness in a pristine body!

"Thanks for making me smile, Mr. Banerjee. I really needed this smile to re-kindle my positive energies. It augurs well for the consciousness if it is full of positive energies during the process of disembodiment."

I simply nodded as I felt the spiritual vibrations in my nerves catalyzed by her beatific smile.

"Let's begin," she said and sat down in *Padmasana*.

She took a few long breaths and closed her eyes. I could see her stomach moving in and out as a part of what is called *pranic breathing*. *Pranic* may be very loosely translated as *something to do with the vital life force*. The rhythmic movements of the *pranic* breathing progressively ceased and very soon she looked lifeless. After having waited for a little more than fifteen minutes, I walked up to the summit. She looked completely lifeless now. I placed a finger under her nostrils. There was no movement of air. The process of disembodiment was over just as she had explained. I brought the body out of the posture of *padmasana* caring not to be rash towards it, and made it lie on its back. Then I turned it over in a manner so that the breasts pressed against the ground. Thereafter, I mounted on the back of the corpse and closed my eyes thinking about Goddess Kali. And then I started the chanting.

35 PUSHED TO THE LIMITS

Recitation of the first few cycles of the mantras went off very well. I was happy with the smoothness of my chanting. The mantras just came to me effortlessly. It was as though my unconscious control over the mantras was infallible. However, my happiness was short-lived. Suddenly my mental screen seemed to fill up with smoke. That smoke was by no means an expression of my thoughts. I immediately knew that *Islakais* and his accomplices had begun their work. A chill ran down my spine. Before I could come to terms with the ugly smoke that billowed all before me, a terrible being emerged from inside it with electric rapidity; it was ugly in the true sense of the word. It was a humanoid with the face giving the impression of half a man and half a lizard. The eyes were red and its skin towards my right appeared burnt with parts of it hanging from here and there. Then it bellowed with all its force. O what a horrible sound came out of its mouth! I saw its tongue. Like the face, the tongue too appeared to be a combination of a man and a lizard. The fork at the end of the tongue was unmistakable. It leaped at me and I leaned backwards. It leaped again and I found myself in quite an inescapable position. But still nothing happened to me. It immediately struck me that all the action was happening on my mental screen and going by usual logic, nothing happening over there could have a material manifestation. The realization gave an instant fillip to my confidence that had just about begun to sap. Thankfully so far my unconscious command over the chanting had not been affected. With the surge of confidence, the chanting became all the more pronounced.

The creature disappeared after some more movements perhaps at the realization that it wouldn't be able to frighten me. Its disappearance didn't give me any comfort for it was clear that *Islakais* would now make dirtier and more formidable efforts to spoil the ritual. So I thought of fuelling my mind with a strong autosuggestion which could possibly prepare me to brave the possible tricks, traps and attacks of *Islakais*. I said to myself – *no matter what the demon tries, you will not be afraid for you are on the path of Dharma. Every time he tries disturbing you or harming you, your focus on your karma will get a boost. After all, the Lord is on your side, so do not worry and keep on chanting.* Alongside the autosuggestion, the chanting went on firmly for my unconscious control over the mantras was really strong. The concurrent thoughts didn't seem to have any effect on the mantras. They were coming and going in a rhythm of their own, apparently separated from the concurrent thoughts by an unconquerable shield.

Soon after the disappearance of the sickening combination of a man and a lizard, the movements of the smoke turned very rapid. A crooked man appeared, again with electric alacrity. He had a robe around him. His face was conical and the body very lean. His eyes flickered every now and then. The long and sharp nose added to the ghastly look. He opened his mouth and made his sharp canines visible. Was he a vampire, I wondered. Slowly he walked towards me. By the time he was in touching distance, the flicker in the eyes had been replaced by a burning redness. I could sense the evil in his gaze. Then he opened his mouth wider and looked to be targeting my shoulders. After a brief spell of fear, I was confident that he couldn't do anything to me. After all, an ethereal being on my mental screen could inflict no physical injury. But I was wrong this time. I did feel the pricks of his canines. The vampire's canines then dug deep into my flesh causing excruciating pain. However, my chanting continued. The autosuggestion that I had made helped. The pain actually raised the intensity of my focus on the mantras. The vampire had his teeth in my body for a long time. Suddenly it withdrew and I saw its mouth full of blood. It was disgusting to see a vampire relishing my blood but the mantras still flowed in and out of my mouth in a brilliant rhythm.

It was not hard to understand that *Islakais* was playing tricks with my mind. I have never been very comfortable with the look of reptiles. Perhaps that's why he sent the half man and half lizard. The idea that a vampire turns one into a vampire by sucking one's blood had been a major source of fear in my early childhood. Many psychologists believe that the fears of childhood never go for good. These fears might turn dormant and sometimes virtually dead but they can come alive in moments of weakness and frustration. Perhaps, the appearance of the vampire and its sucking my blood with the possible result of my turning into a blood sucking monster was yet another attempt of the demon to use my own fears against me. Again, the demon failed.

My inference that he was making weapons out of my fears gave me an inkling as to what could follow. Although I am a staunch Hindu with the highest of regards for Hindu philosophies and rituals, there is one Hindu ritual that I find disgusting and sometimes even frightening. And that is the Hindu ritual of disposing off the dead. Indeed, I have always found cremation of bodies to be aesthetically displeasing. Sometimes the very sight of a cremation ground makes me sick. All the procedures that Hindus follow before and after the body is burnt are difficult to digest. I rather not describe these procedures in detail for I have the least intention of inducing a sickening feeling in myself and possibly in the esteemed readers. The point I am trying to make here is that I feared *Islakais* making use of this weakness to dent my determination and concentration. And he did exactly that.

The smoke cleared off from my mental screen and I saw before me the gate of an electric crematorium. I recognized it immediately. It was the gate of one of the busiest electric crematoriums in Delhi. I hate that place! However, I had to go there, quite understandably very much against my own wishes, to attend the funerals of the relatives of two of my colleagues. What followed next on my mental screen was a mixture of the scenes from these two funerals. The disgusting scenes of the bodies entering the burning chambers weakened my determination and choked my voice. I was still chanting but could clearly sense the unconscious command over the mantras tottering. If I didn't do anything concrete immediately to repulse the dirty efforts of *Islakais*, I was surely going to mess up with the chanting. The more I tried not to be perturbed by the sickening scenes he played on my mental screen, the dirtier and more disgusting imageries he used to raise the feverish tone in my nerves. However, from nowhere a divine sensation emerged in my being. At first, the sensation was a small one, hardly perceivable. Then like a rapid flood of cosmic light it filled my entire being. It soothed me to the core of my existence. The sickening scenes disappeared from my mental screen in a whisker as if the projection system of a terrible movie had suddenly gone awry thereby bringing it to a halt. What a fitting end it was to the terrible sequences that I had had to negotiate so far! I am sure that if those sequences had continued for a little more time, I couldn't have held on to my nerves. But what was the source of this cosmic light, I wondered. The warmth of the light grew still warmer and now I knew what this light was. Surely, it was an emanation of the Lord. It was the Lord who helped me stick to my decision of helping the sorceress, and it was the Lord again who used His divine grace to bring me out of the despicable trap that *Islakais* had laid for me. The Lord's intervention for the second time convinced me that I stood to win! Nothing could come in the way of the successful completion of the *shavasadhana*. I could feel tears rolling down my cheeks ... tears of ecstasy. The Lord's untold kindness had restored my unconscious command over the mantras. However, I knew that the Lord would not stay by my side till the end of the ritual. He wasn't there to act as a permanent shield for me against the onslaughts of *Islakais*. The Lord had intervened to ensure that *Adharma* or sinfulness did not have an unfair advantage over *Dharma*; if *Adharma* had to win, it had to win under equal conditions. With conditions being equal, the truly powerful would emerge as the victorious. I believe it was only because *Islakais* had resorted to filthy means that the Lord intervened. Although the Lord is always on the side of *Dharma*, but He is gracious enough to give *Adharma* a chance too. However, *Adharma* by its very nature tends to use unfair and sometimes highly immoral means. It is then and only then that the Lord guards *Dharma*. I could write volumes on this idea but I guess too much of explication at this point about what I believe to be the nature of God would not be appropriate. So let me come back to the story.

As I had expected, the cosmic light was soon out of my being and I and *Islakais* were left to fight each other. I had grown immensely confident by now for I knew that *Islakais* would not be able to vanquish me by employing means that are too dirty. Whenever he did something that was utterly unjust, the Lord would come to my aid.

Islakais however did not change his ways. He continued to attack my weaknesses in the same unfair way. Although I resisted his efforts with all my might, every now and then the possibility of the physical expressions of the things that were running on my mental screen haunted me. The usual logic that ethereal actions on the mental screen could not have any material manifestations had been defeated by the vampire. So I was now prepared for anything, howsoever illogical it might be.

Islakais now ran an endless sequence of burning dead bodies in traditional cremation grounds. He made the pictures very vivid and yet again I found my powers to resist his evil wanting. Very soon I had begun to crumble under the demon's prowess. I expected my Lord to intervene and protect me as the means employed by the demon appeared grossly unjust. But there was no trace of Krishna now. I counted the moments passing by. But the Lord did not appear. What happened, I asked myself. Had the Lord deserted me? The Lord in His communion with me during the ethereal flight said that He would never desert me regardless of the circumstances I found myself in. Then why was He not coming now when I needed Him the most? Would He allow *Adharma* to have an unfair edge over *Dharma*? I asked one question after the other as the demon's dominance became more and more pronounced with every passing moment. Then I sensed the terrible shakiness with which I was chanting the mantras. Soon the unconscious command over the mantras was completely gone and I was now consciously chanting the cycle. I had to focus very hard on every mantra as spontaneous recitation had made way for mechanical chanting. Meanwhile, *Islakais* made the imageries even more vivid. Shortly, I was at the critical point of my forbearance. I held on to my nerves for some more time with the last trace of hope that the Lord would come to save me from the demon. But He didn't come. In a while I was sure, much to my dismay, that He wouldn't come anymore and that I had been left to fight for myself. The smoke and ash from the burning bodies in my mental screen enveloped me. I shortly discovered that these disgusting imageries were not limited to my mental screen. What was happening on the screen had a material expression as well. I felt the smoke and ash particles touching my exposed skin and hair. The smell of the burning bodies induced nausea of the extreme level. While I still chanted, I feared that if I vomited the recitation would stop thereby bringing the *shavasadhana* to its most unceremonious end. No, I could not afford to vomit. It was at this stage that I made another autosuggestion. I said to myself – *go on with the ritual. You will not stop even if the demon makes you brave your worst fears. Forget about the smoke, forget about the ash, forget about the bodies burning around you, and most importantly forget about the demon. Simply chant ... that is all you need to do. Chant and chant and chant and chant ... not for the purpose of accomplishing any results but for the sake of karma; the shavasadhana might fail but you must not fail yourself by blundering with the karma at hand. Give up the resolve to succeed, if any; banish the hopes to succeed ... simply do what you can do with all your heart. It is time to act on the guiding principle of your life – perform what you believe is the best karma for you to the best of your abilities and leave the results to the Lord.* By the time I finished the autosuggestion, I had breathed in and ingested huge quantities of smoke and ash. Then it struck me in a flash that I was already in the process of braving my worst fears. I was standing in the middle of a cremation ground allowing the materials I loathed most to enter my body. What greater misery could the demon cause to me? If I had successfully braved what felt like the most formidable challenge thrown upon me by the demon, then I could, if I pushed myself a little harder, take on the remaining part of the present challenge and the possible eventual challenges as well with good chances of success. This reasoning strengthened my command over the circumstances and I started reciting the cycle better. Very soon a part of my unconscious competence was restored. The smoke and ash didn't matter in the least after a while. This surge in my inner powers was strong enough to dispel the feelings of nausea.

After a while, the imageries of burning corpses went off. Perhaps, *Islakais* realized that I was no longer vulnerable to such scenes. The mental screen now became full with colorful flowers. I was a little surprised as to why *Islakais* was projecting such wonderful flowers on my psyche. His intention was certainly not to soothe my being with the beauty of the flowers. What was he up to then, I pondered. It didn't take me long to identify the filthiness in the images that I saw on my mental screen now. The scene zoomed out and I saw the same flowers on the top of a shroud covering a body. O how disgusting the ways of the demon were! He was playing with my same fears with a different look. He showed me all kinds of corpses. I was up to the task this time. I did not let those imageries feed on my fears. I was happy to find that I could easily resist what could be hard-to-bear imageries just minutes back. But how did this magic happen? How was it that I could now easily confront images of the dead and cremations? I knew the answer at once. I had actually conquered my fears. The fears and disgust with the Hindu way of disposing the dead were no longer there in my being. I had become immune to them. That's why the Lord did not come to my aid! He wanted me to vanquish the weaknesses of my being. The result of the evil ways of *Islakais* was diametrically opposite to what he had wanted. The imageries now had no effect on me simply because I had no fears which could fuel them to frustrate me.

Islakais now tried the most ghastly pictures.

36 GRACE

My mental screen filled up with more corpses. These were the corpses of my loved ones. No doubt I was very upset. *Islakais* made those imageries more and more vivid. At one point of time it was difficult to make out if I was dealing with virtual or real images. I struggled not to lose my nerves. However, the scenes were turning more and more poignant. Apparently, *Islakais* had understood how distressed I was at the sight of the corpses of my loved ones. As I wondered if I could do something to repulse his terrible ploy, he made the images even more disgusting. Now he showed me scavenging birds feasting on those bodies. He zoomed in on a corpse to show how its face was getting disfigured. Imagine how it feels to see the corpses of the kith and kin being eaten away by birds. My despair reached the limits. The tricks *Islakais* had chosen were working for him for I could sense losing my composure. The rhythm of my recitation also weakened. Once again my unconscious command over the mantras exuded signs of fallibility. Though I was still chanting, I wasn't sure how far I could go on doing so. It was then that I saw the image of my Lord. Most certainly, this was not a projection by the demon. The image was a translucent superimposition on the images run by *Islakais*. At first, I could see the full figure of Krishna. Then the image turned bigger and adjusted itself in such a way so that I could just see its eyes. The ghastly pictures were still continuing to run in the backdrop. It seemed the Lord was trying to tell me something. I tried hard to figure out what. Did the zoomed in eyes convey that I should courageously continue to watch what *Islakais* was showing me while ensuring at the same time that my chanting was not disturbed at all? Were the eyes an indication that He was watching me perform my karma and therefore I should not allow my focus on the karma to go awry? Did the eyes simply appear there to dilute the intensity of the ghastly images behind? Or were the eyes trying to suggest that my end was near and He had come to take me within His fold? No, I could not arrive at any conclusion. As I tried harder to find out the truth, the beautiful eyes of the Lord closed, and then they disappeared leaving the ghastly scenes to continue.

Then a spark of divine inspiration charged my wisdom and I understood at once what the Lord wanted to tell me. The closing of the Lord's eyes indicated that I should close my inner eyes, the eyes that watch the mental screen. Once my inner eyes were closed, I would be spared the sight of the imageries running on my mental screen. Thereafter, the projections of *Islakais* would have no effect on me for I shall get to see nothing. What a great idea! Truly a divine one!

The jubilation died down very shortly as I realized that I simply did not, like every other ordinary mortal, know how to close the inner eyes. For a long time thereafter I continued to confront the disturbing pictures on my mental screen for I had no clue as to how I could follow the Lord's direction.

There happened now yet another flash of wisdom! I remembered having read an article titled *How to Shut Your Mind Off to Negativities* by Ma Rishabha, a noted spiritualist a few months back in an international magazine on spirituality. The article would have gone equally well with the title *How to Close Your Inner Eyes to the Disturbances in the Mind* because for all practical reasons it explained as to how one can, with yogic practice, choose not to see what runs on the mental screen. She had explained that the state wherein one has one's inner eyes closed is a spiritual accomplishment of the highest order. Being in such a state is close to being in a state of thoughtlessness. A large number of spiritual traditions including some prominent Indian schools of thought deem the state of thoughtlessness as the highest state of meditation. Ma Rishabha had suggested a strict regime of constant yogic practices for any spiritual aspirant who wished to accomplish a state wherein one's inner eyes are closed to the distractions of the mind. She explained that one could choose any yogic system that one is comfortable with even if it is a very simple system. The simplest systems of yoga such as singing devotional hymns and chanting the names of God are as effective as any other systems. The memories of that part of the article flashed the solution to my predicament. After all closing one's inner eyes meant nothing but taking one's mind away from disturbing thoughts. Although I have never experienced the state of thoughtlessness, I could sense that constant endeavors to take one's mind away from its thoughts could eventually place the mind in a state of no thoughts. Chanting had been reckoned as an acceptable procedure for achievement of such a state. Though I was not clear, and to be honest I am still not fully clear, as to how chanting of one's Lord's name could lead one to thoughtlessness, I reasoned that the constant repetition of the Lord's name could lead one's mind to a realm where nothing but the Lord's name reverberates. In other words, all existences merge into the existence of the Lord in that realm. And as Lord is all about completeness, and at the heights of spirituality there is hardly any difference between completeness and nothingness, which is also often referred to as *nihil*, chanting could be reckoned an effective method of reaching the *nihil*, which in grosser terms may be explained as a state of no thoughts.

I was thrilled at the realization that if I could focus more and more of my attention on the chanting of the mantras, then I would achieve what the Lord had prescribed. Indeed, closure of the inner eyes was all about taking my attention away from the scenes running on my mental screen to the recitation of the cycle. It was not easy but after repeated attempts, I found myself completely focused on the mantras. Never before had I experienced that level of concentration. The concentration soon appeared to be within the fold of my unconscious competence. In other words, I could now keep my inner eyes closed without any difficulty. The mantras came to me without the slightest disturbance in their rhythm, and my concentration was soon impeccably profound.

The demon and his accomplices now tried to push me down. But I sat firmly chanting the mantras with even greater intensity. The pushes made way for some terrible strikes on my chest. I don't know what Islakais was hitting me with. It felt like a whip. The flogging continued but I didn't feel much pain, perhaps because the higher consciousness I found myself in was also acting as a shield against the demon's assaults. However, I could sense my chest and a part of the upper stomach having become wet. I was bleeding! But then nothing mattered now. All that mattered was the karma at hand. I went on chanting without caring about Islakais and his accomplices, completely assured that I would not lose my balance regardless of how hard they tried to push me down for my level of consciousness was constantly growing and such higher levels of consciousness are too strong for material forces to deal with.

Very soon I lost the sense of time. And thereafter I lost the sense of myself as well. What stayed behind was an infallible equation between the mantras and the deepest layer of my consciousness. It was only when a presence made itself felt, did I get consciously aware of myself again. Unquestionably, the presence was a divine one. It filled my being with bliss and harmony. I was so much at peace that *Islakais* and his accomplices felt like a distant dream. Indeed, the demon was completely out of sync with the state I had accomplished … it was as if the demon and his accomplices never existed. The divine presence turned even more delightful. I was now face to face with Goddess Kali. Her indescribable charm soothed my body, mind and soul. And then I heard the sweet Goddess. Her honeyed words fell into my inner ears. The telepathic cord had indeed been established!

"Biswajit, I am here."

"Ma," I responded with tears rolling down my cheeks, "Ma, you have finally come."

"Yes, Biswajit," she responded in her supernal voice, "you have no reasons to be afraid now. I will absorb all your troubles, make a wish, my child."

"Ma … Ma … Ma … Ma …" My divine joy manifested in words.

"Now, tell me Biswajit, what would you like me to do?"

"Ma, this girl Vaishali …"

"You mean the sorceress friend of yours?"

"That's right, Ma."

"What would you want me to do with her?"

"Ma, I want you to resurrect her and do as she says."

"Whatever you say, Biswajit," the warmth in her tone turned even more pronounced.

Shortly I could feel the movements in Vaishali's body. I opened my eyes and got down from her back. I could not see the Goddess but her supernal vibrations were unmistakable, just as Vaishali had told me. In a while Vaishali got up and paid obeisance to the Goddess. A telepathic communion now ensued amongst the three of us.

"My child," Ma said to Vaishali, "your friend Biswajit has pleased me with one of the most difficult forms of *shavasadhana*. Not many dare to perform this ritual. And many of the intrepid ones attempt it but fail miserably. It is with the blessings of the Supreme Personality of Godhead, that your friend successfully completed the ritual. When I asked him to make a wish, he asked me to bring you back to life and do as you say. So now tell me, my child, what would you want me to do?"

"O Divine Mother," Vaishali said, "there is nothing that is hidden from you. You know what I desire. Yet I shall speak it since you have commanded so. Mother, this demon called *Islakais* and his accomplices killed my parents and is now after my life. And I am sure after the battle my friend so bravely fought against him, he will now also be after his life. So it is my solemn wish, Mother, that you send this demon and his accomplices back to their dark realms and deal with them as you please."

"Your wish is granted, my child," the Goddess said.

Immediately the air was filled with the cries of *Islakais* and his accomplices. That they were being pushed back into their dark realms was easy to sense. The defeat didn't seem to have blunted the intensity of their invectives. It was not long before their cries and vituperations died down. No doubt the demons were back in their dark dimensions.

Ma stayed for some more time and blessed us both.

"I don't have words to thank you, Mother," Vaishali had tears in her eyes, "your appearance has truly spiritualized our lives."

"It is only because of your kindness that this menace is finally over," I said.

"Don't forget the real force that gave you relief, my children," the Goddess said.

"The real force, Mother …" Vaishali appeared somewhat confounded.

"Yes, my child," Ma explained, "I mean the Supreme Personality of Godhead. If He had not been by the side of Biswajit, he would never have succeeded in the *shavasadhana*. So thank Him first, and then thank me."

We did exactly as she said.

"Always keep Him in your heart," she continued, "He is the Supreme Brahman, the seed of all. Now, I shall take your leave, my children. Continue to be on the path of *Dharma* so that you never miss out on the kindness and love of the Supreme Brahman.

Then the Goddess slowly treaded back into her ethereal world. I and Vaishali looked at each other. Both of us were now smiling, smiling right from our hearts!

37 FEEL OF FREEDOM

Vaishali stood up and put the robe around her. Then she slowly walked over to me. On noticing my bleeding chest she tenderly placed her fingers on my wet kurta. Shortly a conversation ensued … a normal conversation and not a telepathic exchange.

"You are bleeding, Mr. Banerjee," the look of concern made her appear all the more attractive.

"Those demons did it," I responded, "but don't worry, I am fine."

"Indeed, I was around and I did spot them launch a physical assault but never thought it would cause you so much pain," Tears appeared at the edges of her eyes.

"The physical pain was not that difficult to bear. It was the mental duress he placed me under that virtually shattered my being. If the Lord had not intervened, I would have surely perished."

She embraced me and wept uncontrollably.

"All is fine, Vaishali," I placed my hands around the sorceress, "I am in no pain now, don't worry."

"Do you realize what you have done for me, Biswajit?"

"Well ..." Before I could say another word it struck me that she addressed me by my first name for the first time.

As she continued to weep, I held her tighter and said, "Do you realize you just called me by my first name?"

"The selflessness of your act has demolished all walls of formality and artificiality between us."

"That's good," I could feel the juices of ecstasy running through my nerves, "it is really nice to see the barriers of artificiality gone."

I wanted time to stop there and never to start again. The embrace filled me with supernal impulses of existence. I drew her even closer and felt her nose and lips on my neck. I wanted to melt into her being and she seemed to share the same desire. Unfortunately, our beings were still within the dimensions of physical space and matter, and therefore the embrace had to end at some point of time and it did. Thereafter, we flew back to *Latika Griha* with our minds full of divine sensations.

The remaining part of my stay at *Prithaka* turned out to be times of unfathomable pleasure! It took the wounds four days to heal. Vaishali did everything she could do to speed up the therapeutic process. She used the choicest of medicinal shrubs to give me relief. And of course she prepared the choicest of dishes for me. I also came to know of a great talent in her that she had kept away from me, and also from the rest of the world, as a closely guarded secret. It turned out that she was a great musician ... a musician of real class. It so happened that one day she just took out a dusty Spanish guitar from one of the wall cabinets and began to play it. I loved the rhythm of the tune she played.

"I didn't know you could play the guitar."

"I learnt it in school."

"What a beautiful piece of music."

"It is an old tune," she smiled.

"Who has composed it?" I asked.

She simply smiled in response and continued to play the guitar.

"You didn't answer me?"

"What Biswajit?"

"Who has composed this tune?"

"Well, the composer is playing it for you, Biswajit."

"You are the composer?" I was taken by surprise for the tune sounded to be the work of a very seasoned musician.

She nodded with the smile still playing on her lips.

"So you are quite an accomplished musician."

"I can't be sure of that, but I do try to pour my heart and soul into my compositions."

"That's quite evident from the tune you are playing."

After my wounds healed, we spent quite a few evenings at *Mayur Paththar*. With the silken *Tarangini* singing her divine tunes and the sorceress smiling beatifically every now and then, each one of these evenings felt like peaks of cosmic ecstasy.

While taking a walk back from *Mayur Paththar* one of these evenings, I shared a concern that had been gaining weight in my mind over the last few days.

"Vaishali, it is perhaps time ..."

"Hmm Hmm … go on," her eyes suggested she knew what I wished to talk about.

"Perhaps my time for return has arrived."

"Indeed," she nodded, "I understand that."

We didn't share another word till we reached the gate of *Latika Griha*.

"It won't feel nice to leave *Prithaka* but …" I said as she opened the gate.

"Well, someday you will have to go, Biswajit," she spoke with shades of dejection, "I can't hold you here forever, can I?"

None of us spoke much thereafter. Suddenly *Latika Griha*, which had over the last few days become a place full of musical vibrancy, had turned into a lifeless domain.

After a rather somber night wherein the idea of separation bothered us both, the freshness of morning was truly welcome. The mood at the breakfast table was good. By now we had come to terms with the truth that separation was on the cards. In fact, the sooner I left the better it would be for our respective vocations. While her practice of sorcery needed solitude for further momentum, the assignments I had left behind in New Delhi required my presence. Some of them were too challenging to be left under the sole charge of my friend for too long. I wondered as to how Saikat was managing all the cases by himself. Just before I left for *Prithaka*, a case on spontaneous combustion had come to us. Although Saikat was confident that he could tackle it alone, I had my doubts. Apart from works of this nature, I was contractually obligated to write at least a dozen screenplays for various production houses. Unless I was back in New Delhi soon, I could be in trouble.

"How's the breakfast?" Vaishali was back in smiles.

"Great as usual," I spoke chewing an eggless cake.

"I will miss these moments so much."

"So will I, Vaishali, but ..."

"I know," she nodded, "you need to get back to work."

"Indeed, I am sure you too have a number of things to do over here."

"Well, I will do what I am meant to do – practice of sorcery."

"I have little doubts that you will be successful on your quest for the truth."

"Both of us are after the truth, aren't we," she said, "but our ways are so much different."

"Yes, Vaishali," I nodded, "your approach appears to be a more direct one."

"Come on Biswajit," she said, "your approach is an equally direct one. So what if you don't practice magic? You look deep into things and then analyze the findings. In fact, there is greater variety in your work."

"You are modest as ever, Vaishali."

She gave me a sweet glance in response.

After breakfast we took a walk to *Tarangini*. The fresh breeze of the rivulet greeted us.

"The breeze feels so different these days," the sorceress took a deep breath with her hands spread.

"Surely it does ... it is no longer laden with the threat of the demon," I responded.

"That's right ... and all this has become possible because of you, Biswajit."

"Not at all, Vaishali," I smiled, "the Supreme Personality of Godhead was the savior, I was merely His agent."

"You are also no less modest, Biswajit," she smiled back.

It was a long walk and by the time we returned it was close to noon.

"When are you planning to leave, Biswajit?" She asked as we were taking lunch. The tonality of her words suggested that she was now completely in sync with the idea that I would have to leave.

"The sooner the better," I replied, "Lot many things are lined up for me in New Delhi."

"Okay," Vaishali nodded, "but I would advise that you avoid the weekend trains. The rush during the weekends is enormous. Although you will be travelling by First Class, yet there is a chance of your journey becoming uncomfortable."

"All right, when do you suggest I should leave then?"

"How about Monday?"

"Monday ... Monday ... today's Friday ... Monday," I ruminated, "I guess Monday would be all right."

"Okay, then I shall send Chinu to get your ticket for Monday."

"That should be fine with me. Will the ticket be obtained easily?"

"I think so, for Monday there shouldn't be much rush."

"So that means I am at *Prithaka* for a little over two days."

"Hmm ... that's right, doesn't sound too good," the disappointment showed in her eyes.

I could hardly word a reply for I was myself unable to gauge my feelings with clarity. Leaving the sorceress behind was certainly not a happy feeling and at the same time the callings from New Delhi were too strong to be ignored.

She was right about the ticket. By the evening my ticket for New Delhi was in my hands. It was time to prepare for the return.

EPILOGUE

We spent a lot of the remaining time in the banks of *Tarangini* and at *Mayur Paththar*. I was happy to see her upbeat about her future in sorcery. She talked about her plans of enhancing her control over the so-called inanimate entities of the universe. Vaishali was also serious about augmenting her understanding of the gamut of consciousness. Sometimes she quoted from my writings. She explained how impressed she was with the idea that science is a subset of philosophy and philosophy in turn is a subset of spirituality, a thought that often finds expression in my works.

While some scientists, mentalists and surrealists have tried to explain why good times pass quickly, I am yet to stumble upon a convincing explanation. But good times do pass quickly for sure and I have, like everyone else I guess, felt it happening on countless occasions in my life. It was evident again from the rate at which time moved towards the end of my trip. Very soon the last evening of my stay arrived. We were sitting on *Mayur Paththar* with our eyes on the silky *Tarangini* slithering along on the bosom of *Prithaka*.

"Which memory of *Prithaka* would be the weightiest for you?" Vaishali asked.

"I guess," I replied after a brief thought, "the first flight from *Latika Griha* to the peak of *Mahachoti* would by far be the weightiest memory."

"Why the first flight to *Mahachoti* and not the *shavasadhana*?"

"Even the memory of *shavasadhana* would be very strong but you would appreciate that by the time I performed that ritual, I had already had innumerable weird experiences, some of which felt nothing short of impossible fantasies! The first flight, I reckon, was the most startling of such impossible fantasies. It was completely unexpected. As regards the *shavasadhana*, I had some idea as to what I would have to face when I performed it. I was mentally prepared for the troubles that would come as a part of the ritual although I had little idea as to what would be the nature of those troubles. But the first flight simply came out of the blue that allowed me to have the first direct feel of the fantastic world of magic. That's why it would be the topmost of all memories."

"Do you remember what followed after we reached the peak of *Mahachoti* at the end of the first flight?"

"Of course, you helped me to a safe area. We sat under a tree and then you came out with many of your secrets one by one."

"That's right, but before I came up with my secrets, I did ask you something. It was a simple question to which you didn't come up with a truthful reply."

I could sense what she was trying to hint at. Before I could word a response, she made the inquiry again.

"Biswajit, what were you looking at before I revealed my truths?" She asked.

"Well ... Vaishali," I struggled to tell the truth.

"Come on now, tell me," there came the beatific smile again.

"I ... I ..."

"Say it ... go on."

"I guess you know what I was looking at? Maybe the telepathic cord had conveyed my thoughts to you."

"Come on Biswajit, we were not telepathically connected at that time. So there was no way I could read your thoughts. Although I can intuit what was in your mind, I cannot be sure. Go ahead and tell me now.

A few deep breaths settled my nerves. But the real strength to speak the truth came from her smile. It conveyed the definite impression that she would not mind in the least if I spoke the truth; rather she would welcome it.

"Vaishali, you were looking stunningly beautiful that night," I finally voiced the truth, "I was particularly drawn by the beauty of your lips. The truth is when you asked me what I was looking at, I was looking at your exquisitely carved lips."

She took some time to respond. The beatific smile turned more beatific and her beauty peaked.

"Don't you find my lips exquisite anymore?" The sorceress drew closer.

Our lips met and then our bodies and then our minds and then our souls. For a while our beings melted into a single existence with our individual identities completely lost. I was nothing but that single existence and so was she. And the reason I call that state *single existence* is that there was just one consciousness and not two. And that consciousness could be felt both as a sum total of two discrete consciousnesses and a non-dual whole with no separable parts. It is the second feeling that we both basked in.

Unfortunately, the non-dual state had to end at some point of time for it was not immune to the forces of matter. However, the spirit of the non-dual state was alive in both of us even after our identities were restored!

I had to start very early next morning to reach *Shyamalpur* in time. The horse cart came around five and I was on my way shortly thereafter. We didn't speak much before my departure for what remained unspoken did all the talking on behalf of our bodies, minds and souls.

As I saw *Mahachoti* receding in the background, I recalled what Vaishali had said about the hill – "... *Mahachoti is the most beautiful and the most spiritual hill around. Tourists take interest in Mahachoti because of its height and steepness. They are so foolish. They are completely unaware that this hill has a heart and a mind of its own. It can talk to you just the way a friend talks to you if your senses are subtle enough to establish a communion with it.*"

Now *Prithaka* sprung its last surprise. I felt as though I received a message from *Mahachoti*. I wondered if my senses had suddenly become subtle enough to hold a communion with it. I soon knew that to be the case. The message came again but it was not clear. I concentrated harder. It came yet again but I still could not hear it clearly. When it came for the fourth time, I could hear it loud and clear.

"Come again," vibrations of *Mahachoti* reached me.

"I shall certainly come again, thanks for the invitation," I sent my thought across to *Mahachoti* and though I wasn't sure that it received it, I was hopeful that the hill with a heart and a mind of its own would sense my feelings.

ABOUT THE AUTHOR

Biswajit Banerjee's life is all about writing, reading, meditating and teaching. He specializes in creative non-fiction and fiction and has written a number of articles, essays, short stories and plays that have been published on various forums. He is also a renowned screenwriter and has been writing scripts for fiction and non-fiction films for a good number of years now for a multitude of government and private organizations including advertisement films and spots, which have been telecast on all major channels in the Indian television circuitry. Biswajit Banerjee is also a very popular teacher. He teaches, amongst other things, subjects such as English communication including creative writing and screenwriting, motivation skills, oratory skills and personality development.

He lives in New Delhi, India, with his family consisting of his parents, brother, sister-in-law, wife, niece and daughter.

Do visit Biswajit Banerjee's Amazon Author's page at https://www.amazon.com/author/biswajitbanerjeepage. You could also visit his principal blog at http://realmofbiswajitbanerjee.blogspot.in/ for all announcements relating to his books, English lessons, articles and spiritual discourses. You can reach out to Biswajit Banerjee at the following:

- ✓ google.com/+BiswajitBanerjeeAuthor

- ✓ http://www.youtube.com/user/BiswajitBanerjee4u

- ✓ https://www.facebook.com/pages/Biswajit-Banerjee

- ✓ https://www.facebook.com/biswajit.banerjee.180

- ✓ https://twitter.com/Biswajitwriter

You could also write to Biswajit Banerjee on his e-mail ID biswajitbanerjeephilosopher@gmail.com .

Printed in Great Britain
by Amazon.co.uk, Ltd.,
Marston Gate.